Praise for Anna Bennett

I Dared the Duke

"Sharply drawn characters, clever dialogue, simmering sensuality, and a dash of mystery make this well-crafted Regency thoroughly delightful." —*Library Journal*

"Readers will enjoy this sassy Regency take on the classic *Beauty and the Beast* tale." —*Booklist*

"A captivating page-turner that will become a new favorite among romance enthusiasts!" —*BookPage*

"Will truly win readers' hearts."
—*RT Book Reviews* (A Top Pick)

"Bennett brings new life to traditional Regency stories and characters." —*Kirkus Reviews*

"Scrumptious . . . I devoured every word! A hot and wounded hero, a heroine you wish could be your friend in real life, and witty scenes that sparkle with life . . . The Wayward Wallflowers just keep getting better!"
—Laura Lee Guhrke, *New York Times* bestselling author

My Brown-Eyed Earl

"Heart, humor, and a hot hero. Everything I look for in a great romance novel!" —Valerie Bowman

THE ROGUE IS BACK
in
TOWN

ANNA BENNETT

St. Martin's Paperbacks

THE ROGUE IS BACK IN TOWN

Copyright © 2018 by Anna Bennett.
Excerpt from *Brown-Eyed Earl* Copyright © 2016 by Anna Bennett.

All rights reserved.

For information address St. Martin's Press, 175 Fifth Avenue, New York, NY 10010.

ISBN: 978-1-250-10094-8

Our books may be purchased in bulk for promotional, educational, or business use. Please contact your local bookseller or the Macmillan Corporate and Premium Sales Department at 1-800-221-7945, ext. 5442, or by e-mail at MacmillanSpecialMarkets@macmillan.com.

Printed in the United States of America

St. Martin's Paperbacks edition / January 2018

St. Martin's Paperbacks are published by St. Martin's Press, 175 Fifth Avenue, New York, NY 10010.

10 9 8 7 6 5 4 3 2 1

For anyone who's felt like a wallflower—
The dance floor is yours. Twirl.

Chapter ONE

London, Fall 1818

"His Lordship requests your presence in his study."

A summons at this ungodly hour? Holy hell. Lord Samuel Travis moaned and pretended he still slept.

A brief pause. "At once."

Sam cracked open burning eyes and scowled at his valet. "Go away, Ralph." He threw an arm across his face to ward off the menacing rays of sunlight that streamed between the curtains. Damn it, he'd passed out in the library.

Ralph cleared his throat. "What shall I tell the marquess?"

Sam grunted. "Tell my brother he can go hang himself."

"Forgive me, my lord, but he was terribly insistent. If you don't go to him at once, I fear he'll be most displeased."

"Then he can hurl a vase against the wall and curse my name. I'll hear his tirade from right here." Sam patted the leather armchair that had served as his bed. Surprisingly comfortable, but then his slumber had been enhanced by copious amounts of brandy. His stomach churned at the thought. "Leave. If I haven't emerged in three hours, return to check if I'm dead. No—on second thought, just send the undertaker."

The valet's boots remained rooted to the floor, and he swallowed nervously. "The marquess said that if you fail to report to his study he shall . . . terminate my service."

Jesus. Sam might have admired his brother's uncharacteristic ruthlessness if it didn't feel like a hundred chickens were on the inside of his head trying to peck their way out. Still, his valet didn't deserve to be a pawn in Nigel's futile campaign.

Sam was *never* going to be respectable enough or gentleman enough or worthy enough. Not in his brother's eyes—and not in his own.

Nigel had assumed that spending six months on the Continent would cure Sam of his rakish tendencies— that if he rubbed elbows with society's upper crust, some of their polish would inevitably wear off on him. It hadn't. Because Sam had returned to London exactly one week ago and had already succeeded in disappointing his brother—in a spectacular fashion.

Groaning, he propped his elbows on his knees and waited for the room to right itself. "We can't allow him to sack you, Ralph. Who else could make me look halfway respectable *and* keep my sordid secrets?"

The valet exhaled in relief. "Thank you, my lord."

Sam pressed a hand to his throbbing forehead. "Just give me a minute."

But Ralph was already circling his chair, assessing the damage from all angles. "Your jacket's wrinkled and there's a small tear near the shoulder." He froze and pressed a hand to his chest. "You didn't remove your boots?"

"Easy, man. It's not a cardinal sin." Which wasn't to say he hadn't committed others in the course of the evening.

"Your boots are on," the valet repeated dryly, "and yet, your neckcloth's gone missing. Have you any notion where—" Clucking his tongue, Ralph plucked it from the top of an unlit lamp. "Never mind."

He snapped the cloth in midair, then held it at arm's length, turning his head as though he dangled a diseased rat. "It reeks of gaming hell. But there's no time to fetch a new one, so we'll have to make do with—"

"No neckcloth." Sam pushed it aside. "My brother will be too preoccupied with skewering me to notice."

"I don't believe I've ever seen him so irate, my lord." Ralph gulped and extended a hand. "May I help you up?"

"I can manage," Sam said with significantly more cockiness than he felt. He gripped the arms of the chair and pushed himself to his feet—

Just as his brother stormed into the room.

The valet cowered behind Sam for two seconds, then decided better of it and fled.

Over six feet of coiled muscle and barely contained rage, Nigel stalked across the library and stood toe to toe with Sam. Looking at his brother's face was like looking into a mirror—except for the eyes. Nigel's were the same icy blue as his, but they perpetually signaled disappointment and disgust. Usually with good reason.

Nigel shoved a rolled-up newspaper at Sam's chest, slamming him back into the armchair. "You've been consorting with that actress again," he spat. "It's all over the gossip pages."

Sam tossed the paper to the floor, dragged a hand down his face, and shrugged. "She ended the affair before I went away. If the rags are still dwelling on it, they must be suffering from a serious shortage of scandal."

"Oh, there's no shortage." Nigel's face was mottled red. "They'll be able to write a whole column based solely on your escapades from last night."

Shit. Sam vaguely remembered losing a vast sum at the hazard tables. Followed by a shoving match with an earl who'd mocked him. And at the very end of the night . . . bloody hell.

"Lord Harborough just paid me a visit," Nigel said through his teeth.

Sam pinched the bridge of his nose and prayed his murky recollection of the encounter with their neighbor was a bad dream. "A friendly call?" he asked hopefully.

Nigel pressed his lips into a thin line and paced as though the sight of his hungover brother was more than he could bear. "You waltzed into his house in the wee hours of the morning and . . . and . . . crawled into bed with his spinster aunt."

Damn. That was beyond the pale—even for Sam. He made a valiant attempt to explain. "Our houses look remarkably similar in the dark. Harborough's butler should really lock the door."

Seething, Nigel stared down his nose at Sam, pinning him to the chair. "You didn't enter through the *door*. You shattered the window of their parlor and crawled into the house like a thief. His poor aunt nearly suffered an apoplexy when she woke and found your head on the pillow next to hers."

Sam cringed. "I thought I was in my bedchamber." He vaguely remembered being dragged out of the house by a pair of footmen and deposited on his own doorstep. "Once I'm presentable, I'll go next door and offer my apologies."

"The *last* thing they want is a visit from you." Nigel clenched his fists. "Besides, I have another sort of penance in mind."

A chill slithered down Sam's spine. His brother had the devil's own temper, but he usually vented his anger with shouted insults, thrown objects, and slammed doors. Nigel's simmering rage was far more alarming.

"What sort of penance?"

"Come with me." His brother's stony expression revealed nothing, but Sam knew better than to poke the bear.

"Fine. Allow me to change, and I'll meet you in your study within the hour."

"I'm through with waiting." Nigel snapped his fingers, and three burly men appeared in the doorway.

Sam jumped out of his chair and braced for a fight. "Who the hell are they?"

The trio stalked across the room and stood behind Nigel, glowering like they'd leap at the chance to throw a few punches. "Hired help. I found them working near the docks."

"Jesus, Nigel. Paying someone to do your dirty work?"

"On the contrary. I'm cleaning house. It's time for you to move out."

Sam blinked. He'd lived in their London townhouse his whole life. Its stately design and elegant furnishings served as the backdrop for every fond memory he had of their father, who'd died barely a year ago. He'd hated it when his sons fought, but he'd always sided with Sam. Always encouraged Nigel to forgive his younger, mischievous brother. But even Father would have had a difficult time defending him this morning.

"Look, I realize my behavior last night was abominable. It won't happen again."

Nigel snorted. "I've heard that verse before, Samuel. It's invariably followed by the refrain of excessive drinking, gambling, and whoring. This time, I'm teaching you a lesson. I want you out."

One of the dock workers cracked his knuckles.

"You're exiling me to the country house?" Sam asked, as though it were a life sentence in Newgate Prison. The truth was, if he laid low for a few months, he should be able to return to London before Christmastide.

"Not the country house," Nigel intoned.

The burly men behind him shifted their feet ominously. The hairs on the back of Sam's neck stood on end. He had to tread lightly here. "I suppose I could let an apartment at the Albany, but I'll need an allowance—"

Nigel barked a laugh. "No. I'm cutting you off. Although, if you're desperate for funds, you could always sell Father's pocket watch. It would fetch a pretty price."

Sam instinctively reached for the gold watch in his pocket, taking comfort from its familiar warmth and weight. "I would sooner die than sell it."

"Suit yourself," Nigel said with a shrug.

Good God. Sam closed his eyes and swallowed

before searching his brother's face, hoping to find a shred of compassion. He hated to beg, but as a younger son with no fortune of his own, he had little choice. "Where would you have me go? Surely you don't mean to throw me out into the street?"

"It would serve you right if I did, but no—I'm presenting you with an alternative."

Sam bit back a curse. "I'm listening."

"While reviewing our father's papers I recently discovered that the estate includes a property in London. It's a small, fairly dilapidated house on Hart Street."

"Sounds charming," Sam quipped. "So, my penance is to move into a vacant tumble-down flat with no servants and no money?"

Nigel crooked his finger at the burly men, and in an instant, two flanked Sam, seizing his biceps in viselike grips. He squirmed but froze when the third man grabbed his collar from behind.

"You have the right of it," Nigel replied, "except for one thing. The house is not vacant. Our soft-hearted father allowed a distant relative to inhabit the property."

"A relative?" Sam managed, in spite of the fact that his collar nearly strangled him. "Who?"

"She died many years ago, but her widower has continued to rely on our generosity. I want him gone." Nigel stared out the library window, his gaze calculating and cold.

"Where will he go?"

Ignoring the question, Nigel said, "Consider it a test—and not a very difficult one at that. You'll do something useful for once. Take possession of the property and send me an accounting of its condition. I have a potential buyer for the house, and the sale would go a long way toward paying off your debts."

"You could have simply asked for my help," Sam said. "Without resorting to force."

"Without *force*, you'd still be in that chair, sleeping off the effects of last night's debauchery."

True enough. "I'll ask Ralph to pack a few things for me and we'll leave immediately."

"You'll leave now. Alone. Don't ask for so much as a shilling until the house is vacated."

Sam started to protest, but his brother turned away as the trio of dock workers dragged him out of the room like yesterday's rotten garbage.

He told himself that the task would be accomplished by day's end. The man who occupied the house would cooperate, Nigel's temper would subside, and Sam could return to his devil-may-care ways.

But as the workers shoved him into the coach with nothing but the clothes on his back, his gut told him something wholly different.

His damned goose was *cooked*.

Chapter TWO

Miss Juliette Lacey paused in the doorway of her uncle's study. Several of the books and journals that she'd shelved the day before were now open, strewn over every available surface. The piles of papers she'd painstakingly organized seemed to have multiplied overnight.

Uncle Alistair paced the room, flitting from book to book like a butterfly in a meadow of colorful blossoms, unable to settle on one. Suddenly he froze, his gaze locked on the portrait of his beloved wife that graced the wall above the mantel. "You mustn't fret, my love," he said earnestly. "All will be well." He paused briefly and tilted his head as though listening intently. "Indeed. I promise I'm working on it."

Julie's heart sank. When he thought he was alone, her uncle, the man who'd generously taken in her and her sisters after they'd lost their parents in a horrific coach accident, had recently begun talking to his wife—who, sadly, had died twenty years ago. He'd always been eccentric, but this latest development troubled Julie more than his habits of inserting the wrong words into sentences and forgetting why he'd walked into a room. She couldn't bear the thought that he was desperately lonely . . . or worse, mad.

Hoping to spare him embarrassment, she breezed into the room as though she'd just arrived. "Did you say something, Uncle?" she said lightly.

He blinked and shook his head, causing the wild, white tufts of hair above his ears to sway. "No, no, my dear," he sputtered. "I was just reading a most edifying letter written by a colleague in New South Wales. The flora and fauna there are remarkable. Like nothing we've seen here or on the Continent."

"Forgive me for saying so, but you haven't seemed yourself of late." Julie walked over and squeezed his sloped shoulder. "Is anything troubling you? Do you feel unwell?"

"Not at all. I'm as pale and hearty as ever. Perhaps because I was never very fit to begin with." He shot her a crooked smile that nearly melted her heart.

"Do you miss Meg and Beth?" Neither of Julie's sisters was in London at the moment. The eldest, Meg, and her dashing husband had removed themselves to their country house, as she was anxiously awaiting her first babe. Beth and her handsome duke had gone to the Continent for their honeymoon and wouldn't return for a few weeks.

So, for now and the foreseeable future, Julie considered herself her uncle's caretaker. After all he'd done for her, the least she could do was to look after him. Besides, she adored him.

"Of course, I miss your sisters, but it's not as though they've left us forever. And I'll tell you a secret, my dear Juliette . . . you've always been my favorite."

"Hogwash." And yet, his confession held a kernel of truth. She'd been only eleven years old when she'd moved into his cozy, chaotic house. Uncle Alistair had been the one to kiss her skinned knees, teach her to play the piano, and tuck her into bed at night. Some days, it seemed she could barely remember her parents' faces. Kissing her uncle's wrinkled cheek, she said, "You're far too charming for your own good, you know."

He waggled his bushy gray eyebrows as he shuffled to his desk. "That's what the ladies tell me."

Julie breathed a little easier. Perhaps her concerns were unfounded. Uncle Alistair talked to himself now and then, but it was hardly evidence of madness. If it were, half of England would surely be carted off to Bedlam.

Still, she reasoned that what her uncle needed was a project. An engaging task to sharpen his mind, ease his loneliness, and impress the intellectuals who looked down their noses at him—and she'd thought of just the thing.

Over the last few days, she'd been debating the best way to broach the topic with him, for he could be terribly stubborn. But the heartbreaking sight of him conversing with Aunt Elspeth's portrait convinced her to speak her mind. "I've been thinking," she began, "that I could help you organize all your research." She waved an arm around the cluttered study. "You've written copious notes and made countless calculations. Wouldn't it be grand if all your papers were sorted and filed?" She spoke in the same hopeful tone a nursemaid uses when trying to convince her charge that Brussels sprouts are tasty.

"Why would I wish to organize my notes?" he said, slightly offended. "I know precisely where everything is. This journal contains sketches and descriptions of moss spores." As he held it up for her to see, several pages drifted to the floor, and she scooped them up and placed them on the corner of his desk. "This shelf," he continued, pointing to a row of books behind him, "houses my daily recordings of temperature, humidity, and precipitation. Pick any date within the last decade, and I will tell you the exact weather conditions."

"I don't doubt your ability to do so," she said—even though she *did* question whether he could locate anything amid scores of unlabeled ledgers. "You've amassed so much valuable information in this room," she said soothingly. "And it's high time you share your considerable knowledge with others."

He scratched the top of his head, clearly confounded. "What are you suggesting, my dear?"

Julie took a deep breath. "I think you should use all of this"—she swept her gaze over the mountains of papers, drawings, and journals—"to write a scientific paper which you could present to the Royal Society."

Uncle Alistair gaped at her for several seconds, then dragged a gnarled hand down his face as he slowly rounded his desk and sank onto the threadbare cushion of a faded arm chair. As he looked up at her, his eyes shone with affection. "I am beyond flattened that you think I might have any knowledge worthy of offering to that esteemed group of scholars, Juliette. But alas, I do not. They have no wish to hear from the likes of me."

She bristled with indignation on his behalf. "Then you must convince them to listen. You underestimate yourself, Uncle. You have plenty of illuminating ideas to share. We simply need to organize your findings so that you'll be able to provide the necessary evidence to support your conclusions."

"Your confidence in me is heartening," he said, "but misplaced."

Julie dropped to her knees before him and clasped his hands. "No, it's not. What if I said this was important to me?"

"It is? Whatever for?"

She swallowed. *Because the world needs more good and brilliant minds like yours. Because you deserve to be respected instead of ridiculed. Because I fear that you're slowly slipping away from me.* "It would give me something to do while Meg and Beth are out of town . . . and it would make me exceedingly happy to see you reaping the fruits of your labors."

"I don't know, Juliette. An undertaking such as this would require months—quite possibly years—to complete."

"And I'll be by your side the entire time. Will you do it?" she pleaded.

He lifted his eyes to Aunt Elspeth's portrait and gazed at it for several seconds, as though seeking guidance. When at last he returned his gaze to Julie, his wizened face was soft with emotion. "You know very well that I cannot deny you. And I'll admit that while the prospect of sharing my findings is frightening, it is also rather exhilarating."

Julie's heart skipped a beat. "Then it's a yes?"

"Yes. But I wish to ask one thing of you in return."

She squeezed his hand. "Of course, Uncle. Anything."

"You must immediately devote yourself to finding a husband."

Oh dear. With a nervous laugh, she stood and shook out her skirts. "But why? I'm happy here with you. Are you so anxious to be rid of me?" she teased.

"Nay, I am eager to see you happy and settled, as your sisters are. It's what your parents would have wanted—God rest their souls—and it would bring me great comfort as well. Young people often fail to inebriate what a precious commodity time is." He paused thoughtfully. "But when you reach my advanced years, you tend to regret every squandered minute."

Julie sighed. "You are a wise man, and I do not doubt the truth of your words. However, finding a husband isn't as easy as selecting a bonnet."

"Nonsense. For someone with your beauty, wit, and charm, finding a suitable mate should be the simplest matter in the world. You have not fully dedicated yourself to the task."

Julie scoffed. "Why do you say that? Because I don't bat my lashes at every man I encounter . . . or giggle at hopelessly insipid jokes . . . or pretend to be in raptures over something as shallow as a pretty pair of slippers?"

He raised a thick brow, skeptical. "I have witnessed your obsession with slippers firsthand."

True enough—blast it all. With a toss of her head, she

said, "That is beside the point. I shall marry. When I find the right gentleman."

But it was rather more complicated than that, due to a minor indiscretion on the terrace at her brother-in-law's masquerade ball. That single foolish, passionate kiss might well haunt her forever—and in more ways than one.

"You are capable of accomplishing anything you put your mind to," Uncle Alistair said firmly. "And seeing you happily wed would bring me great comfort in my old age."

"I promise to do my best to join the ranks of my blissfully married sisters," she said, "in my own time, and on my own terms."

His eyes twinkled at that. "I would expect nothing less, my dear. I, in turn, will give serious thought as to an area of research on which to focus. But to do so properly, I shall require a nap."

Julie released the breath she'd been holding. "Thank you, Uncle. You won't regret it. I've always known you were the wisest, most intelligent man on earth, and the rest of London shall soon know it too."

He chuckled and patted her shoulder affectionately as he made his way to the door. "We shall see about that. For now, I am more than content. Everything I need— my beloved niece, my life's work, and memories of my Elspeth—are all here in this house."

Julie sighed happily as he left, her fingers already itching to tidy the mess. Out of deference to her uncle, she waited until she heard the stairs creak beneath his weight before she attacked the disorderly bookshelf. She'd only just begun when a pounding on the front door made her drop the ledger she'd been holding—directly onto her foot.

Stifling a curse, she grasped the toe of her slipper and squeezed.

Good heavens. It still sounded as though Vikings were attacking with a battering ram. Her uncle needed his rest, and the incessant banging would surely disturb him. What sort of heathen could not wait a short period of time for the butler to make his way to the door before relentlessly beating it like a drum?

Fuming, she released her throbbing toe and limped toward the front hall. "I'll answer the door, Mr. Finch," she called to the butler, who, at the age of seventy, was still surprisingly spry but rather hard of hearing. Besides, given his kind and gentle nature, he would have treated the visitor far too cordially.

Julie, on the other hand, had no intention of coddling the scoundrel.

One hand on her hip, she yanked open the door and opened her mouth, planning to launch into a lecture regarding the proper way to pay a call . . . but the words died on her lips.

The imposing man who stood on her doorstep looked very much like the Marquess of Currington. So much so, that she instantly recalled the scene on the Duke of Blackshire's terrace and blushed, all the way to the roots of her hair. But the man before her wasn't the marquess.

He may have possessed the same breathtaking height, broad shoulders, and soulless blue eyes, but Nigel would never have appeared in public without a cravat and a clean shave. No, this man, with his tanned skin and

mussed hair was infinitely more dangerous than Nigel—
and that was truly saying something.

"Who are you?" he demanded rudely.

"I was going to ask you the same thing," Julie countered. "But all things considered"—she raised her chin,
letting her gaze linger on the exposed skin above his
collar and his wrinkled jacket—"I must conclude that
you're searching for your long-lost valet and have reached
our doorstep in error. Good day, sir." She swung the
door to shut it, but he stopped it with the toe of his boot.

He leaned back in order to stare at the brass numbers
nailed above the front door and shook his head. "No.
This is the house." With that, he angled his way past her
and into the tiny front hall.

Gasping, she took two steps backward. "What the
devil do you think you're doing?"

He arched a dark brow as he slammed the door and
waltzed into the cozy, cluttered parlor. "I'm reclaiming
this house," he announced coldly. "On behalf of my
family."

"Wh-*what*?" she sputtered. "Are you *mad*?"

"No, merely suffering from the king of all hangovers."
He lowered himself onto the faded settee as if it were
an ornate throne. "Which is why I'd rather not engage
in a prolonged debate. I regret to inform you that you—
and any other occupants of this charming residence—
must vacate it. At once."

Chapter THREE

Sam did his best not to stare at the young woman pacing the parlor, tried not to focus on the perfect curl dangling from her nape or the thick lashes framing her eyes. Pretty or no, he had to evict her, and it was best done quickly. It would have been nice if Nigel had warned him that a slender, brown-eyed beauty occupied the house. But her presence was no doubt part of the test.

And Sam wouldn't fail his brother this time. He couldn't—and not just because he'd been tossed out on his ear. It was high time he began to pull his own weight. Who knew? If he managed to reclaim this property for Nigel, maybe he'd start to earn back his brother's trust and heal old wounds. It's what their father would have wished . . . and Sam had to try.

Which meant he needed to deal with the delicate miss who lived here—in a kind but pragmatic, detached manner.

Her cheeks pink with rage, she spun on him, jabbing

a finger toward his chest. "Remove yourself from my settee immediately, you . . . you . . . *beast*."

"Beast?" He stretched his arms over the back of the sofa to show he had no intention of moving. "That's rather harsh, I think."

She stared, incredulous. "*Truly?* Because I was being generous. I could have called you scoundrel, tyrant, reprobate—"

"Perhaps we should begin with introductions," he interrupted. "So we can address one another more civilly."

"I have no wish to address you at *all*. In fact, if you do not leave at once, I shall scream and alert the staff."

"Create a scene if you'd like—it couldn't possibly compare to my exploits from last night." He winced at the memory, then shook his head to erase it. "I am Lord Samuel Travis, and my brother is the rightful owner of this house."

"Miss Lacey?" An elderly servant appeared in the doorway and eyed Sam suspiciously. "I didn't realize you had a guest. Shall I send for tea?"

"No, thank you, Mr. Finch. Lord Travis will be leaving soon."

"Very good. I shall be just outside the parlor if you should require anything." The butler bowed and glared at Sam before taking his leave.

"So you are one of the infamous Lacey sisters," he drawled. Dubbed the Wilting Wallflowers during their first disastrous season, the three sisters were widely known for their sharp tongues, their odd uncle, and their unwavering loyalty to each other. They'd once been ridiculed for their unfashionable gowns and their uncle's odd behavior, but the eldest sister had married a

wealthy earl and the middle sister had landed herself
a duke.

Miss Lacey may have been the only remaining wallflower, but he'd be damned if she looked like one. With
elegant blue silk skimming her curves and lustrous pearls
gracing her neck, she might as well have stepped out of
the latest issue of a lady's magazine. Or, even better, his
wildest fantasies.

"I am Miss Juliette Lacey," she said proudly. "And
you are clearly mistaken. About your brother owning this
house, that is. My uncle, Lord Wiltmore, has lived here
for decades. He is upstairs resting at this very moment,
and I am exceedingly grateful that he did not hear your
outrageous claim, as the mere suggestion that this house
is not his would have left him quite distraught. Fortunately, however, no harm has been done. If you leave
now, I shall be willing to forget that you ever darkened
our doorstep."

Ouch. Sam leaned forward, propping his elbows on
his knees. "I'm afraid you will not rid yourself of me
so easily. You see, my father was the rightful owner of
this residence and, out of the goodness of his heart, allowed your uncle to live here. But my brother recently
inherited the estate—and he has other plans for this
property."

Julie's reasons for gripping the back of a chair were two-
fold. First, she wished to keep herself from throttling
Lord Travis. And second, she needed to steady her wobbly knees in order to keep herself from swooning.

Surely, he was spouting lies. The marquess had sent
him to frighten her. This highly improper visit by a cra-

vatless rogue was merely a bullying tactic, an attempt to manipulate her. Nothing more.

"How dare you barge into our home, threatening us? You say you are suffering from the effects of last night's overindulgence, but I think that you must still be under the influence of very strong spirits indeed if you imagine you can waltz into my parlor and order me and my uncle about."

He dropped his head into his hands—very large, tanned hands—and groaned. When he looked up at her, a hint of compassion shone in his eyes. And it frightened her more than the coldness that had been there before.

"I should have realized that this news would be quite a shock to you," he said softly. "I've been away from London for several months and I fear I have forgotten my manners."

"Manners?" She scoffed, with significantly more daring than she felt. "If the sordid tales about you are true, I cannot think you ever possessed them."

"The tales are mostly correct," he admitted. "Perhaps ninety percent factual. But even *I* am not normally in the business of ousting young ladies from their homes."

"Then why are you here now?" she demanded. She had her suspicions, and her traitorous heart skipped a beat. Perhaps the marquess hadn't given up on her after all.

"It's complicated. But I assure you that I'm not a complete monster."

"No?" she said, not bothering to hide her skepticism. "Am I to suppose then, you are only ninety percent monster?"

He grinned, and the flash of white teeth and the crinkles around his eyes made her breath catch in her throat. Vexing, that. She crossed her arms over her chest in order to resist the urge to fan herself.

"I truly regret," he said sincerely, "that I must be the bearer of this unpleasant news, but—"

"Unpleasant?" she repeated. *"Unpleasant* is a chilly rain during one's morning walk or an irksome pebble in the toe of one's slipper. This news of yours is beyond unpleasant, sir. It's . . . it's . . . perfectly . . . *horrid."*

"Come now." His cajoling tone—the sort men routinely reserved for calming hysterical females—set her teeth on edge. "It's not as though you'll be reduced to living in the streets. I am certain one of your sisters could be persuaded to take in you and your uncle. Besides, for you, the change in living arrangements will only be a temporary situation."

She shot him a fake, toothy smile. "And why is that, my lord?"

Scoundrel that he was, he had the good grace to look mildly contrite. Rising to his considerable height, he raked a hand through his thick sandy brown hair. "I only meant . . . that is . . . I assume you will soon marry and have your own household to run."

"My, my," she said, walking closer. "You seem to have figured all of this out, haven't you? When I choose to marry—*if* I choose to marry at all—is none of your concern. And it is entirely beside the point. Did you honestly think my uncle and I would willingly abandon our home—the same loving home he opened to me and my sisters after my parents suddenly died—for your convenience?"

"It's not as though I'm asking you to abandon a palace." He flicked a glance at the spot beside the window where the wallpaper had begun to peel and at the huge ink stain on the worn wooden floor that the settee couldn't quite conceal.

Julie felt heat creep up her neck. Perhaps it wasn't the grandest of houses or furnished in the latest style. Rather, it was adorned in warm memories and love. Aunt Elspeth's portrait, the mounds of papers, and creak of the stairs were all part of the charm of the place. All part of what made it a home. Uncle Alistair would have preferred to keep the house the way it had always been, but Julie and her sisters had insisted on making a few improvements. "We plan to undertake renovations as soon as my sister and her husband return from their honeymoon."

"Not a moment too soon," he said dryly.

Why on earth was she attempting to defend their home to the likes of him? "You have no right to stroll into this house and judge it."

Dragging a hand down his chiseled cheek, he sighed. "Actually, I do."

She snorted indelicately. "Forgive me if I seem unwilling to take the word of a man who could not be bothered to don a cravat before venturing out of doors this morning."

"Miss Lacey," he said smoothly, "I will not pretend that your poor opinion of me is unwarranted. It does not change the fact, however, that this house belongs to neither you nor your uncle. You *will* vacate these premises, and that may happen in one of two ways."

She batted her lashes mockingly. "Is that so? Please enlighten me."

"Gladly." He moved within a foot of her, so close that

she could see the sprinkling of dark hair above the gaping collar of his shirt. "Either you tell the staff to begin packing your things immediately and inform your uncle of the impending move, or . . ."

"Or *what*, my lord?"

A muscle in his cheek twitched. "Or I will do it for you."

Her heart pounded wildly in her chest and her mouth went dry. He wouldn't be so callous . . . would he?

Feigning nonchalance, she shrugged. "My staff would not take orders from you, nor would my uncle. *I* am the mistress of this house, and I have no intention of leaving it." She strode past him, ignoring the sudden *frisson* of attraction she felt as her shoulder brushed against his arm, and deposited herself on the worn seat cushion of the chair. "If you wish for me to go, you shall have to remove me by force."

Chapter FOUR

Sam cursed under his breath. The gossip rags may have pronounced him London's greatest rogue, but he wasn't so depraved that he'd physically remove a lady from her home.

He may have *briefly* considered tossing Miss Lacey over his shoulder and wrapping his arms around her lithe legs . . . or scooping her out of the chair and cradling her round bottom against his torso . . . but that would never do.

He shook his head to clear the wayward thoughts. What was required here was *finesse*. He was capable of unleashing devastating charm—when it suited his needs. And while the current conditions were hardly optimal for flirtation, he would have to make do.

The coach had barely slowed to a stop this morning before the three henchmen shoved him out, leaving him sprawled on the pavement outside the house with nothing but the wrinkled clothes he'd been wearing the night before. He had no money, no valet, no shave . . . not even a bloody neckcloth.

A week ago, he might have crawled back home begging for mercy and promising to turn over a new leaf.

But he'd pushed his brother too far this time. Even someone as honorable and dutiful as Nigel had his limits, and Sam had crossed them. He couldn't return home to Nigel—or go any other damned place, for that matter—until he'd completed the simple task he'd been given.

Perhaps it couldn't be accomplished in a day or two, as he'd originally hoped. Nigel probably had no idea that the house he wished to sell was occupied by an elderly man and his feisty niece, who happened to be far too beautiful for her own good. Dealing with them would require a bit more patience and persuasion than Sam had initially anticipated.

But persuade them he must. Nigel had given an ultimatum, a final opportunity to prove that Sam could be trusted. That he was capable of more than a life of gambling, womanizing, and excess. That despite considerable evidence to the contrary, he wasn't a complete waste of human flesh. However, before he could hope to convince anyone else of that fact, he had to convince Miss Lacey.

She sat upon her wobbly, faded chair with her arms crossed, her chin held high, and her gaze icy, a warrior queen intent on defending her kingdom.

Sam circled behind her, adjusting the ties of his shirt and smoothing his jacket in a futile attempt to make himself more presentable. Taking a deep breath, he moved to the settee, and sat opposite her.

"I would never forcibly remove you," he began. "And I sincerely apologize for threatening to do so."

She sniffed. "Have you nothing else to add?"

"I was only beginning to enumerate my offences," he replied, even as he scrambled to think of another. "I also regret calling on you in my current disheveled state . . . and the insensitive manner in which I behaved earlier. Most of all, I regret causing those furrows on your forehead."

"How gallant of you to mention it," she said dryly.

"Forgive me, Miss Lacey. That was poorly done. But rest assured, even frown lines cannot detract from your beauty." Good God, he should stop talking before he dug himself even deeper. "A momentary cloud doesn't diminish the brilliance of the sun—it only makes one appreciate it more."

She narrowed her eyes skeptically. "If the apology you offer is sincere, you will leave this household at once."

"I'm afraid I can't."

"It's a very simple matter," she snapped. "You could do it if you wished."

"It occurs to me that we would make more headway if we were to converse in a civil manner. Would you allow me to explain?"

She glanced at a clock with a cracked face perched on the mantel. "I shall give you exactly ten minutes to make your case. After your time has expired, you will leave. If you do not, I shall send for the authorities and alert them that a strange and dangerous intruder refuses to leave the premises."

"Strange and dangerous? Perhaps I'm a bit rough around the edges, but that hardly makes me a criminal.

In fact, I'm attempting to extend an olive branch, in case you hadn't noticed—"

"Nine and one-half minutes," she intoned.

Damn. He expended five more seconds on a slow, seductive smile, confident it would be worth the investment of time.

But she continued to glare at him, rigid as ever.

"I know little of this house's history," he began, "but I will share what I know. You deserve to have all the facts, such as they are."

She frowned, and her lips parted as though she'd speak, but instead she gave him a curt nod.

"My father, the former Marquess of Currington, was unfailingly kind to everyone and generous to a fault. He had an encouraging word and a warm smile for everyone he met, from the lowliest maid to the wealthiest duke. He routinely visited the poor and sick, bringing food and medicine. And he allowed his distant relative— your aunt, I assume—to live here without recompense."

"He sounds like a very decent sort," she said, as though she couldn't quite believe a man of his caliber had spawned such an evil son.

"Decent, yes. But I fear he was not the shrewdest businessman. I can't recall him ever calling in a debt." Sam paused and swallowed so he'd be able to continue discussing his father without his voice cracking. "You wouldn't happen to have any brandy in here, would you?"

"I most certainly would not." She called to the butler who'd apparently been standing guard just outside. "Would you please bring up a tea tray, Mr. Finch?"

She checked the clock. "Eight minutes."

"Are you always so punctual?" he quipped, but he

found himself truly curious about her. Why would a beautiful young miss choose to hide away in a tumble-down house with her peculiar uncle? She must have received marriage offers aplenty, and yet, no man had managed to capture her heart—yet.

"Time is a precious commodity, Lord Travis. Wasting it is akin to throwing guineas into the gutter."

"How eloquently stated." He pressed his fingertips to his temple, willing the pounding in his head to subside. "But you are correct. Life can be snatched away in an instant. My father had the largest heart of anyone I know . . . and, ironically, it was that organ that ultimately failed him."

"I am sorry to hear of it," she said softly. "You must miss him."

"I do." Sam shifted on the settee, taking a moment to compose himself. "When he died, one year ago, my brother inherited his title—and all of the headaches that come with it. My father had not been ill. He'd had no time to put his affairs in order. So, the task of sorting through all his mismanaged accounts, properties, and business ventures fell on Nigel."

"I see. And I suppose that you consider this house one of the *mismanaged properties*."

Damn, but she was sharp-tongued. "I didn't say that. But I won't insult you by tiptoeing around the truth. While reviewing my father's papers, Nigel apparently discovered that this house belonged to my father, which means it is now his. I'm afraid he has alternate plans for the property which require you and your uncle to relocate."

She sat there, still and silent, but she'd heard the words.

The rapid rise and fall of her chest belied her calm exterior. "Is that all?" she asked.

"I beg your pardon?"

She closed her eyes momentarily as though summoning patience. "Have you shared all you know about this house's history?"

He nodded.

"Then allow me to tell you what *I* know of it. Many years ago, my uncle and his young, beautiful bride spent the happiest years of their lives here. She sang as she played the harp in this very parlor every night after dinner, making up her own words to amuse my uncle. But she took her last breaths in the bedchamber upstairs, after giving birth to a stillborn child, and my uncle . . . well, he had the harp removed because the mere sight of it broke his heart." Her voice cracked on the last word.

"I'm sorry," Sam said, surprised he meant it. He didn't know Lord Wiltmore personally, but Miss Lacey obviously adored him. And damn it all if that didn't complicate matters. Ousting a stranger who'd been sponging off his family's generosity for decades was one thing. Now the man had a name . . . and a sympathetic past . . . and a beautiful niece.

"My uncle lived here, alone, for several years," she continued, "channeling all his grief and loneliness into his research. His study down the hall houses the notes representing thousands of hours of meticulous work. He rarely ventured out into society, until . . ."

"You and your sisters arrived?" he provided.

"Yes. You see, no one was eager to take in three orphaned girls with no fortune of their own. A few cousins contrived a plan whereby Meg, Beth, and I would each stay with a different family member, spreading us out over three different counties. But we couldn't bear to be apart and had resolved that we'd run away before we'd dissolve our trio. We had already secretly packed our bags when we received the letter from Uncle Alistair, inviting us to stay with him. This house was our salvation." She swallowed, and her eyes welled.

"Miss Lacey," he said. Crying women were his Achilles' heel. "There's no need to—"

"Please, allow me to finish." She squared her shoulders, blew out a long breath, and composed herself. "This parlor is where Meg taught me all the colorful French words she knew and where Beth tried to show me how to waltz but turned everything around so I learned the gentleman's part by mistake. It's where my uncle made a game of teaching us the Latin names of different animal species, and Meg always won—except for the time that Beth and I cheated by hiding the answers in an embroidery hoop." She glanced up at him guiltily. "Meg still doesn't know about that."

He grinned. "Your secret is safe with me."

She stared at him, impassive. "You say your brother has a paper—a deed, I presume—proclaiming this house to be his. I may not have anything so tangible, but my uncle, my sisters, and I . . . we are the heart and soul of this house."

"I don't believe that houses have souls," he said wearily. "They are built not of flesh and blood, but of brick and mortar." He eyed a fine crack in the ceiling. "And if you want to know the truth of it, this one could use a bit more mortar."

"And *you* could use a bit more compassion. It's hardly

a secret that this house is in need of repair. The stairs creak so that it's impossible to sneak to the kitchen in the middle of the night, and the banister still wobbles from the time I slid down it and broke the newel post—and my arm. This house is neither grand nor elegant . . . but it's *ours*."

Sam stood and raked a hand through his hair. She'd given a pretty speech, but all those stories were a transparent attempt to pull on his heart strings and manipulate him. She wasn't the first person who'd been required to move from one residence to another—people did it all the time. So why did he feel like such a monster for asking her to go?

Planting his hands on his hips, he faced her. "Yes, this has been your home for some time, and it has served you well. Nothing will erase your treasured memories. But my brother was quite adamant. He expects me to take possession of the house."

She narrowed her eyes, and a chill slithered down his spine. "Why did your brother send you instead of a solicitor? Why are *you* the harbinger of this disagreeable news?"

Bloody hell. What was he supposed to tell her? That the task had fallen on him as a penance for climbing into bed with a spinster well into her seventh decade? That it was a test he must pass if he wished to avoid being disowned by his brother—the only close family member he had left, now that their father was gone?

The truth was that until Sam accomplished the task, he wouldn't have a place to rest his head at night.

"Suffice it to say my brother left the job to me," he said coolly, "and I will not fail him. I see no need to summon your uncle immediately, but when he awakens, we must tell him the news. You may be the one to tell him if you like . . . but if you don't, I will."

Spots of color appeared high on her cheeks, and her eyes flashed defiantly. "Heavens, would you look at the time? I'm afraid your ten minutes have expired." She rose from the chair and walked briskly toward the front hall, blue silk swishing around her legs like a lake in a tempest. "I must bid you good day, Lord Travis—and insist that you refrain from calling in the future. You and your deplorable manners and your . . . your *ridiculous* claims are most unwelcome here."

Chapter FIVE

Julie clenched her fists to keep her hands from trembling. She'd never been skilled at bluffing, and yet, she'd rushed headlong into a standoff with this exceedingly masculine, ruthlessly handsome stranger. She'd demanded that Lord Travis leave at once, but he hadn't made the slightest move to do so. Instead, he stared at her insolently, letting his gaze rake over her as though taking her measure.

She swallowed past the painful lump in her throat. What if he refused to do her bidding? She couldn't very well grab him by an impossibly muscled bicep and haul him out. No one in her household possessed the strength to overpower him, and besides, she wouldn't risk injury to any of the staff.

She'd threatened to alert the authorities, but *would* she? Blast it all, as much as it pained her to admit even to herself, Lord Travis *could* be telling the truth. She'd assumed that the house was Uncle Alistair's ancestral family home but had never had cause to ask him about it. What if the house truly *did* belong to the marquess? Alerting the authorities would do naught—but possibly expose her uncle and her as squatters.

The next move belonged to Lord Travis, and Julie held her breath as she waited for him to make it.

He strolled closer, casually, as though he had all the time in the world, and paused before her. "Bold words from a woman in your precarious position. I am attempting to be reasonable, but make no mistake—I could toss you and your uncle out onto the pavement if I wished."

Blood boiling with indignation, she spoke through her teeth. "No gentleman would threaten a lady in that manner."

His amused, heavy-lidded stare did nothing to cool her temper—but it had a most peculiar effect on her belly. "I never claimed to be a gentleman, Miss Lacey. I find the associated rules rather confining."

"Rules like wearing a cravat and dressing modestly in the light of day? I suppose such customs must be quite tedious for you," she said sharply.

"They are." He crossed his arms, leaned against the door jamb, and smiled—the very picture of an unapologetic rake. "My reputation should be proof enough that I am not constrained by society's mores. Something you would do well to remember."

His gaze flicked over her face, lingering a bit too long on her lips.

Her cheeks flamed, but she would not retreat—not even an inch. Instead, she played her last remaining card. "And *you* would do well to remember that I have two powerful brothers-in-law. Neither the earl nor the duke would be pleased if they knew you were here, harassing me." It was true. And though neither was within one hundred miles of London, Lord Travis needn't know it. "They are fiercely protective of their kin, and no one with a smidgen of good sense would dare to raise their ire."

The corner of his mouth curled into a wicked smile. "I've never been accused of having good sense, but your point is well taken." Thoughtful, he sauntered to the mantel and picked up one of Uncle Alistair's odd treasures—a drinking cup with a stem resembling a griffin's claw. Running a finger over gilt silver, he inspected the cup as though debating its value. But she knew what he really was about—he was marking his territory.

She wanted to launch herself at him and rip the cup out of his hands. He had no right to touch her uncle's prized possessions or frown at the thin layer of dust covering the knick-knacks in his collection or arch a superior brow at her.

But he *might* very well have a right to the house. So she bit her tongue.

"It occurs to me that each of us has something to lose," he drawled. "You stand to lose your home, and if your irate brothers-in-law unleash their anger on me, I stand to lose my perfectly straight nose."

A dozen retorts danced on the edge of her lips, but she remained silent.

"However, if we were to work together," he continued, "perhaps we'd be able to minimize our losses."

Julie blinked in disbelief. "I don't see how we could possibly—"

Mr. Finch entered the room, carrying a tray laden with

a steaming teapot, assorted china, and a plate of scones. "Here you are, Miss Juliette," he said, setting the tray on a table. "Will you be needing anything else?"

"No, thank you. I shall ring if I require assistance of any kind." The words had barely left her mouth before Lord Travis swooped over the tray, plucking a scone off the platter like some audacious bird of prey.

When faced with trials and tribulations, her first instinct was always to turn to her sisters. But they were married now, starting their own families. Meg and Will had their hands full with their adorable seven-year-old twin adopted daughters and were also expecting their first baby together. After Meg suffered a few fainting spells, the doctor ordered her to rest as much as possible until the babe arrived that winter. Julie would not risk upsetting her sister in her fragile condition and certainly didn't want to be the reason her devoted husband had to leave her side.

Beth and Alex were also unavailable for the next few weeks while on their honeymoon—in an undisclosed location. Their butler knew how to reach them in case any emergency should arise, but Julie was loath to spoil this idyllic time for the couple. After all they'd gone through to find each other, Beth and Alex deserved a few weeks of newly wedded bliss. Indeed, they deserved a lifetime.

Julie could handle this on her own. All she had to do was put off Lord Travis for three or four weeks, until Beth and Alex returned. She would delay using all manner of tactics. She would feign naiveté, create a diversion, and drag her slippers at every opportunity. Anything to spare her sisters this headache—and spare herself some embarrassment.

Because she had a terrible, sinking feeling that her current dilemma was somehow tangled up with her previous indiscretion with the marquess. It seemed an unlikely coincidence that the man she'd foolishly kissed—and even more foolishly believed to care for her—now claimed to own the house she occupied.

Perhaps if she pretended to be amenable to working with Lord Travis, she could sort it all out before her sisters or anyone else learned what she'd done—and how she'd humiliated herself.

Lord Travis had helped himself to a second scone and was plunking sugar cubes into his tea. "Shall I pour for you?" he asked.

"Is there anything left?" she replied wryly.

"Forgive me. I hadn't broken my fast, but I'm already feeling more human."

"If only you could behave like one," she muttered uncharitably.

"Do not count on it, tigress," he said, handing her a cup of tea.

Her hackles rose. "Tigress?"

Shrugging, he said, "You're formidable, like a tigress guarding her cubs."

She rewarded the observation with an icy glare but was rather pleased on the inside. She'd been aiming for formidable. "Earlier, when you said we should work together, what did you have in mind?"

"I thought we might make certain accommodations for each other. Compromise."

Julie stiffened. Compromising was not her forte. As the youngest daughter, she was used to having her way. When she was a child, her parents had indulged her, and after they died, her sisters and Uncle Alistair tried to fill the awful void by granting her everything she wished. Not expensive baubles, of course, since they hadn't two shillings to rub together, but something more precious— the freedom to make her own choices and control her own destiny.

Which was why she found the idea of bending to accommodate an unapologetic scoundrel so distasteful.

He set down his tea cup and frowned. "Are you unwell, Miss Lacey? You look rather green."

"I am merely dismayed by the situation in which I find myself."

"You would rather not strike a bargain with the likes of me," he said.

"I confess to being less than enthralled by the prospect . . . but I'm listening. What exactly do you propose?"

"I could be persuaded to allow you to remain here for a short period of time, while you consult with your sisters and make arrangements to relocate your household."

Time was precisely what Julie needed, but Lord Travis was putting the cart before the horse. "I have no intention of distressing my sisters or Uncle Alistair with your dubious claim—at least not until you have provided some proof."

He had the audacity to look affronted. "Proof?"

"Surely you did not expect me to begin packing my trunks without seeing a deed?"

"My brother is the Marquess of Currington," he said proudly. "And you may take him at his word. I've never met a more honorable man."

Julie swallowed. She'd thought the marquess was

honorable too. So much so that on the night of the duke's masquerade ball, she'd allowed him to claim her for a waltz, fetch her a glass of champagne, and lead her onto a moonlit terrace. She'd basked in the warmth of his appreciative gaze and nearly melted when he told her she was far too beautiful to dress as Artemis—that she should have been Aphrodite. He'd made her feel special and desired, and in that moment, she'd desperately wanted him to kiss her.

And he had.

But she'd expected him to call the next day—or perhaps the day after—to ask Uncle Alistair's permission to court her.

And he hadn't. Clearly, she was no Aphrodite, but rather a mere girl who'd imagined she might have a future with a handsome marquess.

"I am not impugning your brother's character," she said, hoping her voice didn't betray her. "If he has recently discovered the deed to this property, as you say he has, you should have no trouble producing it."

Lord Travis stretched out his muscled legs and crossed his boots at the ankles. "I'll produce it soon enough. And though my brother is extremely anxious to take possession of the property, I will petition him on your behalf."

Hope warmed her chest. "You will?"

"Certainly. I'll send word to him at once, asking him to provide the proof you seek."

"Why on earth would you need to send word? Simply go and ask him in person." Maybe once Lord Travis finally left her parlor, she'd be able to think clearly—and formulate a proper plan to keep Uncle Alistair in his home.

"I cannot," he said flatly.

"What is stopping you?"

"You'll recall that we agreed to work together," he said, ignoring her question.

"Are you in need of a coach? Never fear, I will hire you a hackney cab." She would personally transport him on a royal litter in order to rid herself of him.

"I don't require transportation, Miss Lacey. I require temporary lodgings."

Chapter SIX

Miss Lacey gripped the arm of the settee and gaped at Sam as though he must be jesting. "Why can't you simply return home—or to whatever other unsavory place you stayed last night?"

Er, return to the bedchamber of his neighbor's spinster aunt? That was entirely out of the question. As was returning home. Sam considered telling Miss Lacey that his older brother had all but disowned him but was reluctant to confess what a monumental disappointment he'd turned out to be. "It's rather complicated."

"You think me incapable of comprehending?" she countered.

"My brother believes the task of vacating this house is best accomplished while I am here. He wishes me to personally oversee the process."

"Do you always blindly follow your brother's orders?" she replied, clearly hoping to goad him.

"No. In the past, I have not. But in retrospect, I should have—I'd have saved myself a great deal of trouble."

"If you think I will allow you to stay here, you are mad."

"Why won't you?"

"*Why?*" She snorted indelicately. "I fear the list of reasons is too long to enumerate."

"Then give me three," he challenged.

"I beg your pardon?" She stared at him as though he'd sprouted horns.

"Give me three reasons I may not stay here."

"I am under no obligation to explain anything to you, however, the reasons are so glaringly obvious that I shall indulge you." She smoothed her skirt and raised her chin, then counted off on a slender finger. "For one, I am an unmarried miss and you are . . . you're known as . . ."

"London's greatest rogue?" he provided.

She rolled her eyes in a manner that suggested she was wholly unimpressed with the dubious title. "Something like that. Suffice it to say, my reputation would be thoroughly and irrevocably ruined. Never again would I be able to show my face in polite society."

"Your reputation would only be compromised if someone were to learn I was here—and no one will," he added emphatically.

She narrowed her eyes, clearly skeptical. "You are not known for being discreet. In fact, your exploits are rather legendary."

"Thank you," he said, only because he wanted to see

if he could make the adorable little lines on her forehead reappear—and, indeed, he could. "Shall we proceed to reason number two?"

"By all means," she mocked, counting off a second finger. "Furthermore, you cannot stay here because your presence would, no doubt, distress my uncle greatly. He is getting on in years and possesses a sensitive soul. I will not subject him to undue stress."

"Your uncle would only object to my presence if he knew the real reason I was here. He won't."

"Falsehoods may come easily to you, Lord Travis, but I am not similarly blessed. What lie would you concoct to explain the necessity of your staying with us?"

"I prefer to call it massaging the truth, Miss Lacey, and I'll admit to being something of an expert. We could tell your uncle that I am a distant relative—which is apparently true—and tell him that I've just returned from the Continent—which is most definitely true—and that I cannot stay in my own home because my brother has undertaken extensive renovations."

She stared at him for a moment, then burst into laughter.

Maybe it wasn't the most convincing lie, but as she wiped tears of mirth from her cheeks, he had no choice but to defend it. "Some people are highly sensitive to noise, dust, and the like. In fact—"

"I said my uncle was getting on in years, Lord Travis," she interrupted. "But do not mistake him for a fool. He would never believe such a ridiculous story."

"You underestimate my powers of persuasion. A falsehood is only ten percent idea."

"And the other ninety percent?"

"Execution. Making people *believe* through one's words and actions."

"My, you must be very proud of your powers of manipulation," she said dryly.

He shrugged. "Persuasion is a valuable skill, and it is not always used for sinister purposes. It *can* be employed for good."

She arched a perfectly formed brow. "So now I am to believe you are naught but a misunderstood philanthropist?"

He shot her a wicked grin. "I wouldn't go that far. My point is, the problem of your uncle objecting to my presence here is easily overcome. Perhaps we should move on to the third reason you think I cannot stay here."

She rose from the chair, walked to the window, and gazed thoughtfully at the street. "The most important reason is . . . I do not trust you. I have heard the rumors about you. You are reckless and debauched. You think of no one but yourself. And that makes you far too dangerous to be a guest in this house."

Her words, though true enough, stung more than they should have. But his first loyalty was, and always would be, to his brother. "I understand your reluctance to place your faith in me, but I would never physically hurt or threaten a lady. You are safe with me."

Miss Lacey shook her head, causing the curls at her nape to bounce like springs. "There are other dangers. If you stayed in our guest bedchamber, you would have unfettered access to this household. My uncle, his research, and all his . . . quirks."

"If you are worried that I will reveal family secrets, you may rest assured I will not. I have no interest in maligning you, your uncle, or any member of your family. My only goal is to assist my brother who has requested that you vacate this house—at your earliest convenience."

"And what would you do if I said you were not welcome to stay here?"

"I would have no choice but to call on your brother-in-law, the Duke of Blackshire, and inform him that my brother is the rightful owner of the property and wishes to take possession of it immediately."

"You can't go to Alex," she replied, a hint of panic lacing her voice.

Sam resisted the unexpected urge to comfort her. "Why not?"

"He and my sister are on their honeymoon and cannot be reached. Even if they could, I would not spoil this idyllic time for them."

"Fine. Then I would go to your other brother-in-law, the Earl of Castleton."

"No," she said firmly. "He and my sister have concerns of their own at the moment. Make no mistake, Will would return to London as quickly as possible if he suspected I were in danger, but he should be with Meg right now. I won't allow you to trouble them."

"Then your choice is clear." He rose from the settee and stood behind her, keeping a respectful distance between them. "You must let me move into the guest bedchamber."

"*Moving in* sounds as though you'd be setting up a permanent residence." She frowned and her voice trembled . . . as though she was finally realizing she had no other option.

He should have felt victorious—or at least satisfied

that his powers of persuasion hadn't failed him. But as he admired the graceful curve of her neck and the smooth skin of her cheek, he felt no triumph. Only hollowness. And guilt.

"I won't stay a day longer than is necessary," he said, keeping his voice light. He let his gaze drift around the cluttered, shabby parlor. "This isn't exactly my idea of a holiday."

"Fine." She rubbed the tops of her arms as though chilled. "Let's make sure we're both aware of the terms of our deal."

"Shall we put it in writing? Sign our names in blood?" he quipped.

"Tempting, but that won't be necessary. I only want your word."

"Very well," he said, surprised but pleased that his word counted for something with her. "What are your terms?"

"First, you will ask your brother to produce documentation showing he has the legal right to this property. A solicitor of my choosing will then review it. If—and only if—your brother has a claim to it, we will discuss our options."

Sam gave a curt nod. Nigel had been adamant that the house should be vacated, but for now Miss Lacey needed a glimmer of hope. Hell, she deserved at least that much for tolerating his damned company.

"In the meantime, you may stay here, but no one can know. That means no one will be permitted to visit. Furthermore, you may not come and go as you please. If you should venture out, Mr. Finch will not permit you to reenter our home."

Good God. "I shall be a prisoner in this house?"

"On the contrary," she said. "You are free—nay, encouraged—to go at any time. However, if you do, you shall not come back."

"But I don't have any of my things with me," he sputtered. "Not even a change of clothes."

"What a pity. It seems your stay with us may be shorter than you'd anticipated." She blinked innocently.

"I don't intend to change my plans. If I'm not permitted to send for additional clothes, I shall avail myself of your staff to wash the ones I have with me."

She smiled as though she'd just declared *checkmate*. "And what will you wear while your clothes are being laundered?"

He *knew* he shouldn't say what he was thinking—but damned if he could stop himself. "*Nothing*, Miss Lacey. Because of the terms you've laid out, I shall be forced to take my meals, go about my business, and conduct my daily activities as naked as the day I was born."

She blushed crimson all the way to the roots of her hair. "You are beyond the pale."

"Parts of me are," he said with a shrug. "As you shall soon see for yourself."

Chapter SEVEN

Julie clenched her fists, closed her eyes, and counted to three in her head. When she thought she might be able to speak in a civil tone, she said, *"Fine.* I will make one exception. When you send word to your brother requesting the deed, you may also ask your valet to bring you a bag."

"If you are certain," Lord Travis said lightly, as though it mattered not to him. Did *nothing* matter to him?

Worrying her bottom lip, she added, "Can you trust him to be discreet?"

Sam barked a laugh. "There is no valet in London who's more discreet. Ralph could be tortured within an inch of his life, and he *still* would not reveal the depths of my depravity." More seriously, he added, "He's an honorable man, and if I ask him to safeguard a secret, you may count on him to take it to his grave."

"I doubt it will come to that, but I must remind you that my reputation and my family's name is at stake."

Heavens, she was already regretting her decision. She was regretting a great many things that had taken place that morning.

"I understand," he said soberly. "And I will not forget it. Now, if you don't mind, I'll make use of your writing supplies and send a message to my brother's house at once."

When he would have walked past her toward the desk in the corner, she boldly pressed her palm to his chest, effectively stopping him in his tracks. Through the soft cambric of his shirt, she felt hard muscles and warm flesh. But she felt something else wholly unexpected—his heartbeat galloping wildly beneath her fingertips.

She searched his vexingly handsome face, trying to make sense of it. The centers of his eyes turned dark, and his lips parted as though he were on the verge of . . . that is, it almost seemed as if he were about to . . . *nonsense*.

But there was no denying the pounding in his chest—it mirrored her own. Could he be more nervous than he let on . . . or was he was as affected by their proximity as she?

Either way, it was imperative that she remained focused. Which meant banishing these sorts of dangerous, wayward thoughts.

He dropped his gaze to her hand resting on his chest and arched a brow. "I thought we'd concluded our negotiations."

"There's one more important caveat," she said firmly.

"Ah, like any skilled negotiator, you're aware that the devil is in the details."

She smiled sweetly. "I rather thought he was in my parlor."

"Well done, Miss Lacey," he said, grinning. "What else do you wish to stipulate?"

"It's simple. Uncle Alistair may not know what you are about. If he should have even an inkling that you are here for the purpose of tossing him out of his house, he'd be utterly distraught. We will tell him that you're—"

"Juliette!" a gravelly voice called from the hall. "It sounds as though you have a visitor. Has someone come to call?"

Julie backed away from Lord Travis as though she'd touched a hot stove instead of a man's chest. "Yes, Uncle," she said with forced cheer. "We're in the parlor."

How had matters spiraled so out of control? She gripped the back of the settee as a tidal wave of panic threatened to sweep her away.

Lord Travis grasped her upper arms, instantly steadying her. "We'll tell him the house renovation story," he said reassuringly.

"What? No." They required a more convincing explanation.

"Trust me." Releasing her suddenly, he turned and began rooting through Beth's old sewing basket on the floor.

"What are you *doing*?" she hissed.

"Looking for a cravat." With a mumbled curse, he yanked a large piece of fabric out of an embroidery hoop and threw it around his neck. It was much too short to tie into any semblance of a knot, but he did his best to tuck the ends into his collar.

Julie pressed a palm to her forehead, beyond exasperated. "Are you mad?"

"Who is it, dear?" Her uncle shuffled across the wood floor outside the parlor.

"Here he comes," she whispered, as she valiantly attempted to straighten Lord Travis's makeshift neckcloth and smooth the lapels of his jacket. Pasting on a smile, she called out, "Someone I'd like you to meet."

"Why, this sounds promising." Lord Wiltmore toddled into the parlor wearing a grin that split his wizened face. "I know I implored you to find a husband this morning, but I didn't expect you to accomplish the feat during my nap."

"Now, Uncle," she scolded affectionately, "you mustn't embarrass me when we have company." She cast a furtive, desperate look at the man who wanted to toss them both out onto the street. "I'd like you to meet Samuel Travis."

"My lord." Sam extended a hand. "The pleasure is mine."

The old man frowned as though trying to recall the name and put it with his face. "Are we grievously acquainted?"

Sam blinked, then recalled that Wiltmore was known for bungling his words. Very aware of Miss Lacey's gaze trained on him, he smiled at the old man as though the sentence he'd uttered was completely coherent. "I have not had the pleasure. However, I understand that we are distant cousins. My grandmother's sister-in-law was your father's aunt." Jesus, he had no idea what he'd just said.

"You don't say." Wiltmore scratched his head, causing the snowy white tufts of hair over his ears to stand on end.

Sam nodded confidently, wishing to hell that the embroidery fabric didn't feel like burlap against his neck. He didn't dare venture a glance at Miss Lacey, who was surely steaming like a teapot.

Wiltmore sank slowly into an armchair upholstered in faded blue brocade. "Your grandmother's sister-in-law was . . . Harriet?"

Sam breathed a sigh of relief—the conversation would have turned extremely awkward if Wiltmore had announced his father had no such relative. At last, *something* today had gone Sam's way. "Yes, I believe Harriet *was* her name—God rest her soul. My grandmother always spoke fondly of her." He rocked on his heels and waited. Lies were similar to wine—once uncorked, they required time and space to breathe.

"Well, this is an unexpected but most pleasant surmise," Wiltmore said, his expression jovial. "My nieces and I haven't much family. Not that I'm complaining, mind you. I'm beyond blessed to have them in my life." He beamed at Miss Lacey like she was the center of his world.

"The feeling is mutual, Uncle." She whisked a wool blanket off a stool, draped it across his lap, and patted his sloped shoulder. "Your nap was exceptionally short today. Would you like to rest your eyes a bit longer? Lord Travis and I could leave you in peace . . ." Her voice trailed off as if she realized that any attempt to delay the inevitable was futile.

"Heavens no, my dear! I'm far too curious about our long-lost cousin." To Sam, he said, "Sit, please, and tell us all about this newly discovered branch of our family tree."

Miss Lacey wrung her hands. "There's not much to tell, is there, Lord Travis?" Good God, she was a noticeably nervous liar . . . which meant she was also a hopelessly *horrible* liar.

Sam sat on a stool opposite Wiltmore and cleared his throat in what was meant to be a signal to Miss Lacey that she should leave the *storytelling*—as it were—to him. "Your lovely niece is correct, in that my side of the family is small. My father died a year ago, and now only my older brother Nigel and I remain."

At the mention of Nigel's name, Miss Lacey stiffened visibly, but she needn't have worried. Sam had no intention of telling Wiltmore that his brother was a marquess. He'd discover that in good time. For now, Sam was sticking to the truth as much as possible—or, at least, some convenient version of it.

"I'm sorry to hear of your father's passing. He couldn't have been very old, and it's especially sad to lose a man who's in the prime of his life." Wiltmore offered his condolences so sincerely that Sam couldn't help but like him. He was the sort of affable, quirky fellow that anyone would wish to have for a grandfather.

But this was no social call, and Sam would do well to remember it.

"Thank you," he said. "I do miss him."

"It's odd, the things you miss about a person, isn't it?" Wiltmore stared straight ahead, as though looking through a window to the past. "My Elspeth used to cut her scone in two. She'd always balk at the size of it, saying she couldn't possibly eat the whole thing, that she only wanted to nibble on a bit of it. But about five minutes after finishing the first half, she'd invariably come back and devour the rest. And when I'd tease her, she'd say she had no choice in the matter—that the remaining half had been calling out to her." The dreamy smile lighting the old man's face said he was still head over heels in love with Elspeth. He shook his head, blinked, and continued. "What do *you* miss—about your father?"

Sam examined the threads of the muted gold carpet, debating how much to reveal. He supposed it couldn't hurt to indulge the old man this once. After all, he needed to gain Wiltmore's trust, and sharing a glimpse of himself could go a long way toward that end.

"My brother and I are only a year apart in age," he began, "but we are a world apart in temperament. Nigel is good and honorable and decent, and I am . . . well, I'm not. My father was the bridge between us, always able to help one of us cross to the other's side. Within minutes of a knock-down, drag-out fight, he'd make us laugh so hard that we'd forget what we'd been arguing about. I miss many things about my father . . . but more than anything, I miss the way he could span the gap between Nigel and me." Sam reached into his pocket, pulled out the watch that had once belonged to his father, and absently rubbed his thumb over the warm gold casing. The watch was Sam's most prized possession—not because of its significant monetary value, but because his father had treasured it. "My mother gave him this." Sam held the watch up by its chain, admiring the way it glinted in the sunlight. "Not long before she died, as she gave birth to me."

Sam looked up to see Wiltmore nodding sadly and Miss Lacey hanging on every word. Their scrutiny left him feeling uncomfortably exposed—like he'd walked out his front door without putting on his trousers.

"Grief's tentacles wrap around us in unexpected ways," Wiltmore said sagely. "A situation will arise, and I'll think, Elspeth will know what to do. Or I'll read an amusing passage and bookmark the page to show her. And each time, after I recall that she's left this world, my heart breaks a little more."

Standing beside his chair, Miss Lacey sniffled. Sam instinctively reached for the crisp handkerchief in his jacket and handed it to her.

Her brow creased as though she couldn't quite believe a scoundrel like him was capable of the smallest kindness. "Thank you."

"Of course." Sam tucked the watch in his pocket and mentally reminded himself why he was there.

Wiltmore reached up and squeezed Miss Lacey's hand as he continued to address Sam. "I'd like to say the pain lessens over time, but . . . you know the way of it." Smiling weakly, he shook his head, mentally scolding himself. "Enough of that. From where do you and your brother hail?"

"We live here, in town." It took Sam a moment to realize this was precisely the opening he needed to launch the fib about renovations driving him out of his own home. "However, I—"

"Lord Travis has very recently returned from the Continent," Miss Lacey interrupted—damn it all.

"On a Grand Tour, were you?" Wiltmore slapped his knee, enthused. "You must tell me your impressions of

the great masterpieces and ruins. I'm particularly interested in artifacts—did you bring any home with you,
perchance?"

Sam didn't have the heart to tell the old man that
he'd spent far more time in pleasure haunts than he had
at archaeological sites. "No, but I did climb Mount
Vesuvius."

Wiltmore gasped. "Fascinating!"

Sam supposed it had been. But not even the steady
diet of culture, art, and antiquities could fill the hole in
his chest. All he'd wanted to do was return to the place
where his father's memory was strongest—home.

And when he had, nothing was the same.

"Yes," Sam replied, thoughtful. "The ruins at Pom-
peii were a potent reminder that life can change in an
instant. The eerie, unnatural stillness of that city made
me long for the bustle of London . . . and I returned to
England's fair shores at the first opportunity."

Wiltmore's eyes gleamed as though he were imagining it all and, at the same time, formulating a long and
varied list of questions.

Which meant Sam must make his move *now* and tell
his renovation tale before Wiltmore launched his first
question. "Interestingly, when I arrived home I found
that—"

"—he had developed a new appreciation for the sciences," Miss Lacey interjected.

What the *devil* was she doing?

"Wonderful!" The old man nodded appreciatively.

"Yes." She hazarded a glance at Sam then quickly
looked away. Lord Travis has decided to devote himself
to . . . research."

Holy hell. Desperate to reverse the conversation, he jumped in. "Actually, I haven't completely decided on a course of action—"

"Which is why Lord Travis would like to act as your assistant."

Chapter EIGHT

Sam loosened the bloody embroidery cloth around his neck. "I'm afraid I'm not in *any* way qualified to—"

"Nonsense," Miss Lacey said, cutting him off once more. "You're being far too humble, my lord."

"I have many faults, Miss Lacey," he said through clenched teeth. "But an excess of humility is not one of them."

"Never fear," she said, not daring to look at him. "Your lack of experience is not a deterrent. You will help my uncle organize his research, and he will serve as your mentor. Perhaps your experiences abroad will even shed light on certain subjects—or support my uncle's findings. It's such an exciting proposition, don't you agree?"

Sam blinked at her, dumbfounded. She *really* should have left the lying to him.

An aversion to dust and noise was far more believable than his sudden, newfound passion for science.

"It's an extremely generous offer, but I cannot accept.

I would only be in Lord Wiltmore's way . . . slowing things down," he stammered.

"A slow, methodical approach is actually best," Wiltmore countered. "And it *would* be immensely helpful to have someone to discuss my findings with. Juliette is a wonderful listener, but I fear that one of these nights she shall keel over from boredom."

"Never," she quickly assured him. "However, Lord Travis would offer a fresh perspective."

Sam should have responded in the negative, but from the moment that her uncle had spoken her given name—Juliette—he'd been driven to distraction. The lilting, intimate sound of it echoed in his head like a melody begging to be sung . . . or like a poem that left a lump in one's throat.

"I quite agree," Wilmore said magnanimously. "Lord Travis, you are welcome to join me and wade into the scientific waters any time you wish."

"Please, call me Samuel," he replied, grateful that the old man hadn't immediately dragged him to his study and begun reading scientific treatises. "I will give the matter serious thought."

"Oh, come now," Juliette scolded. "You'll never learn anything worthwhile while acting in half-measures. You must immerse yourself in research in order to make genuine progress." She swallowed nervously, then turned to her uncle and pressed on. "In fact, now that I think on it, Cousin Samuel should stay here with us for a few days. What better way for him to begin his apprenticeship than by diving in?"

Good God. The last thing in hell he wanted was to be someone's apprentice. But he *might* enjoy spending time with Juliette. Perhaps she'd let him mentor *her* in a few choice activities . . .

"I have no objection," Wiltmore said, snapping Sam to the present. "The house has felt terribly empty since Margaret and Elizabeth married and set up their own households. Juliette shall soon do the same, I hope. And then, it will be only Elspeth and I again—just like old times. However, in the meantime, it would be grand to have another man in the house." In a stage whisper he added, "Someone I may sneak a cigar with."

"Don't you dare," Juliette said, softening the admonition with a kiss to her uncle's cheek. "You know cigars don't agree with you."

Wiltmore winked at Sam. "Now you see why I must sneak them. In any event, I look forward to learning more about your branch of the family tree and furthering our complacence. You must make yourself at home here—you are kin, after all."

Juliette clamped her lips together clearly struggling to remain silent in the face of such a distasteful falsehood. One would have thought her uncle had just announced they were descendants of Attila the Hun.

"Thank you, my lord," Sam said as graciously as he could—considering he'd been strong-armed into serving as a research assistant by a woman too clever and attractive for her own good. Sam leaned forward and shook the old man's hand, effectively sealing the deal.

"Juliette will have a room prepared for you." The old man smiled proudly. "She runs this household quite efficiently and will happily see to your every need."

Sam arched a brow at her. Couldn't help it. He was

already mentally enumerating his needs—most too wicked to mention.

She pretended to ignore him, but a telltale blush stole up her neck like an incoming tide.

"Would you like to clear a space in your study where you and your new apprentice can conduct your research?" she suggested to her uncle. "I could send Mr. Finch in to assist you while I ensure Cousin Samuel is settled."

"A capital idea, my dear!" Wiltmore pushed himself to his feet and ambled toward the door. "Imagine," he said more to himself than to anyone else, "what a serendipitous thing, having Samuel appear on our doorstep this afternoon. Elspeth, do I have you to thank for this seemingly fortuitous event?"

Juliette busied herself with plumping and straightening the pillows on the settee—as though it were perfectly normal for a man to carry on a conversation with his dead wife.

Dear Jesus. The rumors about Wiltmore being mad were true.

And Sam was going to be spending several hours a day with him, which meant he'd soon be ready for Bedlam too.

Sam managed to contain his anger until Wiltmore left the parlor—then shoved himself out of his chair and strode to the settee beside Juliette. "What the *devil* were you thinking, volunteering me as your uncle's apprentice?"

"Shh," she said, casting a nervous glance at the door. "He'll hear you."

"You should have discussed the idea with me beforehand," he sputtered.

"It popped into my head at the last moment. And I think it was rather brilliant." She leaned back against a worn cushion, beaming with triumph.

Sam sat beside her, closed his eyes, and imagined being cooped up in the old man's stuffy study for hours on end, listening to tedious lectures concerning God only knew what—the digestive systems of mollusks . . . the mating habits of beetles . . . He broke into a cold sweat. "I can't do it. I was never a very apt student."

She picked an invisible piece of lint from her skirt. "I cannot say I'm shocked. But a short apprenticeship is hardly cause for alarm. Heavens, you'd think I'd enlisted you to fight with the British army."

"Enduring enemy gunfire might be preferable to deciphering scientific formulas," he muttered, raking a hand through his hair.

Smiling with false sweetness, she said, "You are most welcome to join the cavalry any time you wish."

He moved closer, forcing her to meet his gaze. "You'd like that, wouldn't you?"

She shrugged her delicate shoulders. "I certainly wouldn't attempt to stop you."

"And the moment I stepped foot outside this house, you'd no doubt barricade the door."

She tilted her head, pretending to consider his words. "It's difficult to predict what I would do. However, if you'd like, we can put your theory to the test."

Damn, she was beautiful—and too stubborn by half. Her full lips were pressed into a straight line, and her captivating eyes sparked with defiance. But she knew very well that he wouldn't walk out the front door. He wouldn't shirk his responsibility or fail his brother—not this time.

"I'm afraid you won't rid yourself of me that easily . . . Juliette."

Her composure fled instantly, and her cheeks flushed pink. "I-I have not given you leave to address me by my given name."

True, but Miss Lacey sounded too prim and starchy. Juliette, on the other hand, perfectly captured her grace and passion.

He stretched an arm behind her, resting it on the back of the settee. "I shall be living here—assisting your uncle, apparently—for several days at least. Given the circumstances, I see no reason to stand on ceremony. Besides," he said glibly, "we're cousins."

"*Cousins?*" she repeated, incredulous. "Apparently you've lost track of where your falsehoods end and reality begins. Have you forgotten that our *supposed* mutual relation—your dear great aunt Harriett—is a figment of your imagination? Merely one of the many lies you told my uncle?"

Sam swallowed. No, he hadn't forgotten.

And he sure as hell wasn't having cousinly thoughts at the moment.

Juliette was so close that the citrusy scent of her hair enveloped him, and the slight pulse beating at the base of her throat entranced him. Though she may have been his adversary, all he wanted to do was to brush aside the errant chestnut curl that skimmed her shoulder and press his lips to the satin skin of her neck.

Maybe a few days trapped in this house wouldn't be as torturous as he'd feared.

She leaned toward him, giving him an excellent view of her round breasts straining against the confines of her silk gown. "Have you heard a word I've said?" she demanded.

He lifted his eyes to hers. "I have. You don't want me to address you as Juliette."

"And you will respect my wishes?" she asked warily.

"Of course." He stretched out his legs and crossed them at the ankles. "But since I'm averse to addressing you as Miss Lacey, I shall have to think of another name for you. Something more fitting."

"Your manners leave much to be desired," she said, clearly piqued.

He rubbed his chin thoughtfully. "Don't fret. I've already conceived of the perfect name."

With a toss of her head, she sniffed. "Congratulations, but I have no interest in hearing it."

"No? Suit yourself then . . . *spitfire.*"

Julie narrowed her eyes. "Perhaps other women of your acquaintance are charmed by your utter lack of decorum, but allow me to assure you that I am not similarly affected." She'd had the upper hand for all of two minutes before Lord Travis had managed to wriggle under her skin again.

"Forgive me." Despite a valiant attempt to keep a straight face, his eyes crinkled in a vexingly appealing manner. "Like it or not, we have an arrangement of sorts. I thought we should be on more familiar terms."

"We do *not* have an arrangement," she countered, even as she dragged her gaze from his impossibly muscled thighs.

"Fine," he amended. "We are working together for our mutual benefit."

"No, we're perpetrating a lie because you've placed me in an untenable position."

"I wish it didn't have to be this way." He stretched, letting his arm rest on the back of the settee behind her, and his fingertips brushed against her shoulders—incidentally perhaps . . . it was difficult to be sure. Either way, the slightest touch had made her body thrum. "But we might as well make the best of the situation . . . *vixen*."

Her eyes widened. "Stop that at once."

"I was only jesting," he said, grinning.

But he did have a point about their temporary alliance, blast it all. Regrettably, they would be spending an inordinate amount of time together, and until she could prove that Uncle Alistair was the rightful owner of this house, she had no choice but to trust Lord Travis. With one careless action or word, he could ruin her. Indeed, the shattering of reputations was all in a day's work for an unapologetic rogue.

But she had no intention of falling victim, to either him *or* his charms.

"I am willing to form a truce with you," she said, striving to keep her voice icy.

"Excellent," he said smoothly. Hopefully. "There's no reason we can't make the next few days . . . pleasurable."

Oh dear. "I'd prefer *amicable*."

"Why split hairs?" he said, as if there were no distinction at all. "In any event, allow me to extend the first olive branch and make a gesture of good will. Simply tell me what you would like me to do."

"Very well." She sat a little straighter and folded her hands in her lap. "You may begin by acting the part of a gentleman."

"Happy to oblige." He pulled in his legs and squared his shoulders. "How am I doing so far?"

She cast a critical eye over him, from his slightly long sandy brown hair to the toes of his expensive boots. "Marginally better. However, there is still the matter of your cravat. I'm certain I don't need to tell you my sister's embroidery cloth is hardly an acceptable substitute."

"You are correct," he intoned formally. "I shall remove the offensive garment at once."

Good heavens. As he grasped the cloth from behind his neck, she reached out with both hands to hold it in place. After all, a makeshift cravat was better than none at all. "That won't be necessary," she said quickly.

But she was too late.

As he yanked the cloth free, it slid from beneath her fingers, leaving her palms on the tanned, warm skin of his neck and chest. Lord help her.

Stunned, she momentarily froze while Lord Travis lightly circled her wrists with his hands and tugged her closer.

"I'm trying to act like a gentleman," he said hoarsely, "but it's damned difficult in the face of so much temptation." He stared at her lips, and her traitorous heart leapt in response.

"It wasn't my intention to encourage you," she whispered—but made no move to pull away.

"Perhaps not," he breathed, "but you have earned yourself another name nonetheless . . . temptress."

Chapter NINE

"I know what you're doing," Julie said coolly, as though touching a man's bare neck was as commonplace for her as mending a sock.

"Tell me what I'm doing," Lord Travis murmured, "because I have no idea." His large hands still circled her wrists loosely, and his dark eyes searched her face.

"You are addressing me in a most indecorous manner, using highly improper names, so that your earlier request—to call me Juliette—will seem more palatable by comparison."

"Is it working?" His deep voice, low and intimate, sent odd shivers through her body.

"Of course not. You shall not bully me into changing my mind."

"Then I shall have to persuade you using other means." His heavy-lidded gaze suggested he intended to employ his wickedest methods—and she wished she wasn't desperately curious as to what they might be.

"I am not easily manipulated, Lord Travis," she said, conveniently ignoring the fact that she was almost sitting in his lap.

"A moment ago, you called me Samuel," he countered.

She sniffed. "I addressed you as *Cousin* Samuel. Besides, we were in the presence of my Uncle. I was merely keeping up the charade."

"Fine. You may call me anything you like. Scoundrel, rake, sinner—take your pick."

"I think not." She tried not to stare at the light stubble on his chin. Tried not to think about what it might feel like beneath her lips. "You would probably consider any of them to be compliments."

"No," he said soberly. "But I've become accustomed to such labels."

"Are they true?" The question had tumbled out of her mouth of its own accord. And yet she held her breath, awaiting his answer.

"Yes, they're true." He tugged her closer and touched his forehead to hers. Their breath mingled in the space between them. "At least ninety percent of the time."

"So you are a rogue ninety percent of the time," she repeated softly. "What are you the rest of the time?"

He released one of her wrists and brushed a thumb along the curve of her cheek. "I suppose that's what I'm trying to find out."

His words, spoken so earnestly, melted away her willpower, and she sank into his chest. His lips were a hair's breadth away from hers. He slid his hand to her nape and traced little circles on her sensitive skin. The lightest of touches, and yet, she felt it throughout her body.

Her belly somersaulted, her heart pounded, and the tips of her breasts tingled deliciously.

"Juliette." He closed his eyes and tilted his head—
Knock. Knock.

Good heavens. They had a visitor. At the front door. While Julie was on the verge of kissing a notorious rogue. On the settee in her parlor.

Leaping off of him, she called, "I'll answer the door, Mr. Finch." While she frantically straightened her dress and smoothed her hair, she cast a pleading glance at Lord Travis. "I'm going to send the caller away. All I ask is that you remain silent and out of sight. No one may know you are here."

He had the nerve to look amused. "A moment ago you were about to kiss me. Now I am a source of embarrassment?"

She rolled her eyes dramatically. "You know very well that I—"
Knock. Knock. Knock.

Pressing a hand to her chest, she ordered, "Just stay quiet and do *not* move from that spot."

"Yes, ma'am," he said obediently. Then he clamped his mouth shut, leaned back on the settee, and sprawled his legs as though he was relaxing in his gentlemen's club. As though he hadn't been wielding his considerable charms in an attempt to seduce her—and evict her at the very same time.

She must have been mad to even *consider* kissing him. But there would be plenty of time for self-recrimination and hair shirts later.

The first order of business was ridding herself of this visitor.

Quickly, she moved around the corner to the front door and placed a hand on the handle, pausing a moment to collect herself. She hadn't been expecting callers, and yet, the second of the day was apparently on her doorstep.

Taking a deep breath, she pulled the door halfway open and saw Meg's dear friend—the governess who'd introduced Meg to her now-husband, the Earl of Castleton.

"Charlotte!" Julie exclaimed. "What are you doing here?"

The governess angled through the small opening, pulled Julie into a warm hug, and giggled. "Not the most gracious of greetings, but I shall forgive you. Your lapse in manners is no doubt due to a lack of companionship. You must be terribly lonely with both of your sisters gone." She released Julie and immediately began untying her bonnet. As if she intended to stay a while.

Oh dear.

Julie forced a chuckle and tried to block the entrance to the parlor. "Yes, please forgive me. But we're actually quite content—Uncle Alistair and I, that is. I mean, who else could I possibly be referring to?" Good lord, she was a dreadful liar.

"I can't imagine." Charlotte shot her a curious look. "Are you feeling well? Has anything of import happened here since Beth left on her honeymoon?"

"No!" Julie replied—a bit too vehemently. "Uncle Alistair and I have decided to undertake a project of sorts."

"Oh? That sounds interesting. You must tell me all about it." Charlotte hung her bonnet on a hook in the hall and inched her way toward the parlor—and the rake who'd taken up residence on her settee.

Julie slid in front of her. "I would love to, however, I promised Uncle Alistair I'd help him with . . . something . . . in his study."

Charlotte slid her shawl off her shoulders and draped it over another hook. "Perhaps I could assist as well. Or at least pay him a quick visit. How has his health been?"

"Fine," Julie assured her. "Or rather, the same."

Frowning, Charlotte peered past Julie into the parlor. "Have I come at an inconvenient time? I could return tomorrow if you wish."

"No. I mean, you needn't bother to return. All is well here," Julie said with false brightness. "In fact, I—"

Charlotte planted her hands on her hips, narrowed her eyes, and glared down her nose. Every inch the quintessential governess, she intoned, "Miss Juliette Lacey, step aside at once and permit me to enter your parlor so that we may enjoy a cup of tea like two civilized persons instead of conversing in the hall like heathens."

Julie swallowed. Her friend's curiosity had been piqued, and sending her away would only raise her suspicions. But if Charlotte had any inkling that a half-dressed bachelor was lounging in the Lacey sisters' parlor, she'd take it upon herself to string him up by his boots *and* march Julie straight to the nearest convent.

"You are a dear to worry about me," Julie said soothingly. "But I am not a six-year-old in need of minding."

"No, you are my best friend's youngest sister, and we both know that a little minding wouldn't be amiss."

"Charlotte, you're being ridic—"

Before Julie could finish, Charlotte swept past her toward the parlor.

Oh no. The whole morning had been a nightmare, and surely this was the moment Julie would wake up screaming. Because the second her well-meaning friend laid eyes on Lord Travis, all would be lost. Charlotte would alert Meg, who'd feel the need to return to London at once in spite of her doctor's orders to avoid travel. Then Meg would write to Beth, who would cut short her honeymoon so she could lend her support. And both her sisters would be distraught over the news that Uncle Alistair might soon be displaced—forced to leave the home that was as much a part of him as his wizened face, kind smile, or his untamed, white hair.

Charlotte would never be taken in by the falsehood that Julie had created. The perceptive governess would see right through the tale of Lord Travis's apprenticeship as easily as she saw through a far-fetched excuse for a student's tardiness.

Dear God. Julie took a step back, closed her eyes, and braced herself for Charlotte's reaction. She would soon discover that Julie harbored a disheveled rogue in the parlor.

It would take the governess all of five seconds to deduce he was recovering from a night of excess, or worse—from an interrupted morning tryst. He had the arrogant, devil-may-care look of a man who'd been forced to make a hasty departure through a bedchamber window.

The sight was sure to shock Charlotte, and Julie prepared for anything from a gasp to a scream to a swoon.

"Julie . . ." Charlotte said curiously as she entered the parlor. "What, in heaven's name, is going on here?"

Wringing her hands, Julie rushed into the room behind the governess. "I know it looks bad, but it's not what you—"

The settee was empty. The window was open. A warm but gusty breeze blew sheet music, letters, and Uncle Alistair's scribblings all over the room.

And the rogue was nowhere to be found.

Chapter TEN

Sam hit the floor behind the settee and stifled a curse. He was too old, too jaded, and too damned hungover to hide from would-be chaperones. Especially when he hadn't even *done* anything terribly improper with Juliette—at least not by his standards.

He'd *wanted* to do plenty, though.

And she had too, in spite of herself. The telltale signs of desire were all there. Her slender fingers had curled into his shoulders, her breath had hitched in her throat, and her eyes had turned dark.

For a few moments on the settee, she'd almost forgotten that she hated him.

But the knock on the door had broken that tenuous spell.

He'd listened intently to the muffled conversation, and when he'd realized Juliette was unable to turn the caller away, his first instinct had been to flee. He couldn't say why, exactly. *His* reputation would not have suffered if he'd been discovered with Juliette. He certainly didn't give a fig what anyone thought of him.

But he didn't want to make more trouble for her. He was causing her enough already.

Besides, they had a deal of sorts.

So he'd bolted for the window and had one foot slung over the sill when he remembered what she'd said—that if he left the house, she wouldn't allow him back in. There hadn't been time to close the window before the visitor, Charlotte, pushed her way past Juliette, so Sam had left it open and dove to the floor, where he was reduced to spying on their slippers and eavesdropping.

"Papers are blowing everywhere!" Charlotte exclaimed. "And what did you mean when you said it's not what I think?"

"Did I say that? It was rather stuffy in here this morning, so I opened the window a crack." Juliette's pretty pink slippers padded across the room, the window slammed shut, and the lock clicked. As if there were any doubt as to how badly she wished to be rid of him. She was probably smiling ear to ear, thinking of him landing headfirst in a shrub outside.

"That was more than a crack, Julie. A sheep could have leaped through that opening without any trouble at all. Look at this mess!"

Sam held his breath as both women fluttered about the room, retrieving papers. It was only a matter of time before his hiding spot was discovered, and Juliette would be humiliated. He made himself as small as he could—which was not small enough for the settee to conceal him entirely. And when Juliette stooped to pick up some sheet music by his head he gave her a mock salute—nearly causing her to jump out of her skin.

She fumbled with the papers in her hand and quickly steered Charlotte away from him. "Let's not fuss over this now," Juliette said. "Please sit, and tell me why you've come."

"I confess the governess in me will have a hard time relaxing so long as the room is untidy."

"You are forgetting two things," Juliette said. "First, you are not *my* governess, and second, it's your day off. Honestly, Charlotte, the world won't fall apart just because a few papers are out of place."

"If you say so," the governess said, clearly skeptical. She rounded the settee, and sat next to Juliette.

The ensuing clink of china and silver reminded Sam that he was still hungry, and he hoped Charlotte wouldn't eat all the tarts. At least he'd avoided detection—for now. He carefully rolled onto his back and tried to make himself more comfortable among the dust balls on the hardwood floor. He had to agree with the governess on one point—the place could use some tidying up.

"You're sure you haven't been too lonely?" Charlotte asked.

"I miss my sisters," Juliette confessed, "but how could I be sad where they're both so blissfully happy?"

Charlotte sighed. "I can't believe you're the last remaining Lacey sister."

"Don't say that!" Juliette coughed as though part of her scone had caught in her throat. "Meg and Beth are married—not dead."

"Yes. Well, your turn is coming. I can feel it," the governess said confidently.

"I am in no hurry to join their ranks," Juliette assured her.

"Oh, I know. But that's just when you're most likely to be swept off your feet. I predict you'll have many gentlemen vying for the honor."

"That's kind of you to say, but I am content for now. Uncle Alistair needs me, and I want to help Meg when the baby arrives, and Beth—"

"Go to a ball with me tonight," Charlotte interrupted.

"*What*?"

"Lady Breckinridge is hosting. I realize it's terribly short notice, but simply don a beautiful gown and come with me. I am confident you shall not regret it."

"How can you be so confident?" Juliette asked suspiciously.

"It's my understanding a certain gentleman will be in attendance," the governess replied, causing Sam's ears to perk up. So Juliette had set her cap for someone. It shouldn't surprise him—that's what young, gorgeous unmarried misses did. What *did* surprise him was the stab of jealousy in his gut.

"I don't know who you could possibly be referring to," Juliette sputtered nervously. Odd, that.

"Oh, I think you do. I'm talking about the—"

"Do not speak his name!" she blurted. "That is, I would rather not discuss him."

The governess chuckled softly. "Fine. But you needn't be coy. I saw the two of you waltzing at the masquerade ball. The dreamy look on your face as he twirled you around the dance floor spoke volumes."

Sam checked the urge to snort. Had Juliette's expression been dreamy moments ago? When he'd been on the verge of kissing her? He wished to hell he could have that moment back—he wouldn't waste it a second time.

Juliette sniffed. "Your romantic imaginings are completely unfounded."

"You are a deplorable liar," Charlotte countered, causing Sam to nod in hearty agreement. "But you needn't worry. Your secret is safe with me. I wouldn't dream of mentioning your beau to your sisters . . . as long as you agree to accompany me to the ball tonight."

Just when it seemed Julie's day couldn't get any worse, her sister's dearest friend and confidante had resorted to *blackmail*.

But Julie couldn't possibly attend a ball tonight. Not if it would mean leaving Lord Travis alone in the house with Uncle Alistair—it would be a classic case of the rogue guarding the henhouse. No, it would never do.

And yet, Julie *had* to get rid of Charlotte—quickly. As long as Lord Travis was sprawled on the floor behind them, every minute of the governess's visit was fraught with danger. Especially when she might unknowingly spill Julie's history with his brother, the marquess. The rogue already had her back against the wall. Revealing her tryst with his brother would be akin to handing him a pistol.

And all of that aside . . . she didn't want Lord Travis to know. She didn't want him to know that she'd allowed the fickle marquess to pull her close and whisper her name and brush his lips over hers. That she'd melted into him and sighed as he slid his hands around her waist . . . and lower, over the curve of her bottom.

She certainly didn't want Lord Travis to know she'd

foolishly imagined that his brother might care for her and respect her and properly court her—when that hadn't been the case at all.

To make matters worse, she'd almost kissed the rogue. Surely Sam's resemblance to the marquess was to blame. In that moment, she'd been remembering the heady feelings on the terrace with Nigel—when he'd promised her the moon. Or had she?

Gathering her wits, Julie exhaled slowly. "Charlotte, I'd love to attend the ball with you—"

"Excellent, then it's all settled."

"—but I can't. I told Uncle Alistair I'd assist him in his study this evening."

Charlotte clucked her tongue. "A poor excuse. He will likely be asleep before the ball begins."

Drat. "Perhaps, but I think I should stay with him all the same. He's been a little wheezy of late."

"Then instruct Mr. Finch to send him some willow bark tea before bed. He will be fine," Charlotte said, adamant. "It's been weeks since you enjoyed the social whirl. I know how you love a fancy ball, and tonight you shall—with me. Of course, if you refuse, I could write to your sisters and tell them you've been despondent ever since the masquerade ball when you and—"

"Stop!" Julie's heartbeat pounded in her ears. "I will go with you."

Charlotte clapped her hands in glee. "We'll bring the carriage 'round at nine o'clock."

"You are shameless. And I can see why you're such a good governess," Julie added grudgingly. "You have an impressive talent for imposing your will on others."

"Thank you." Charlotte stood and smoothed her skirt. "On that note, I shall take my leave."

Julie's heart leaped into her throat—again—as she prayed that the rogue behind the settee would continue to go undetected. "In spite of your bullying, I know that you mean well," she said, slowly guiding Charlotte toward the front door, "and I adore you for it. Now, tell me which of your gowns you intend to wear this eve—"

Cough.

Oh no. Lord Travis must have succumbed to the dust.

Julie held her breath as the governess whirled back toward the parlor, eyes narrowed. "What was that?"

Pressing a hand to her chest, Julie cleared her throat, then coughed a little for good measure. "This? Just the remnants of a head cold. Nothing to be concerned about."

Charlotte arched a brow and pursed her lips, skeptical.

"Honestly, I am fine." Julie inched toward the door, but Charlotte's slippers remained rooted to the floor.

"Something strange is afoot here," she said softly.

"You've been reading too many gothic novels." Julie laughed nervously as she handed Charlotte her bonnet and opened the front door. "Now enjoy your afternoon, and I shall see you in a scant few hours."

Once Charlotte was gone, Julie sagged against the front door, willing her heartbeat to return to normal. She replayed their conversation in her head, wondering how much of it Lord Travis had been able to piece together. When she thought she could face him again without bursting into flames, she made her way back to the parlor.

He stood leaning over the settee, his muscled arms braced on the curved back, looking far too attractive for someone who'd spent the last half hour lying on the floor.

"So," he drawled, "you have a beau. You might have told me earlier. You know, before I almost kissed you."

Chapter ELEVEN

"I don't have a beau," Juliette countered, but she wouldn't meet Sam's gaze.

"Your friend seems to think you do. Or, at the very least, that the gentleman has captured your affections." Sam hoped it was someone worthy of her. Someone who'd appreciate her loyalty and passion and not try to snuff it out.

Juliette began scooping the remaining papers off the parlor floor. "Charlotte is mistaken. But if I *did* have a beau, he would be no concern of yours. You may be staying here for a short while—a *very* short while—but that doesn't give you the right to pry into my personal affairs."

Sam stooped, retrieved a page of sheet music from beneath the settee, and handed it to her. "Perhaps not," he said. "But you cannot blame me for being curious."

"There is a whole host of things I could blame you for," she retorted. "And curiosity is the least of them. I

hope you realize we had a very close call just now. Charlotte knows something is amiss."

He shrugged. "No harm was done. You'll go to the
ball with her this evening, and all will be forgotten."

Juliette snorted. "I'm not going to the ball."

A tiny part of him was relieved. He didn't relish the
prospect of being stuck in the house, twiddling his
thumbs while she danced the evening away in the arms
of another man. But the governess had seemed adamant.
"You should go," he said half-heartedly.

"And leave you here to your own devices? I think not."

Ah, so that was the crux of it. "You don't trust me."

She froze and pinned him with an icy stare. "You've
given me no reason to trust you."

True enough. He wondered what it would take. "So
you plan to beg off?"

She sighed. "I'll wait a couple of hours and send word
to Charlotte that I've developed a headache."

"A headache?" he repeated, scoffing. "She's already
suspicious. You'll need a better excuse than that."

"By all means, give me your suggestions. I've told
more lies in the course of this day than I have in the
past two decades. I might as well end it in a spectacular
fashion."

He rubbed his chin, thoughtful, and realized he
needed a shave—badly. "Allow me to give the matter
some thought. I'll formulate some creative yet believable excuses for you to avoid the ball, and you may take
your pick. But in the meantime, I'd like to send word to
my valet and request a change of clothes."

Juliette blinked. "Yes, of course. I will show you to
your room myself, explain to the staff that you're Uncle

Alistair's temporary assistant, and have a luncheon tray sent up. I think I should like an hour or two of solitude as well. It's been a terribly long day already."

Sam resisted the impulse to gather her in his arms and massage the tension out of her shoulders. He couldn't forget why he was here and what he had to do—evict her and her uncle from their home. Maybe one day she'd find it in her heart to forgive him, but the chances were admittedly slim.

She placed the stack of papers she'd collected on top of the pianoforte and inclined her head toward the door. "Come with me."

He noted the wobbly newel post and the wallpaper peeling at the seams as he followed her up the staircase. But he was soon all-too-pleasantly distracted by the graceful line of her neck and the seductive sway of her hips. When they reached the landing, she led him to a doorway at the corner of the house and waved him in. "I'm certain the accommodations are more modest than you're accustomed to. But in the event that you are dissatisfied, you are free to leave at any time."

He leaned against the doorjamb and folded his arms. "You'd like that, wouldn't you?"

"Of course I would. I'd like nothing better than to have my life return to the way it was this morning—before the hour you arrived on my doorstep."

"Life doesn't work that way, spitfire. We can never go back." What he'd give for the chance to undo some of his misdeeds or to have one more heartfelt conversation with his father.

"No, I suppose we can't." The faraway, wistful look in her eyes made him think she might have regrets too.

He wanted to pull her close and tell her not to fret. Instead, he jabbed a thumb toward the small desk beneath the window. "Do you mind if I avail myself of pen and paper?"

"Please do. And do not forget to ask your brother about the deed. I would like to put this matter behind me as quickly as possible."

She obviously assumed that her uncle's right to the property was superior to any claim Nigel had to it—and for the briefest moment, Sam wished that were true. "Of course. I understand." Impulsively, he reached for the wayward curl that dangled from her temple and swept it away from her cheek. "You should rest. Everything seems less onerous after a nap. Even me."

She seemed to consider this a moment. "Then I should *definitely* nap. But first, I shall have a word with Mr. Finch."

"To have him send up a tray?" Sam was famished.

"Yes," she said, too sweetly. "While I am at it, I shall attempt to explain your presence in this house and—not coincidentally—request that he count the silver."

With that parting shot, she spun on her heel and left him standing there, more than a little smitten with a woman who obviously, and rightfully, detested him.

"Miss Juliette." A gentle but insistent nudge on her shoulder roused her.

Julie rolled onto her back and stretched. "Hmmm?"

"You'll be wanting dinner tonight, won't you?" Her maid, Lucy, scurried across the bedchamber and flung open the doors of the armoire.

"Eventually," Julie murmured. Sparring with the

rogue for the better part of the morning had stirred a whirlwind of emotions within her. She'd spent hours in her room fretting over her predicament before surrendering to exhaustion. And the moment she'd drifted off to sleep, wicked dreams had plagued her. He'd cupped her cheek, his smoldering stare melting away her defenses. She'd kissed him with abandon, letting him lay her back onto the settee and cover her body with his. The warm, solid weight of him had thrilled her, but also made her ache—as though she were positively starved for more of him. Even though she was awake now, her whole body felt flushed and alive and undeniably aroused.

Which was not at all appropriate, given the circumstances.

Lucy held up a red brocade gown—one of Julie's finest. "How's this?"

Reluctantly, she sat up, rubbed the sleep out of her eyes, and considered the dress draped over her maid's arm. The daring neckline, sensuous silk, and decadent color all seemed a bit too much for dinner at home—even though a tiny part of her would have loved to see Lord Travis's face as she walked into the dining room wearing it. "Let's save the red silk for a special occasion." She gestured to the gown hanging on the post at the foot of her bed. "The dress I wore earlier will be fine. I just want to rest a bit longer."

"That will never do. Dinner will be served in a quarter of an hour. And Lord Travis is expecting you." Lucy raised her brows cheekily. "He's a handsome devil, isn't he, miss?"

Julie ignored the question and pressed a hand over her pounding heart. "A quarter of an hour? What time is it?"

"Why, it's almost eight. I thought it best to let you rest up before the ball—which happens to be the perfect occasion for the red silk."

"Ball? But I—" Blast. She'd intended to send a note to Charlotte earlier. Julie leapt out of bed, hurried to the window, and swept aside the curtain with dread. "It's already dark. I wasn't planning to attend the ball, but—"

"No?" Lucy approached from behind and began adjusting Julie's corset. "Lord Travis said you were going with Miss Winters."

Good heavens. The rogue had the audacity to convey her plans to the members of her staff? "Lord Travis doesn't dictate my schedule," Julie said, just as Lucy tugged hard on her corset laces, forcing the air from her lungs. "Not so tight, please."

"Forgive me, miss. I'll loosen this a bit, but the red silk fits you like a glove. We wouldn't want to spoil the lines of the gown with a sagging corset."

Julie turned to face the maid. "The red silk? I thought we'd decided it was going back into the armoire."

"That was before you recalled you were attending the ball." Lucy frowned, clearly confused.

Julie capitulated. "Fine. I'll wear the red silk, but I'm not yet certain I'm attending the ball. I feel a headache coming on."

"Wait till you see yourself in this gown," Lucy said, unceremoniously throwing it over Julie's head. "It will cure your case of the doldrums."

There was no sense in arguing with Lucy, who seemed determined to play either the role of fairy godmother or brothel madam—Julie wasn't certain which. As the maid continued to fuss over her, pinning her curls into submission and debating the merits of pearls versus rubies, Julie considered her own options for the evening. She hated the thought of leaving the rogue alone in the house with her uncle, but Charlotte was bound to be suspicious if she begged off at this late hour. Perhaps more dangerous, however, given the salacious nature of her dreams, was the prospect of spending the entire evening in Lord Travis's company.

"There," Lucy announced proudly. "You look stunning, miss."

Julie turned toward the looking glass and gaped at her reflection, momentarily mute.

"What do you think?" the maid prompted.

"It's all a bit much, isn't it?" Torrents of curls cascaded over one bare shoulder, and a single teardrop pearl was suspended above her breasts, which felt scandalously exposed. The fashionably low neckline of the red brocade gown was fraught with peril. "I feel as though one wrong tug on my hem could result in me revealing much more than is seemly."

The maid waved a dismissive hand. "All the young ladies are wearing such dresses this season."

"Well, I suppose it's some comfort to know I shall not be the only one whose vanity ultimately led to death by humiliation," she replied dryly.

Lucy clucked her tongue. "Goodness, would you look at the time? You're late for dinner. Go join your uncle and Lord Travis. I'll bring a shawl and reticule down to you before you depart for the ball. You're going to have such a grand time! I assume Lord Travis shall be joining you?"

"He certainly shall not!" Julie shuddered at the

thought of the unkempt if devilishly handsome rogue accompanying her and Charlotte into Lady Breckinridge's ballroom. "That is, I am sure he's eager to begin his research with my uncle." Julie blushed to the roots of her hair and prayed that the lying would grow easier over time.

"I see," Lucy said doubtfully. "Do try to enjoy yourself, regardless. You deserve to be the belle of the ball—and you look too beautiful to while away the evening straightening the shelves in your uncle's study."

"Thank you," Julie said sincerely. She exited the room as gracefully as possible, so as not to unduly test the staying power of her gown's neckline. Thankfully, it proved steadfast as she descended the staircase, and she breathed a little easier.

Lord Travis's deep voice came from the direction of the dining room, which meant he and Uncle Alistair awaited her. She paused only a moment before she walked into the cozy if slightly shabby room, her head held high. "Forgive me for keeping you waiting," she said breezily. "I fear I overslept." She moved behind her uncle's chair, bent forward to kiss his cheek—and immediately regretted it.

In hindsight, she shouldn't have complained to Lucy that her corset was too tight.

And she most definitely should have insisted on wearing a dress that utilized more fabric.

With one careless motion, she'd unduly tested the limits of her gown. The bodice shifted, her neckline dipped, and blast it all, one breast slipped free of her corset and shift.

Heaven help her. She frantically adjusted her neckline, yanking the fabric to cover herself. But the damage had already been done. Uncle Alistair was entirely unaware of the slip, but the rogue . . . he'd no doubt seen *everything*.

She wanted to crawl beneath the table and remain there till the entire household slept. Perhaps then she could flee to her bedchamber and lock herself inside for the next decade. But mortified or no, she would not run away from Lord Travis. Closing her eyes briefly, she willed her heartbeat to slow and steeled herself before meeting his gaze.

When she did, she almost forgot her abject humiliation—for the sight of him nearly took her breath away.

Gone was the unshaven, half-dressed rake with mussed hair. In his place stood a tall, impeccably-attired gentleman whose golden-brown hair curled just over his jacket collar and gleamed in the candlelight.

Devastatingly attractive, he looked so much like his brother, Nigel, that Julie might have mistaken him for the marquess—if not for the telltale, wicked gleam in his eyes.

"Good evening, Miss Lacey," he said, his voice impossibly rich and smooth. "There's no need to apologize for your tardiness."

Uncle Alistair chuckled. "I should say not. Every young lady is entitled to make a bland entrance. Isn't that right, Samuel?"

The rogue winked conspiratorially at her uncle before launching the full force of his gaze on her. "The entrance you just made was . . . was . . ."

"Spit it out, man," Uncle Alistair encouraged.

The corner of Lord Travis's mouth curled into a smile that had no doubt seduced scores of innocent maidens. "Let me put it this way. Even if I had been starved of food for an entire fortnight, your entrance would have been well, *well* worth the wait."

Chapter TWELVE

Sam had known—and bedded—many beautiful women in his lifetime.

But he'd never known anyone who compared to Juliette Lacey. True, some women may have been more classically beautiful or more fashionable. Some may have been more sought after.

None, however, possessed Juliette's courage and confidence.

Despite the myriad challenges she'd faced today—most of which had admittedly been spawned by him—she hadn't once swooned or cried or crumpled to the floor.

Even now, when he was certain she wanted to crawl beneath the table, she stood her ground, looking him directly in the eyes.

He wished he could tell her that she had absolutely nothing to be ashamed of. That the glimpse of her nakedness was akin to a glimpse of heaven, and that nothing on earth—no glorious sunset, no work of art—could compare to her beauty. He wanted to tell her to hold her head high. That her daring red gown matched her fiery personality perfectly, and that it was vibrant and unapologetic—just like her.

Instead, he resolved to be a gentleman. At least for the evening. He rounded the end of the table and pulled out her chair, inviting her to sit.

Ever so carefully, she lowered herself onto the seat.

"Why, my dear, you look even lovelier than usual." Wiltmore raised his wineglass toward Juliette in a toast.

"Thank you." She smoothed her napkin across her lap and sipped her wine tentatively, as though doing her best to remain in control in spite of everything. Sam admired that about her. "You look very handsome yourself, Uncle."

"Samuel tells me you plan to attend a ball this evening with Miss Winters."

Juliette shot a withering glance at Sam before pasting a smile on her face and addressing her uncle. "I'm not yet certain of my plans. Charlotte was quite insistent, but I had my heart set on remaining at home tonight. I think I shall tell her that I've developed a headache."

As a footman circled the table serving the first course, Wiltmore shook his head, causing his hair to sway wildly. "That will never do. A headache is far too common an excuse."

"That's what I told her." Sam ignored her incredulous expression and tested the soup, which was delicious.

"A good excuse is less vague and more prolific," Wiltmore expounded.

"Precisely." Sam nodded in agreement. "It must be serious enough that no one will dream of questioning it but not so grave as to cause undue alarm."

Juliette leaned back in her chair and tilted her head in mock interest. "How fortunate it is you are here to enlighten me. Tell me, Cousin Samuel, what excuse would you suggest I give to my sweet friend Charlotte?"

Sam set down his soup spoon and pretended to ponder the question. He'd given the matter some thought while she rested. "Tell her you woke from your nap to find that a particularly horrid spot had suddenly surfaced on your face, and, as a result, you cannot possibly show yourself at the ball." He smiled, wholly satisfied with his efforts. "Do you see what I mean? It's believable without giving your friend reason to worry."

Juliette sniffed. "I would never forgo a ball because of a silly spot, my lord. I am not that shallow—as Charlotte is well aware."

"Very well. We'll need another excuse." Sam drummed his fingers on the table for a few moments, then snapped them triumphantly. "You could tell her that you have seven chapters left in a book you must read before returning it to the lending library—which you intend to do first thing tomorrow morning."

"And what shall I say when she inquires as to the title of the book?"

Wiltmore slurped his soup. "One must anticipate those sorts of oblivious questions."

Sam shrugged. "Make something up."

"No," Juliette said glumly. "Charlotte reads extensively. She'd go looking for the title and discover my lie."

"Never fear." He rubbed his chin as he stared at a hairline crack in the plaster ceiling, hoping for sudden inspiration. "There's one more possibility."

"Which is?" she asked, arching a brow hopefully.

"Simply tell her you've developed a headache."

She tilted her head, perplexed. "And what of your earlier advice—that I should avoid such a common excuse?" Her dress shimmered in the candlelight, and her skin seemed to glow from within. The whole effect was damned dazzling, but Sam did his best to appear unaffected.

"My earlier advice has been trumped by another important theorem: that the best falsehood is the most obvious one," he said.

"Is it, now?" Her eyes sparked with unspoken retorts—barbs she'd no doubt throw if her uncle weren't sitting between them, observing their exchange with keen interest.

"Yes, obvious is best in most situations—at least ninety percent of the time."

"Ninety percent," she repeated through her teeth.

"Quite right," Wiltmore agreed. "It is the same with science. The answer is usually right in front of us. The truth is what's left after we sweep away all the extraneous stuff and distractions. Elspeth reminded me of that principle this morning."

Sam glanced at Juliette over the rim of his glass, but she avoided his gaze. Something told him that the old man hadn't been speaking metaphorically when he'd mentioned his late wife.

"Aunt Elspeth was a wise woman," Juliette said softly. "And speaking of extraneous stuff, there is much we can sweep away in your study. We will begin working in earnest tomorrow. Now that Cousin Samuel is settled," she said pointedly, "the two of you should discuss some of the various topics you've researched. Perhaps he'll be able to help you narrow your focus to the one that will best suit our purpose."

"And what purpose is that?" Sam asked, eyeing the lamb cutlets that the footman offered.

Wiltmore waved a dismissive hand. "Juliette has the wild idea in her head that I should organize and present my findings to the Royal Society."

"Why is it a wild idea?"

Wiltmore blinked as though the question befuddled him. "It's a highly prestigious organization."

"Formed of men—and perhaps a few intrepid women—who are no more worthy than you," Sam said. "They put on their breeches the same way. Not the women, of course. But certainly the men."

"But it's an esteemed group," Wiltmore countered, "whose members have devoted their lives to the sciences and the dispute of knowledge."

"Then that's something else you have in common with them," Sam said. "And another reason they should be delighted to have you join their ranks."

"Do you really think so?" Wiltmore's fuzzy gray eyebrows shot up his forehead.

"I do." Sam sliced into the tender cutlet. "It sounds as though there's some work to be done, but I've no doubt you're up to the task."

In truth, Sam had no idea whether the old man was up to the task—or if he was even in possession of all his faculties. But Sam had little tolerance for exclusive clubs and pretentious societies. Maybe because he'd been tossed out of his fair share.

"Interesting," Wiltmore murmured to himself. "Perhaps this won't be an exercise in fertility after all."

Sam nearly choked on his lamb and reached for his wineglass. Across the table, Juliette covered a smile with her napkin.

And beamed at him as though he'd just performed a minor miracle. Once he'd managed to swallow properly, he smiled back at her. And the look they shared raised the temperature in the dining room by ten degrees.

Sam knew better than to misinterpret the approval in her shining eyes. She was grateful that he'd encouraged her uncle. But his body responded as though she were sending an altogether different signal, making him very glad for the cover that the tablecloth provided. Her gown was the perfect foil for her innocence, leaving just enough to the imagination.

The problem was, his imagination was a bit *too* good. He could feel his palm sliding over silk as he settled his hand at the small of her back. He could smell the citrusy fragrance of her hair and taste the sweetness of her lips.

He wanted her. And though she was principled, she was also passionate enough that he *might* be able to seduce her, given ample time and opportunity. In her case, it would take more than a few pretty words and accidental caresses to do the trick, but he was up to the challenge.

Whether he *should* employ his roguish charm in order to bed her was a different matter entirely. The situation with Juliette was complicated. As far as she was concerned, he was the villain intent on stealing her uncle's house. And regardless of what transpired between Sam and her, he would do what his brother asked of him.

The tenuous truce lasted throughout the remainder of

dinner, until a knock sounded at the front door and Juliette nearly jumped out of her seat. "Is it nine already?"

Wiltmore leaned forward and addressed Juliette in a stage whisper. "Will you plead a headache, my dear? It would be a terrible waste of a dress if you did not offend the ball."

"I think I must go for a short time, at least," she said. "If I were to decline the invitation at this late hour, Charlotte would no doubt march in here and drag me away by my hair. Mr. Finch, did Lucy retrieve my shawl?"

"Indeed. Your gloves and reticule as well. Everything is on the table by the door. Miss Winters and her aunt await you in their coach."

"Would you please tell them I'll join them in a moment?" Juliette closed her eyes briefly as though she required a few seconds to collect herself. When she opened them, she turned to her uncle. "You should retire early tonight—you've a busy day tomorrow. And Cousin Samuel"—she narrowed her eyes at him—"I trust you shall find a book or a solitary card game or some other form of innocuous entertainment for the evening."

Sam nodded soberly, even though the chances of him reading a book that evening were approximately as great as the odds of the moon falling out of the sky.

Wiltmore scratched his head. "What's this? Samuel's not joining you?"

"No," Juliette said, too adamant for Sam's liking. "He's not."

"Well, my dear, you mustn't fret," the old man said, sympathetic. "Charlotte will make a fine companion. Besides, you'll be swarmed by gentlemen wishing to claim you for a dance."

Sam didn't doubt it for a second. But the bloody young bucks vying for her attention were going to be interested in much more than a dance. He happened to know because he *was* one of those young bucks.

He gripped his dessert fork till it bent.

The thought of other men ogling her sensuous curves, whispering seductive words in her ear, luring her onto the moonlit terrace . . . Damn it all to hell.

She gracefully rose from the table and Sam stood as well. "Allow me to escort you out."

"Enjoy yourself," Wiltmore said, waving from his chair. "I look forward to hearing all about the ball to-morrow."

"Sleep well, Uncle." As she squeezed his shoulder affectionately, Sam tucked her other hand securely in the crook of his arm, ignoring the sharp look she gave him.

The moment they were out of earshot, she warned, "You may not come near the door. Charlotte or her aunt may see you."

"I know," he said, savoring the pressure of her hand on his arm. "I just wanted a moment alone with you. To tell you . . ."

To tell her *what*, precisely? That she was the most beautiful, captivating creature he'd ever known and the vision of her in her daring red gown would haunt him forever? That he wanted to haul her to his bed and show her all the glorious things her body could feel? Or that maybe—just maybe—he could be more than a rogue. For her.

"Charlotte is waiting." She released his arm and tugged on her gloves, the simple act nearly as arousing as if she'd slipped off her stockings in front of him. She blinked up at him with sooty lashes, her lips parted expectantly. "What did you want to say?"

He took the shawl from the table, draped it over her bare shoulders, and impulsively took her hands in his. "The gentleman that Charlotte spoke of earlier . . ."

Her breath hitched as though she was instantly on her guard. "Yes?"

He swallowed. "I hope . . . I hope he's deserving of you."

She looked away. "Please remember our bargain. And do not speak to my uncle about the house. What you did at dinner—bolstering his confidence—well, thank you for that."

"Do not worry about him. Enjoy yourself this evening." *And stay away from rogues like me.*

The fortifying breath she took made her breasts swell above the tight bodice of her gown, and he nearly groaned at the sight.

"Good night . . . Sam." She smiled softly before gliding toward the door and making her exit.

Sam. The sound of his name on her lips echoed in his head, filling it like a concerto—and giving him a sliver of hope.

But holy hell. Dressed in that gown, she may as well have been Red Riding Hood, blindly running into a ballroom full of wolves. He couldn't remain in the house wondering who she was with and whether the cad would try to hold her hand or kiss her lips.

Someone needed to keep the wolves at bay—and it might as well be him.

Chapter THIRTEEN

Julie had planned to contract a splitting headache no later than ten and return home. But once she arrived at the Breckinridge Ball and was thrust into the swirl of glittering gowns, sparkling jewels, and boisterous laughter, she realized that Charlotte was correct—Julie *had* needed a few hours of dancing and revelry.

A few hours to feel young and free and admired.

She'd been avoiding the social whirl since her encounter with Nigel at the masquerade ball, and each time she declined an invitation, it became more difficult to accept the next. Charlotte had provided the much-needed shove, and now that Julie was there, she had to admit she was enjoying herself.

She'd danced every set of the evening so far and was now waltzing with a dashing army officer whom her friend had introduced. He had impeccable manners and a charming smile, but for some reason, she kept comparing him to Sam.

Her dance partner didn't have Sam's razor-sharp wit or confidence, and he lacked the ability to leave her breathless with a mere arch of his brow.

But as long as she was in the officer's arms, twirling around the dance floor, she didn't have to think about scientific papers or property deeds or broken promises—and it was a heavenly respite.

"May I call on you, Miss Lacey? Perhaps tomorrow?" The young man's question yanked Julie back to the present. The music had ended and he was walking her back to the perimeter of the dance floor where Charlotte and her aunt stood.

"Of course you—" What was she saying? As long as Sam was staying at their house, she couldn't dream of entertaining visitors. "Actually, my uncle hasn't been entirely well."

"I'm sorry."

"Oh, I am certain he shall recover fully. But he's not been himself of late."

The soldier smiled weakly. "I understand," he said, clearly pained. "However eager I am for your company, I would not wish to disturb your uncle's rest."

"Please, do not think—"

"Good evening, Miss Lacey." The commanding voice came from behind her, but she already knew who it belonged to—Nigel.

Her dance partner made a hasty, awkward departure, leaving her alone with the marquess.

"Good evening, Lord Currington," she said smoothly. As if he hadn't passionately kissed her over a month ago and neglected to call on her ever since.

And now, to add insult to grievous injury, he'd sent

his brother to evict her and her uncle from their home. She didn't want to believe he was capable of such a thing. Perhaps it was Sam who was lying . . . but she didn't want to believe he could be so callous either.

"You look exquisite tonight." Nigel's eyes gleamed with appreciation, and Julie's belly flipped. The resemblance to his brother was remarkable, but Nigel was more serious, more reserved. Unlike Sam, he couldn't afford to squander his days sleeping off the previous night's excesses. He couldn't afford to spend his evenings in gaming hells and brothels.

Nigel's title required him to be responsible and honorable. Which begged the question—why hadn't he behaved honorably where Julie was concerned?

She inclined her head slightly, determined to remain aloof. She would not let him see how much he'd hurt her, how desperate she'd been for him to call.

"Dance with me." Part command, part plea, the words made her heart flutter in her chest.

"I should return to my friend's side. I've hardly spoken to her since we arrived." Julie had no intention of letting him wound her again—and as vulnerable as she felt, it wouldn't take much. Besides, how could she dance with the man who would toss her uncle out of his house?

He dropped his chin and stared at the ground, clearly disappointed. "Your rebuff is no more than I deserve. But I wish you'd give me the opportunity to explain."

Julie bit her tongue. He'd had a month's worth of opportunities, chances to seek her out, and hadn't bothered. What could he possibly say that would explain his failure to call on her or to at least send a note? "A ball is hardly the optimal time or place," she said icily.

"Permit me to take you for one turn about the room. Then I shall return you directly to your friend Miss Winters." His pale blue eyes searched her face, beseeching her to say yes.

"Very well," she said, too curious to refuse him. Perhaps a few minutes in his company would help her move on—or to at least ascertain whether he really did have a superior legal claim to her uncle's house.

She took the arm he offered and allowed him to guide her toward the refreshment table near the far wall.

They walked in silence for a few moments, and at last he whispered, "I haven't been able to forget you."

Her skin tingled at his admission, but she was no ingénue, easily manipulated by a few huskily spoken words. "No? I confess I'm surprised."

"Please, don't be too harsh with me. I've been tortured by the memory of that night on the terrace."

She glanced around to make sure no one had overheard him. *"Tortured?"* she asked, incredulous. "I suppose that is why you've decided to toss my uncle out of his home?"

He blinked slowly, then frowned. "What are you talking about, Juliette?"

"Do not play coy with me," she whispered. "You sent your brother so you wouldn't have to sully your own hands."

"My brother? You and your uncle live in the house on Hart Street?" He shook his head as if to clear it. "I had no idea."

Julie was reluctant to take him at his word, but a sprout of hope took root in her chest nevertheless. Perhaps the whole thing was a huge misunderstanding. Nigel would fix it, and Uncle Alistair would be free to remain in his home with his beloved Elspeth. "But . . . how is it possible you didn't know?"

"I own a great many properties, Juliette," he said, his tone slightly patronizing. "I cannot know the details of each and every one."

"But now that you are aware," she began cautiously, "that my uncle has lived in the house for decades, will you allow him—and me—to stay?" She held her breath as she awaited his answer.

He looked over his shoulder, pulled her closer, and whispered, "We are surrounded by curious ears. Perhaps we should continue this discussion outside?"

Alarms sounded in Julie's head. The last time she'd ventured outside with the marquess, she'd succumbed to temptation, and the slightly heady feeling she had from the pressure of his hand on hers suggested she was no more capable of resisting him now than she was then. But she simply had to discuss the matter of her uncle's house with him—and who knew when she'd have another opportunity?

"We may not tarry long," she said hesitantly, "or Charlotte will become concerned."

"We wouldn't want that." Nigel's gaze slid from Julie's face, lower, to the swells of her breasts. "But it will be infinitely easier for us to talk where we have a modicum of privacy."

"And all we will do is talk," she said pointedly.

"Of course." His eyelids grew heavy and a smile

spread across his handsome face. "What else would we do?"

Sam sat across a chessboard from Wiltmore in the man's cluttered study, half irritated and half amused that a man in his seventh decade was beating him. Handily.

But in fairness, his mind wasn't entirely on the chess match. He flicked a glance at the clock on the mantel and made his last—fatal—move.

"Checkmate," Wiltmore said, his face splitting into a crooked grin. "But you were a worthy opponent. Almost as skilled as Juliette, isn't that right, Elspeth?" He looked up at his late wife's portrait as though the young, smiling woman might respond.

Sam coughed, suddenly uncomfortable. "I shall leave you to savor your victory. I'm for bed." He stretched his arms as though exhausted, gave a polite bow, and headed toward the stairs.

But instead of ascending the staircase, he sneaked past it, toward the front door. The house was quiet, and Mr. Finch was nowhere to be seen.

It was the easiest thing in the world to slip out of the front door, unnoticed.

Glad that he'd dressed in his finest jacket for dinner, Sam strolled down the street looking for a hackney cab to take him to the Breckinridge Ball.

A quarter of an hour later, he paid the driver with a few coins his valet had delivered and hopped out of the cab in front of an elegant, brightly lit Mayfair townhouse.

During the short drive, he'd debated his options. He could walk through the front door, make his way into the bustling ballroom, and do his best to remain out of

Juliette's sight—so she wouldn't discover that he'd left her uncle's house and broken his promise to her.

Or he could skulk around to the back of the house like a common criminal, wander onto the terrace, and peer through the windows, hoping for a glimpse of her. He might even learn the identity of the man who'd captured her affections.

Neither option was particularly appealing, but since he wasn't in the mood for socializing—at least not with anyone besides Juliette—he settled on the skulking route. With a little good fortune, he'd satisfy his curiosity and be back in her uncle's house before she returned from the ball.

Chapter FOURTEEN

Julie allowed Nigel to steer her around a group of elderly matrons sipping lemonade and past a pair of debutantes standing awkwardly on the edge of the dance floor. Knowing all too well what it felt like to be in their slippers, she cast them an encouraging smile.

A mere year ago, she'd felt invisible. And on the rare occasion that she and her sisters *had* succeeded in capturing the attention of the ton . . . it was for all the wrong reasons. Society's elite had mocked them for their hideous gowns and their loyalty to their eccentric uncle.

But not tonight.

Tonight, in her daring red gown, Julie was the opposite of invisible. It had been disconcerting at first, being on the receiving end of so many admiring glances. Men who'd once scorned her now stared with undisguised appreciation. Women who'd snubbed her now looked upon her with grudging respect.

Julie soaked it all in . . . but wondered why the one

man whose attention she'd craved hadn't sought her out until tonight.

Very aware of Nigel's hand at the small of her back, she allowed him to guide her out of the ballroom doors and into the cool evening air. A few lanterns hung from the boughs of a tree, illuminating a stone bench in the corner of the terrace.

"Shall we sit?" he said smoothly.

Julie swallowed, wishing that the terrace wasn't quite so deserted. Walking onto a moonlit terrace with Nigel was a bit like walking into a bakery while trying to slim down. Decidedly ill-advised.

And yet, she couldn't say no. She needed to understand why he'd neglected to call on her. She needed to convince him to let her uncle stay in his home. Above all, she needed to know if Nigel was truly as heartless as he seemed.

Nodding, she walked to the bench and sat on one end, careful to keep some distance between them.

"Here we are . . . again." Nigel shot her a conspiratorial smile.

"I can only stay a moment," Julie said, hoping to signal there would be no encore of their previous dalliance. "You said you wished to explain. I'm listening."

"As I said, I've been unable to forget you." He reached for her hand. "The memory of that night haunts me—the feel of you in my arms, the taste of your lips—"

Julie pulled away. "I was there," she said dryly. "The things you said . . . and the things we did . . . well, I thought that they meant something to you."

"They did." He scooted closer on the bench while gazing earnestly into her eyes. "I meant everything I said . . . about wanting you."

"And yet, you did not call on me or even write me a note. What was I to think?"

"Juliette," he breathed, smoothing a curl away from her face. "You must have faith in me. It is difficult for someone like me . . . that is, a marquess must necessarily put duty before pleasure."

She blinked, trying to follow his reasoning. "Allow me to make sure I understand correctly. You're so consumed with your *duty* you cannot spare an hour to call on me?"

"No." He looked down, his handsome face shadowed by regret. "But duty requires me to marry strategically. No matter how much I might want to follow my heart, I must think of what's best for my estate."

Blood pounded in her ears and her hands clenched the edge of the bench. "What's best for your estate," she repeated evenly.

"And for my family name. I'll admit it's not fair, and I wish to God it weren't the case, but . . ." He sighed, as though he were relieved to have that bit of unpleasantness off his chest.

Julie resisted the urge to run back into the ballroom. His words stung more than they should have.

"And why, precisely, am I unsuitable? Is it because my father was a vicar?"

Nigel swallowed uncomfortably. "That's part of it— yes. And of course, there's the matter of . . ."

She knew what he was going to say, and yet she wanted him to say it. "There's no need to prevaricate. Tell me."

"Your uncle." He reached for her hand again, but Julie felt dazed, detached from her body. "It's natural that you would care for him, but surely you understand that his unconventional mannerisms make him rather—"

She snapped her gaze to his. "Charming? Refreshing? Brilliant?"

"Of course, all those things. But also odd. Forgive me for being so blunt, Juliette. The last thing on earth I'd wish to do is hurt you." He raised her hand and pressed a kiss to the back.

Her whole body went numb. At last, she knew the truth—Nigel thought she wasn't good enough.

Oh, she knew he was mistaken—dead wrong, in fact—but hearing him speak the words was a slap in the face nonetheless. He was the man she'd allowed to kiss her, the man she'd foolishly imagined she might give her heart to.

Worse, if he and his brother were to be believed, he possessed the deed to her uncle's house.

And she had to tread very carefully if she wished to ensure her uncle could remain there.

She raised her chin. "You knew who I was, before you . . . that is, before we . . ."

"I did." He had the good grace to look contrite. "But I was powerless to resist you, Juliette. I still am. You must know that I would do anything for you."

Anything, perhaps, but risk sullying his reputation. Still, he looked so vulnerable and sincere . . . *this* was the opening she needed. "If that is true, I have but one request, and it is simple. Allow my uncle to remain in his home."

His icy blue gaze sharpened, as though he realized

their conversation had taken a turn from romance to business. "You could have asked me for pretty poetry or jewels, but instead, you ask a favor for your uncle."

"Do not forget that I live there too."

He shrugged. "Yes, but either of your sisters would be happy to take you in, would they not?"

"Of course, but . . ."

He stood and paced the terrace in front of the bench, the heels of his boots clicking on the smooth slate. "Your devotion to your uncle is admirable, and I wish I could help. Truly, I do. But it's a complicated legal matter. I could probably consult with my solicitor, but . . ."

"But what?" she countered.

"I'd like some assurance that you aren't simply taking advantage of my tender feelings for you."

A shiver ran the length of her spine. "What are you suggesting?"

He paused and faced her, his expression wounded. "Only that I would wish for some encouragement—a sign that you return my feelings. Do you?"

She stood and laced her fingers together to keep her hands from trembling. "I don't know. After we . . ."

"Kissed?" he said huskily.

"I thought I cared for you." She'd relived that kiss a hundred times over, savoring the genuine affection in his eyes. But perhaps it had only been desire.

"And now?"

"I find myself in a predicament." She folded her arms, rubbing the exposed skin above her gloves. "My heart remembers our kiss fondly, but my head says I deserve a gentleman who respects me."

"Oh God, Juliette, I do. I hold you in the highest

esteem." He placed his hand on her shoulder, and steered her away from the light of the lanterns, beneath a vine-covered trellis. "Have I told you how beautiful you look tonight? Or that when I saw you dancing with those other men, I thought I'd go mad with jealousy?"

After weeks of wondering what, if anything, Nigel felt for her, his words were a balm to her pride. But they weren't enough. Not after the things he'd said. "Did you expect me to sit in my parlor, waiting for you to call and facing disappointment day after day?"

His hand slid from her shoulder down her arm, and his heated gaze dropped to the swells of her breasts. "Of course not, darling. But you must know that I did not forget you—not for a moment. Give me some more time, and I'll find a way for us to be together."

The combination of his impassioned speech and ardent stare had a potent, heady effect. "And what of my uncle's house?" she managed.

"I'll see what I can do," he murmured, as his hands slid down her back, coaxing her hips closer to his.

One kiss, she thought. *One kiss to see if the magic is still there.*

Breathless, she turned her face up to his—

—just as the trellis above them crashed down.

Chapter FIFTEEN

Shit.

Sam crouched behind a trellis overrun with vines, unbelieving, as Juliette stood on the Breckinridges's terrace . . . with his brother.

A gurgling fountain nearby had drowned out most of their conversation, but in the light of the lanterns, Sam could see the besotted expression on Nigel's face as he gazed at her with undisguised desire. He could see his brother's hands caressing her skin.

And he almost retched at the sight.

It couldn't be coincidence that Nigel had sent him to toss Juliette and her uncle out of their house. But even if Nigel wasn't the saint Sam had imagined him to be, he was no scoundrel.

Sam was the one who was regularly featured in the gossip rags—*he* was the one who was a source of constant disappointment. Not Nigel.

And yet, the evidence before him was hard to refute.

Nigel and Juliette had formed some sort of attachment . . . and now Sam was in the middle of it. Which
was the very last place he wanted to be.

Still, he couldn't drag his eyes away from Juliette's
face. Beneath her cool façade he detected a hint of distress, and an odd tingling at the base of his spine wouldn't
let him leave her, just in case she needed him.

So he watched as Nigel steered her away from the lanterns, closer to Sam's hiding spot behind the trellis. Too
close, damn it.

He had to move, quickly. He crouched and began
crawling toward the cover of a waist-high hedge—then
stopped short.

The shoulder of his jacket caught on the trellis's frame,
holding him prisoner.

Nigel and Juliette were only yards away and would
surely spot him if he didn't free himself quickly. He
pulled harder, willing to sacrifice his jacket if it meant
he could escape undetected and save all involved a heap
of embarrassment.

But he remained stuck.

He had no choice but to throw his whole body into
the effort. Holding his breath, he counted to three and
prepared to lunge.

One, two, three . . .

Crash. He managed to pull himself free, but took half
the damned trellis with him in the process. The other
half listed toward the terrace, balancing for one hopeful moment before tumbling down, directly toward Juliette. Panic flooding his veins, he scrambled to his feet
to rescue her from the mess—

But of course he was too late.

Nigel shielded her, letting the falling posts and scraps of wood bounce off his back. Sam took a step toward them, then froze.

Neither Juliette nor Nigel had seen Sam on the other side of the rubble—Nigel was too preoccupied with pulling ivy leaves out of Juliette's hair; she was busy brushing the dust off his jacket.

As they fussed over each other, Sam slowly retreated.

Juliette didn't need him.

And if Nigel discovered he'd been spying on them, he'd skewer Sam alive.

So he stayed in the shadows as he rounded the corner of the house, keeping his head low. He paused as a few curious guests who'd heard the ruckus spilled out onto the terrace. Listened as they proclaimed his brother a veritable hero for protecting Juliette.

Sam sighed, wishing that for once, *he'd* been the one to save the fair maiden.

He would have liked to be the one checking her for scrapes and telling her not to fret about his ruined jacket—that he'd sacrifice a hundred jackets to keep her safe.

In truth, he was more like the villain in her story—the one who'd darkened her doorstep, bringing distressing news about her uncle's house. The one who'd failed to keep his end of the bargain and then managed to knock down the trellis on top of her.

He shoved his hands deep in his pockets as he left the gardens and strode in the direction of Juliette's house. It was a long walk, but he welcomed the chance to expend some pent-up energy—and think.

If the ball guests had spotted Sam alone on the terrace

with Juliette, they would have assumed he was in the process of seducing her . . . and, in all likelihood, they would have been correct.

But when the guests had discovered Nigel with her, they didn't appear to suspect anything untoward. Rather, they likely assumed that Juliette had merely wanted a bit of fresh air and that Nigel had been good and honorable enough to escort her to the terrace and protect her from all manner of falling objects.

Sam had no one to blame for the unfavorable comparison but himself. He'd earned his bad reputation with every drunken night, every short-lived affair, every reckless throw of the dice. Likewise, Nigel's good name was the product of a lifetime of doing the right thing: making top marks at school, following the rules, doing his duty.

Why then, hadn't Nigel been forthright with Juliette about her uncle's house?

He'd only told Sam that the house was occupied by a distant relative, so perhaps he hadn't realized the connection to Juliette. But the note Sam sent him that afternoon had made the circumstances perfectly clear.

Sam had said the house was occupied by Lord Wiltmore and his niece, who wished to see proof of Nigel's legal right to the property before they vacated it. Sam had also asked his brother to grant Juliette and Wiltmore some time—time to adjust to the news and make other living arrangements.

And Nigel hadn't responded. Yet.

Sam rubbed the back of his neck and walked faster down the dark, mostly deserted street. Given all he'd seen and heard tonight, he had to assume that he was being manipulated and played the fool by either Nigel or Juliette. Maybe both.

He didn't want to believe either capable of such treachery. Nigel was his flesh and blood—the wiser, older brother he'd always idolized. And Juliette . . . well, she was someone he'd thought could become his friend. Or something more.

But at least one of them was lying to Sam.

Whoever the guilty party turned out to be, Sam was going to be gutted.

He shrugged to himself, shaking off his uncharacteristic melancholy. He was better off not caring. Nothing he could do would change his brother's opinion of him—much less society's.

And someone like Juliette could never see past his unsavory past and his myriad sins.

To hell with them both.

If a tiger couldn't change his stripes . . . neither could a rogue.

The moment Julie stepped through the front door of her uncle's house, she kicked off her heeled slippers and rubbed the arches of her feet, nearly moaning with relief. She couldn't recall a night when she'd danced so much, twirling around the parquet floor into the wee hours of the morning.

But the joy she should have felt was dimmed by her frustration with Nigel. The disaster with the trellis had prevented her from receiving the answers she sought.

He'd certainly made her no promises where her uncle's house was concerned . . . but she did have the distinct impression that the marquess was open to negotiations.

Which was, in itself, troubling.

Julie picked up her slippers, hoisted the hem of her dress, and tiptoed toward the parlor, mildly disappointed that Sam had not waited up for her. Ridiculous, that.

She'd danced with half a dozen handsome men, all of whom were eligible bachelors and infinitely more suitable for her than Sam.

And, at the moment, she could barely recall their names.

Sam was the one who'd tried to spare her embarrassment after her dress debacle at dinner. He was the one who'd made Uncle Alistair believe his research was worthy. He was the one who'd said she deserved a gentleman—even though she'd been certain he wanted to kiss her.

She walked slowly toward the staircase, navigating carefully around small tables and the stool at the pianoforte, and—

"Good evening, Juliette. Or should I say morning?"

Chapter SIXTEEN

"Sam?" Juliette waited for her eyes to better adjust to the dark parlor and took two steps toward the settee. "What are you doing?"

"Having a glass of brandy. I nicked it from the study." His sounded weary. Jaded.

"Is everything all right? Why are you sitting here in the dark?" Julie moved closer, relieved to see he still wore his jacket and cravat. Not a glimpse of sinewy forearms nor tanned neck to be found, thank heaven. She tamped down a vague sense of disappointment.

"Everything is as it should be. Your uncle retired hours ago, and the house is quiet. But I couldn't sleep."

She tossed her slippers on the floor and lit a lantern on the mantel. "You could have enjoyed your drink in the study—I daresay my uncle wouldn't have minded."

"I started to," Sam said. "But I couldn't stand being watched."

Julie sank on to the settee next to him and frowned. "Watched? By whom?"

"Elspeth." He crossed his long legs at the ankles and rested the bottom of his glass on his taut abdomen while she endeavored not to stare.

"You couldn't bear to be in the room with my aunt's portrait?" she asked, teasing.

"She was judging me," he said flatly.

"Is that what she told you?"

"She didn't need to say anything—it was in her eyes."

"I never met Aunt Elspeth, but by all accounts she was a kind soul. I cannot think that she'd be the sort to judge you."

He shrugged. "Everybody does. I don't blame them. That's just the way of things."

Julie wondered how much he'd had to drink. He seemed to have his wits about him, but *something* was different. If anything, he seemed more sober. More genuine.

Reluctant to bid him good night, she asked, "How did you and my uncle spend the evening?"

"We played chess. Chatted about a variety of topics."

She prayed Sam hadn't mentioned anything that might have alarmed her uncle. And her curiosity was piqued. "Topics such as . . . ?"

"Mummies. Wombats." He took a swig of brandy. *"You."* He stared at her as though issuing a challenge.

Her blood heated, but she didn't look away. "Me?"

"Yes. Infinitely more interesting than mummies and wombats—to me, at least."

Julie winced at the thought of all the embarrassing

childhood stories her uncle might have shared. "I hope he didn't reveal too many of my secrets."

"Do you have many?" He looked straight into her eyes—as though the question had crossed a line from playful banter into a high-stakes game of truth or dare.

A chill raced over her skin, heaven help her. "None that are particularly scandalous." If one discounted the wholly improper kiss she'd shared with his brother.

He nodded thoughtfully—perhaps doubtfully. After a few moments, he shot her a mischievous smile. "Your uncle told me that you wanted a pet dog so badly you fashioned one out of a mop."

"Unfortunately, I can confirm that. Her name was Moppet. Imagine my horror when I walked into the kitchen one morning to discover our cook using Moppet to clean broken eggs off the floor."

"You must be scarred," he quipped. "Haunted by the image."

"You've no idea." She let her neck rest on the back of the settee and stared at the ceiling, contemplative. "I never did get a puppy."

"A pity. A puppy might have kept you out of trouble."

Oh dear. "What else did Uncle Alistair tell you?"

"Not much," Sam said noncommittally.

Julie smiled and breathed a sigh of relief—until he raised a finger in the air. "Although he did mention that you've been singing bawdy songs since the tender age of twelve."

Heat crawled up her neck, and she made a mental note to scold Uncle Alistair for speaking so freely with Sam. "In my defense, I didn't realize the songs were naughty until Meg threatened to wash my mouth out with soap.

I'd found an old book of poems and made up my own tunes—I thought I was a budding singer."

"You are welcome to perform naughty songs for me any time you wish." He arched a wicked brow.

She shook her head vehemently. "I'm certain you've heard them all before. I wouldn't want to bore you."

He stretched out his hand and let the back of it graze her bare shoulder. "You could never, ever bore me, Juliette."

His low, husky voice and his heavy-lidded gaze made her belly do cartwheels. Suddenly, the settee seemed fraught with delicious danger. What was it about Sam that made her want to misbehave?

From a young age, she'd worked hard to rein in her impetuous nature. She'd learned that nice girls didn't swim naked or run barefoot through the fields or climb trees. And when she was a bit older, she'd learned that proper young ladies didn't flirt with scoundrels or read risqué novels or entertain gentlemen in their parlor without a chaperone—especially in the wee hours of the morning.

But Sam seemed vulnerable. Tonight, he wasn't the rogue regularly featured in the gossip rags. Rather, he was the man who'd spent the evening listening to her uncle's rambling, embellished stories because he wished to understand her.

But she could barely understand herself.

A scant hour ago, she'd been on the verge of kissing his brother, and now . . .

. . . all she could think of was kissing Sam.

She made one last, valiant attempt to do the right thing. "It's late. I should say goodnight."

"Don't." He traced the shell of her ear with a finger-tip. "Don't go."

"Sam," she said, suddenly finding it hard to breathe. "I'll admit I'm tempted to stay. But I fear I'd regret it tomorrow."

"Of course you would. You *will*." He set down his brandy and slid closer, cradling her face in his hands. "But I promise you'll enjoy tonight."

He dragged the pad of his thumb across her lower lip . . . "Every."

Pressed his forehead to hers . . . "Single."

Speared his fingers into her hair. "Second."

Oh my. She had no doubt he'd deliver on the prom-ise. But the intensity of his gaze and the hint of gruff-ness in his voice told her that perhaps this was to be something more than mere passion. He was offering her a glimpse of his true self. The mysterious ten percent that the rest of the world had never seen.

"Give me a sign, Juliette. Or tell me to go. But don't torture me like this."

She pressed a palm to his chest and felt his heart beat-ing wildly. Slowly, she brushed her lips over his.

He went very still. As though he were afraid that the pressure of her lips on his was merely a dream and he might wake at any moment. As though one sudden move could break the tenuous connection between them.

But he needn't have worried—nothing could make her turn back now.

He tensed as she boldly twined her hands around his warm neck but remained stoically frozen.

More determined than ever, she teased the corner of his mouth with her tongue, savoring the tangy taste of him. Beneath her palms, his shoulder muscles twitched in protest of his self-imposed restraint.

But she sensed he was close to his breaking point, teetering on the edge. She could see it in the sheen on his brow and the fine lines around his mouth.

So she decided to take a page out of Uncle Alistair's research papers on the mating habits of exotic animals . . . and let instinct guide her. She grabbed Sam's cravat, pulling him toward her as she reclined on the settee.

She fell back against a silk pillow, breathless. His hips pressed against hers, pinning her to the seat cushions and shifting her gown. Her breasts spilled out of the top of her bodice, but she made no move to cover herself from his gaze.

"Jesus." He devoured her with his eyes as he braced himself above her, his hair dipping across his forehead like he was some gorgeous fallen angel.

"Kiss me, Sam," she breathed.

With a feral grin, he lowered his head. "Gladly, temptress."

Chapter SEVENTEEN

Sam didn't know what game Juliette was playing, but the hell of it was, he didn't care.

Let her flirt with his brother one minute and play the seductress with him the next.

Maybe her goal was to make Nigel jealous.

Maybe she wanted to experience a torrid affair before settling into the role of a proper wife and marchioness.

Or perhaps she meant to bend Sam to her will—to try and manipulate him in an attempt to keep her uncle in his home.

The truth was, Sam didn't give a damn about her motivation. Didn't mind if tonight was simply the means to an end for her.

He'd take what she was willing to give—and savor every glorious moment.

Chestnut curls framed her heart-shaped face, and her skin glowed in the soft light of the lantern. The tips of her breasts peeked out of her dress, tempting as ripe strawberries.

She gazed up at him, her bow-shaped lips parted expectantly.

And he knew he'd die if he didn't have her.

Stifling a curse, he slanted his mouth across hers and kissed her like he'd wanted to from the start.

No more tentative brushes or gentle touches. This kiss was hot. Unbridled. Raw.

With a groan, he urged her lips apart and greedily explored her mouth with his tongue. Most demure misses would have run for their smelling salts, but not Juliette. She met him thrust for thrust, parry for parry. Rather than lie back and wait to be ravished, she arched her body toward his and curled her fingers into his shoulders.

He drew her lower lip between his teeth and nibbled. Grabbed a handful of curls at her nape and kissed her deeper, harder. Till they were both panting and breathless.

Everything about her felt right. Her breath, warm on his cheek. Her skin, satin smooth against his lips. He kissed a path down her neck and lower, over the swells of her breasts, and drew a taut tip into his mouth. Growling, he ripped the silk sash off her gown and slid it across her stomach. Let it trail between her breasts and across the pink tips, pleased to see her eyes close from the sheer bliss of it.

When her eyes fluttered open, she said, "This is madness. I know I should tell you to stop . . . but I don't want you to. Does that make me very wicked?"

"You are only ten percent wicked," he said smoothly.

As if he weren't aroused to the point he might explode. "But I happen to adore this side of you."

The blush spread over her fair cheeks. "I must go soon. Perhaps five more minutes."

"Then we shouldn't waste any time." He grasped her arms and gently pulled her up, so they sat facing one another. With her delightfully mussed hair and exposed, luscious curves, she was half innocent, half seductress.

He hauled her across his lap so that she knelt astride him, then cupped her bottom, reveling at how perfectly she fit in his hands. Holy hell. She was right—this *was* madness. And yet, he pulled her closer, willing time to stop.

Sam had experienced more than his fair share of erotic encounters. And while this one rated rather low on the wickedness scale, he'd never been so aroused—so attuned to the level of his partner's pleasure. Every hitch of her breath, every soft sigh, was a beacon guiding him toward what she liked best.

He savored the honeyed taste of her skin. Slid his hands over her hips and between her legs, stroking her through the silky layers of her gown.

"Sam," she whimpered.

Reluctantly, he sat back and brushed a curl away from her face. "What is it, siren?"

He shouldn't care so much—not when she could be playing him for the fool. But the vulnerability in her eyes broke down his defenses.

And made him forget he was supposed to be a rogue.

She raised a palm to her forehead. "I don't know what we're doing here. That is, I *do* know. And I fear we're making a mistake."

"Why?"

"For any number of reasons." The worry lines on her forehead said she was already regretting this night. Already regretting *him*. Maybe she was worried Nigel would discover what they'd done. Perhaps she feared Sam would expose her, ruining her reputation.

"You don't have to explain," he said. Mostly because he was certain that any reasons she gave would wound him further.

"Forgive me," she said, leaving Sam unsure as to whether she was speaking to him or some all-seeing deity. She looked down and shook her head as though she couldn't quite believe the extent of her wantonness. Suddenly self-conscious, she began to pull up the bodice of her gown.

Sam could feel the chasm between them growing. He could feel her drifting away. And he wasn't ready to let go.

"I understand," he said—even if he didn't fully. "But would you grant me one favor before you go?"

She met his gaze, wary. "That depends."

He cupped her cheek in his hand and drank in the sight of her heavy-lidded eyes and swollen lips. "Let me kiss you. One last time." If she wanted nothing to do with him tomorrow, he needed one more chance to imprint himself on her, body and soul.

"But we already—"

He dragged a thumb across her bottom lip. "Please. Just a kiss."

Julie considered the request. Where Sam was concerned, "just a kiss" was akin to labeling Stonehenge as "just some rocks" or Windsor Castle as "just a residence."

But Lord help her, she wanted him. Her entire body still tingled from his touch, and there was an odd ache deep in her core which she suspected only he could ease. She was very aware of his muscled thighs beneath her bottom and the hard length of him straining against his trousers.

She felt utterly alive and free.

Every moment alone with him was temptation personified. She'd been trying valiantly to suppress her wanton side, and in less than a day, he'd succeeded in awakening it. So much so, that every part of her desired him. She could not deny him.

She could not deny herself.

"Very well," she said, her voice husky to her own ears. "Just a few moments longer. And then I must go."

He swallowed and nodded like she'd given him a precious gift. One he didn't intend to waste.

With heartbreaking tenderness, he pulled her face to his. Their noses touched and their breath mingled sweetly. "I want to savor this," he murmured. "I want us both to remember."

As if she could possibly forget the brush of his warm, calloused hands over her skin or the way every inch of her thrummed in response to the pull of his mouth on her breast. As if she could forget his scalding kisses and the heady knowledge that London's greatest rogue desired her.

He teased her lips apart, tasting her like she was the rarest, sweetest chocolate. Holding her like she was the most precious jewel.

She wondered how two people could be so perfectly in tune. How he could know just what she liked—and what she needed.

He kissed her deeply and drew her hips closer to his, so that she rocked against him. "Do you see what you do to me, Juliette?" he whispered against her lips. "Do you see how much I want you?"

"Yes." Of their own accord, her fingers unbuttoned his waistcoat, and she slipped her hand inside, skimming the hard contours of his chest and the flat planes of his abdomen.

He cupped her bare breast in his large hand and tweaked her nipple with his thumb, whispering naughty things in her ear. "If I could, I would taste every inch of you. I would touch you until you came apart in my arms."

Oh dear. This was bad—very bad. She should be shocked or scandalized. Instead, she found herself intensely curious. And aroused.

This would never do. As she was under the spell of his knee-melting kiss, she was powerless to resist him . . .

And so, it was time to end their tryst.

She pulled back and scrambled off his lap, still dizzy with longing. Clutching her gown to her chest, she stood—and instantly felt the loss of intimacy and warmth.

He blew out a breath as he stood and paced in front of her. Meanwhile, she attempted to straighten her bodice and slow the beating of her traitorous heart.

She scooped her slippers off the floor and wrapped her shawl around her shoulders, as if restoring her modesty were just that simple. "That's better."

He arched a brow, skeptical.

In a transparent attempt to regain her footing, she assumed a conversational tone. "I see that your attire is much improved from this morning."

He leveled a glare at her. "Thank you. I think."

"So your valet paid a visit this evening?"

"He did. I made sure he was very discreet."

Then she asked the question she really wanted to know. "Did you also ask your brother to provide the deed to this house?"

He narrowed his eyes and stared at her, his expression unreadable. "Aye. I wrote to Nigel."

"And?"

"He hasn't responded. Yet."

Julie nodded briskly. "Thank you. I hope we're able to put the matter behind us. Soon." Even as she spoke the words, she knew it wouldn't be that easy. For better or worse, after tonight—and the kiss—she'd never see the world in quite the same way.

With a doubtful snort, he shoved his hands into his pockets and took a step closer. "Who can say what tomorrow holds, vixen? I suppose that will be up to my brother . . . and you."

Her heart tripped in her chest. His tone was half accusatory, half hurt. As if he suspected there was something between Nigel and her—when she wasn't at all certain herself. "It doesn't feel as though I truly have a say in the matter," she said.

He leaned closer, the brush of his shoulder against hers instantly reigniting her desire. "Don't fool yourself, Juliette," he said, his breath warm on her cheek. "You *do* have a decision to make. And I will have to live with your choice. Even if I don't like it."

Chapter EIGHTEEN

"Miss Juliette, you're finally awake!" Lucy exclaimed.

Julie sat up with a start. "What time is it?"

The maid clucked her tongue as she yanked open the doors of the armoire. "Well past noon. But don't fret, miss. A few extra hours of sleep were no doubt necessary after your eventful night."

A chill skittered down Julie's spine. "What do you mean?"

Lucy cast a confused look over her shoulder. "Only that you were at a ball, dancing the evening away. Did you enjoy yourself? I'll wager you had a slew of admirers thanks to your lovely red dress."

Heat crept up Julie's neck. "I suppose I did have more dance partners than usual," she said vaguely. "Where are my uncle and Sam—er, Cousin Samuel?"

"I'm not certain, but they broke their fast hours ago." The maid plucked a pink sprigged morning gown from the armoire and held it up questioningly.

Julie shook her head as she scrambled out of bed and reached for her corset. "The green striped, I think." It was her most modest gown, and it seemed to her that a little extra fabric wouldn't be amiss after last night. "And let's hurry, Lucy. I feel badly for leaving my uncle alone with Cousin Samuel all morning."

"I'm sure the gentlemen are capable of entertaining themselves, but never fear, we shall have you ready in a trice."

True to her word, Lucy quickly laced Julie's corset and morning gown, then attacked her hair with a brush. "So many tangles," she said with a *tsk*. "If I didn't know better, I'd think you'd been caught in a windstorm."

Oh my—a windstorm wasn't responsible for the knots. "I must have had a restless night," she said, avoiding the maid's gaze in the vanity's mirror.

Julie's scalp tingled at the memory of Sam spearing his fingers through her hair. He'd cradled her head in his large hand, taking complete control of their kiss. He'd stoked her passion till she burned for him.

Even now, in the cold light of day, she could feel the power of that desire. Sweet as sugarplums and rare as a shooting star, it had spiraled within her until she was floating. Being with Sam was a sliver of ecstasy she wasn't likely to forget.

But she knew one thing for certain. There could be no more midnight trysts in the parlor—or anywhere else, for that matter.

Because the price she might pay for a few minutes of heaven was steep, indeed.

"There," Lucy said with a satisfied smile. "A simple but elegant twist."

"It's perfect." But Julie barely spared a glance at her hair before leaping out of her seat and stepping into a pair of slippers.

"Shall I have a tray sent up?" the maid asked.

"I'll wait for luncheon." Julie was already heading out the door of her bedchamber, thinking about what she had to do. What she had to say to Sam.

The little deal they'd made yesterday had been a very bad idea. An idea fraught with danger. If anyone discovered that he was staying there and that she'd been alone with him . . . She shuddered at the mere possibility.

And while she hated the thought of distressing Uncle Alistair with the news about the house, perhaps it was preferable to bringing shame upon her entire family.

This wasn't like the one time she'd secretly taken in a stray cat and hid him in her room, sneaking scraps of food and bits of yarn upstairs when no one was looking.

Rogues were far more difficult to hide than cats.

Whatever the consequences were of tossing Sam out of the house, well . . . she'd just have to face them.

Perhaps she should write to Meg in spite of her oldest sister's delicate condition. Though Julie was loath to relate news that would upset her sister, she had no doubt that Meg and her doting husband, Will, would know just what to do about Julie's predicament.

And if it happened that Uncle Alistair wasn't the rightful owner of the house, Will would probably offer to buy it from Nigel outright. He'd do anything to make Meg happy.

Julie sighed, wondering if she'd ever inspire that sort of devotion in a man.

She glided into the empty parlor and quickly checked the settee for lost hairpins, handkerchiefs, or any other potentially incriminating evidence of her dalliance with Sam. She slid her hands beneath the silk cushions. Nothing.

Crouching, she checked the floor and carpet around the settee—all clear, if one discounted the dust balls.

Everything was as it should be. Sunlight streamed through the windows, the pillows were plumped . . . almost as though their interlude hadn't occurred at all.

Oddly disappointed, she made her way to the study—for Uncle Alistair and Sam must almost certainly be there.

She paused outside the closed door and listened. Male voices, punctuated by the occasional chuckle.

Perhaps she'd been too hasty in judging Sam. Maybe he was holding up his end of the deal right now, playing the part of dutiful research assistant. She could open the door to find him hunched over a table beside her uncle, busy transcribing, organizing, and filing.

Tentatively hopeful, she turned the handle and walked in.

To find her uncle standing on a chair, brandishing his cane like sword.

Dear God. A frantic cry escaped her throat.

Her uncle spun to face her, smashed a glass lamp with his cane, and teetered, arms flailing wildly.

The cane hit the floor. His eyes wide with terror, he listed toward the sharp corner of his desk. And like a scene straight out of a nightmare, Julie's feet wouldn't move.

Everything was happening too fast. The edges of her

vision blurred. The white tufts on Uncle Alistair's crown waved as he fell, headfirst, toward the solid desktop.

Julie screamed, bracing herself for the inevitable thud of his skull against oak—

But Sam leaped over a globe and caught him. Just before impact.

Uncle Alistair groaned. Sam grunted under his weight and staggered toward an arm chair, where he gently sat her uncle on the worn cushion. Breathless, Sam leaned over, his hands on his knees.

"What the devil were you thinking, walking in here like that?" he gasped.

A roar filled her ears. "What the devil am *I* thinking?" she asked, incredulous. Oh dear, the room began to tilt a little.

"Yes, Juliette. You barged in here and screamed like the house was on fire."

She took two steps toward Uncle Alistair and instantly regretted it. Blast it all, she was going down. She heard herself moan just as the world went black.

Dear Jesus. Sam lunged toward Juliette and caught her under the arms just before her knees would have hit the floor. Heart in his throat, he laid her on the carpet, cradling her head in the crook of his arm. What the hell was wrong with him? She'd had a terrible fright and instead of comforting her, he'd yelled.

No wonder she preferred Nigel to him.

"Alistair," he called over his shoulder. "Do you have any smelling salts?"

The old man scratched his head. "Heavens no—

don't need them. Juliette doesn't succumb to fainting spells."

For a scientist, his powers of observation were sorely lacking.

"I think she just did."

Chapter NINETEEN

As Sam looked down at her pale, still face, panic raced through his veins. He put his cheek near her parted lips. Felt her breath faint upon his skin. Said a prayer of thanks—his first in a decade or so.

"Juliette." He gave her shoulders a light shake. "Can you hear me?"

Her lashes twitched, but her entire body remained limp. Frighteningly so.

"Juliette, please. Say something." He caressed her forehead and shook her some more. No response, so he turned to Alistair. "Have you any water in here?"

He pushed himself out of his chair, mumbling. "'Water, water, everywhere, nor any drop to drink.'"

Sam blinked. *"What?"*

"Samuel Taylor Coleridge."

"Juliette's fainted," Sam reminded her uncle. "We don't need poetry. We need water. What's in that jar over there?" He pointed toward the window.

Alistair retrieved it, unscrewed the lid, and handed it to Sam. "Water," he announced.

"Perfect." Sam tilted the jar toward Juliette's lips.

"Straight from the Thames."

"Good God, man! She can't drink this." Sam jerked the jar back, and the river water sloshed, soaking the front of her dress.

Her eyes fluttered open, and she pressed a hand to her chest. "Sam?"

At the sound of her voice, his heart squeezed in his chest. "I'm here." When she strained with the effort to sit, he scooped her into his arms. "I have you."

Savoring the feel of her body snuggled against his chest, he walked toward the open window and sat her on a cushioned bench.

"I'll go find Mr. Finch," Alistair said. "And request a proper glass of water."

"Thank you, Uncle," Juliette said. "But there's no need. I shall be fine."

"I'm sure you shall, but since I'm feeling rather superfluous at the moment, I may as well be of nervous."

Juliette started to protest, but Sam whispered, "Let him go." Surprisingly, she didn't argue but allowed him to keep his arm around her as he sat beside her on the bench.

She waited until Alistair shuffled out of the room, then looked up at Sam, her forehead creased in confusion. "Would you please tell me what just happened?"

"I almost made you drink water from the Thames," he confessed with a shrug. "Thankfully, I spilled it on you before it passed your lips."

"I *suppose* I should be thankful," she said, understandably doubtful. "But what happened before that?"

"You fainted." He tilted her chin up with one finger and searched her face. He'd never noticed the charming sprinkling of freckles on the bridge of her nose or the flecks of green in her eyes. "How are you feeling now?"

"A bit embarrassed. I don't faint, you see."

"No. Obviously not."

She smiled at that—and instantly brightened his whole damned day. "I'm feeling fine, honestly. It was just a shock—to walk into the room and find Uncle Alistair standing on his chair waving his cane. Why on earth would he do that?" Her gaze snapped to his. "Please don't say we have mice."

"None that I know of," Sam assured her. "We were simply conducting an experiment."

"An experiment," she repeated, skeptical.

"You're the one who wanted me to be his research assistant," he reminded her. He lightly massaged her nape, pleased that she permitted the intimate touch. But maybe she was still more dazed than she realized.

She frowned, thoughtful, then pulled away. Damn it all.

"Let me make sure I heard you correctly. You allowed a man in his seventh decade to climb onto a chair?" she asked, incredulous.

"I see your fighting spirit has returned—I suppose that's a good sign." He crossed his arms smugly. "In response to your question, I not only *allowed* him to climb onto the chair, I *encouraged* it."

She slapped a palm to her forehead. "What sort of experiment was it, exactly? Were you investigating how long it would take before my uncle fell and broke his hip? Perhaps you planned to measure the quantity of blood that would spill from his head wound?"

Sam winced. In retrospect, the chair probably *had* been a bad idea. But it wasn't his nature to back down once he'd taken a stand. Time to dig in his heels. "Must you be so morose? I wouldn't have let Alistair harm himself. You forget, I caught him *and* you before either one of you suffered grave consequences," he said proudly.

She shook her head in disbelief—apparently not quite ready to profess her undying gratitude. "What, precisely, was the point of that foolhardy exercise?"

"Physics."

"I beg your pardon?"

Assuming his best stodgy professor tone, he said, "It's a branch of science devoted to understanding the universe—forces, energy, that sort of—"

"Thank you, Sir Isaac. I *know* what it is." She rolled her eyes dramatically. "What were you testing?"

"I could explain . . . but it would be easier to show you." He plucked Alistair's cane off the floor, tossed it in the air, and caught it with one hand. Pointing the end of the cane at a stack of documents, he said, "Crumple one of those papers into a ball."

"What?" she said. "They could be important."

"Don't worry. You won't be destroying any secrets of the universe," he said dryly. "Alistair and I went through them earlier. That whole stack is destined for the dustbin. You see, we were working, while you lounged in bed all morning recovering from last night's mischief."

"How gentlemanly of you to remind me," she said, blushing prettily.

He grinned at that. "I would be wounded if you were to forget our mischievousness."

Casting a nervous glance at the door, she shot him a pointed look. "Where were we? Oh, yes. I'll crumple a paper." She formed a lopsided ball and held it up. "Now what?"

"Toss it at me."

She arched a brow. "Where?"

"At me," he repeated.

"You'll have to be more specific. Your shoulder? A knee?"

"It's not a duel, for God's sake. You're not likely to maim me with a paper ball."

She propped her fists on shapely hips. "We'll see about that. Just so you know, I'm aiming for your head."

"Perfect." Chances were the ball wouldn't make it half the distance to him. "Do your worst."

She wound up, preparing to launch. "It's a rather big target."

He held the cane like a cricket bat and prepared to swing. "Shall we make a wager?"

Her arm cocked, she froze. "What sort?"

"If you can hit my head, I'll . . ." He looked around the study and pointed at a bookcase stuffed with a multitude of jars, their contents unidentifiable. Bordering on grotesque. "If you hit my head, I'll organize and clean that entire shelf."

Her eyes lit up. "I like the sound of that. Perhaps we'll finally rid this room of its faint putrid odor."

"But if you miss my head," he continued, "you will owe me . . ."

She narrowed her eyes. "Owe you *what*?"

"More mischievousness." He held his breath, awaiting her answer.

Willing her to say yes.

Chapter TWENTY

Julie casually tossed the ball from palm to palm, weighing her options.

She should refuse Sam's wager, of course. The stakes were too high. Mischievousness, indeed.

But whenever she and her sisters played cricket, she was invariably the bowler—and she would match her skills against anyone's—even the rogue's.

Besides, she'd been purposely avoiding that shelf in Uncle Alistair's study for months. Though she'd never asked him what was in the jars, the contents looked similar to moldy cheese, rotting meat, or poorly preserved body parts.

And Julie had a strong, unfortunate tendency to gag whenever she looked that way.

"I'll take your wager," she said impulsively. "But you may not move your feet."

"Fair enough." A feral grin lit his face. "And the mischievousness?"

The thought of being alone with him again—like she had been last night—made her belly do a somersault. Or perhaps the sight of his rolled-up shirtsleeves and sinewy forearms was responsible for the butterflies.

"*If* mischievousness is required," she stipulated, "it shall be at a time and place of my choosing."

Shrugging, he said, "As far as I'm concerned, there is no bad time or place. In fact, sometimes the most unusual places are the best. Dark pantries, sunny fields, cozy libraries—"

"You've made your point," she interrupted—even though she *was* curious about the other suitable locations. "I suggest you prepare yourself."

"Ready." He once again raised the cane like a cricket bat as she pulled her arm back and threw.

"Here you are!" Uncle Alistair shouted, rushing into the room holding a goblet of water.

Startled, Sam turned.

Just as the paper ball hit him squarely in the ear.

"Damn it!" He raised a hand to his ear—which was already turning pink.

"What's the problem?" Uncle Alistair handed Julie the goblet, and she raised it toward Sam in a silent toast.

"Forgive my outburst. All is well," Sam replied, glum. "I was merely demonstrating our experiment for Juliette."

"Ah, it's quite simple, my dear. I was attempting to hit the paper balls into the dustbin using my cane but was having difficulty achieving the required acceleration and distance. In an effort to lessen the impact of the force of gravity, I—"

"Risked life and limb by standing on a wobbly old chair?" she provided.

His shoulders slumped. "I suppose it was foolish of me," he said, chastened. "But I confess I cannot recall the last time I felt so . . . so . . . young."

The triumph she'd felt moments ago fled. Oh, she was still happy that Sam would have to clean the bookcase, but she should have realized that her uncle needed more than his work and the occasional game of chess to make him feel fulfilled.

He needed joy.

Even though Julie hadn't understood it, Sam had. And he'd done something about it.

"I'm glad you enjoyed yourself." Julie set down the glass and gave her uncle a fierce hug. "I probably shouldn't coddle you so much, but I cannot help worrying about you."

"Ach." He waved a hand dismissively. "It's not exactly a hardship to be coddled by my lovely niece, and someone must look after me. I don't know what I'd do without you and Elspeth." As he gazed lovingly at her portrait, Julie shared a furtive glance with Sam.

His expression—a mix of sympathy and concern—gave her a lump in her throat.

Until that very moment, Julie hadn't realized how alone she'd felt. With her sisters out of town and still unaware of Uncle Alistair's new habit of talking to Aunt Elspeth, she'd been doing enough worrying for all three of them.

But now, Sam was here. He saw what was going on . . . and he seemed to understand.

It was nice, but it wasn't enough to change her mind.

After all that had transpired between them last night—kisses and caresses, not to mention various stages of disrobing—Julie couldn't permit him to spend another night in her uncle's house.

For the sake of her reputation, she had to make Sam leave. She'd ask him nicely, and if he refused, she'd enlist the help of her sisters and their powerful husbands.

Besides, it was hard to think clearly as long as he was lounging about in his snug trousers and tailored jackets. She'd concoct a story to tell her uncle—something to explain Sam's sudden departure—before her uncle formed too close an attachment.

But for now, she would let him enjoy a bit of fun.

"Would you like to continue your experiment?" she asked.

"What?" Uncle Alistair smiled sheepishly. "You'd allow it?"

"I would," Julie began, "as long as Cousin Samuel remains close enough to the chair to help, should you require a bit of steadying. I'll throw the paper balls."

Sam grinned wryly. "Fine. As long as I may take a turn standing on the chair also."

They spent the next half-hour playing cricket in Uncle Alistair's study. Julie must have thrown two dozen paper balls before her uncle's cane finally connected with one, and it only floated a few yards before joining the rest of the balls in the pile littering the carpet.

But it didn't matter. She hadn't seen such unadulterated happiness on his face since Beth's wedding, which though not so long ago, seemed like an age.

When he grew tired of batting and relinquished the

chair to Sam, Julie threw the balls faster, and he hit one so hard that it flew out the open window.

"By George," her uncle shouted gleefully. "You've succeeded in proving my theory."

A bit breathless from her exertions, Julie propped her hands on her hips. "Which is?"

"That gravity is easily overcome by youth, exuberance, and a vigorous swing," he said, eyes twinkling with satisfaction.

Sam hopped off the chair and dusted his hands. "If my science classes at Eton had been more like this, I'd have been a far better student."

Uncle Alistair yawned. "After that scholarly endeavor, I think we all deserve a bit of a rest."

"I don't know about *all* of us," Sam teased, scratching his head. "You and I may have been working since the sun came up, but Juliette has barely had time to wipe the sleep from her eyes."

Julie launched another paper ball at him, but he easily swatted it away with his hand.

Turning to her uncle, she said, "Shall I have a luncheon tray sent up to your room?"

"That would be frightful, my dear. Thank you." As he cheerfully hobbled out of the room, Juliette followed and located Mr. Finch to request the tray.

When she returned to the study, Sam stood, arms crossed, in front of the shelf he'd promised to clean, his expression grim.

"Luncheon is served," Julie informed him. "If the sight of those jars hasn't completely robbed you of your appetite."

"I'm not the squeamish sort." He rubbed his chin,

thoughtful. "But I expect the task will test my limits. Better to eat before. I think."

She shrugged and led the way toward the dining room. "Suit yourself. I trust your ear has made a complete recovery?" she teased. "Or shall I summon the doctor?"

"You should have warned me of your bowling prowess," he grumbled.

"Then you might not have agreed to the wager," she countered, smug.

Scoffing, he lowered his voice to a growl. "I don't scare easily, temptress. And you could have increased the stakes. I would have wagered far more for the chance to be with you again."

Julie quickly checked the corridor to make certain no one had overheard him and jabbed a finger at his hard chest. "You may not say things like that. What if one of the staff had been about?"

"I don't think they would have been horrified at anything I said. It's not as though I mentioned kissing, or pressing my body to yours, or caressing your bare—"

"Stop," she hissed. "Now you're simply trying to humiliate me."

"Juliette," he said, smooth as silk. "Nothing could be further from the truth. This is my attempt at flirtation."

She gave an unladylike snort. "You missed the mark—by a mile." Well, maybe not a mile. She had to admit her heart was pattering, and his almost-mention of her breasts had caused her to shiver delightfully. "I must say I'm glad that we'll be dining alone, however."

He settled his hand at the small of her back and whispered low in her ear. "So am I, vixen."

"You misunderstand," she said quickly. "I only want to talk about the house and the deal we made yesterday."

"I don't think we should talk until you've had a chance to break your fast," he said. "A lack of food most certainly contributed to your fainting spell earlier." He handed her a plate and pointed at the buffet laden with platters of sandwiches, salads, and fruits. "Eat."

Julie started to object, but the smell of roasted chicken tickled her nose and reminded her she was famished. So she filled her plate and sat across the table from Sam, surprised they managed to dine like two civilized people.

Indeed, they spent the entire meal chatting pleasantly, without exchanging barbs, casting aspersions—or debating property rights.

But she could not forget why he was here and the threat he posed to her uncle. Sam might have wormed his way into Uncle Alistair's heart, but he still meant to take possession of the house.

Julie's fork froze halfway to her lips. What was it that Sam had said only moments ago? That he'd wager the highest stakes for the chance to be with her again?

That kind of leverage could be valuable, given the precarious situation she found herself in. What if she agreed to be with him again in exchange for his help?

It wouldn't be a hardship to allow him a few kisses . . . a few liberties. And she wouldn't permit him to compromise her thoroughly, just to give her another taste of passion . . .

No. It would never do. She was not some sort of strumpet. And her sisters would be beyond appalled that the idea had even popped into her head. Heaven forfend they ever discovered the wicked nature of her thoughts.

"You must tell me what you are thinking right now," Sam drawled over the rim of his glass.

"Nothing," she said a bit too sharply. "Only that I need to mend the hem of my russet day dress." Gads, she was a horrid liar.

He arched a brow and nodded knowingly, blast it all. "And that's why you're blushing?"

"Not exactly," she said icily. "But I'm under no obligation to share the subject of my thoughts with you."

"Am *I* the subject, Juliette?" He folded his arms and leaned his elbows on the table, his eyes gleaming seductively. "Because I don't mind telling you that you're the subject of mine."

Goodness, the dining room was warm. Julie started to fan herself with her napkin, then pretended she only meant to wipe her mouth with it. "There is an important matter we need to discuss," she said primly. "After all that transpired last night, I've realized that the deal we made was ill-conceived. I must insist that you leave. Today."

Chapter TWENTY-ONE

Sam trained his gaze on Juliette and kept his face impassive. He was trying to pretend their delightful luncheon conversation hadn't just taken a very bad turn, when in truth, it had careened off the road into a ditch.

"Let me see if I understand you properly," he said. "You were content to let me remain under this roof as long as we were bickering, but now that we've declared a truce, you are insisting I leave?"

"We may have ceased our bickering, but we are still adversaries," she clarified.

"Were we adversaries last night, Juliette?"

"Yes," she said unequivocally—as though she were valiantly trying to convince herself. "I merely lost my head for a moment. And now I realize that the deal we made will never work."

He leaned back in his chair. "Do you want to know what I think?"

"No, I do not." She shifted in her seat, the questions

in her eyes belying her words. "Your thoughts are invariably wicked and best kept to yourself."

Undaunted, he grinned. "I think you are afraid."

She snorted. "Of *you*?"

"Not of me. Of the way I make you *feel*."

"You give yourself too much credit." She glanced away and pressed her lips together. "However, I cannot risk a repeat of last-night's performance."

"There will only be a repeat performance if you wish it." And he hoped to hell she did. "You have nothing to fear from me." He paused to let that sink in.

"You want to take my uncle's house away from him."

"My *brother* is the one who wishes to take possession of the property," he reminded her. "And this *is* his house."

She rubbed the tops of her arms as though she'd suddenly taken a chill. "I've yet to see proof."

"I'm working on it." He stroked his chin, thoughtful. "But you could always ask Nigel yourself."

Her gaze snapped to his. "What are you implying?"

He shrugged. "Nothing. I'm merely stating that you don't need me to intercede on your behalf. You could go directly to the source . . . and ask my brother yourself."

Sam watched her expression carefully. He wanted to ask why she hadn't told him about her relationship with Nigel.

And whether she was in love with him.

"How could I ask the marquess?" She blinked innocently. "Proper young ladies do not call on gentlemen."

"True." They did not venture onto moonlit terraces with them either.

Sam swallowed the bitter taste in his mouth. Clearly,

Juliette harbored feelings for Nigel. If she didn't, she'd have been more forthcoming with Sam.

If he was a gentleman, he'd step aside. Nigel and Juliette had obviously formed some sort of attachment before Sam had even met her.

And Nigel was infinitely more suitable for her. There wasn't a miss on the marriage mart who'd pass up an honorable marquess in favor of a wicked rogue. Sam might be acceptable for a secret dalliance or midnight tryst, but he wasn't the kind of man that respectable matrons invited into their drawing rooms. He wasn't the kind of man that noble gentlemen allowed to court their daughters.

Juliette was too good for him.

The problem was that he'd had a taste of her—her fire, her passion, her light—and now, it was impossible not to want more.

"I have a duty to my brother, and I will not fail him." He looked at the sandwich crust on his plate, the stem of his goblet—anywhere but the wounded expression on her face.

"So, you are dutiful when it suits you," she said dryly.

"I don't want to hurt you or your uncle. As it turns out, I'm fond of you both. But Nigel wants to sell this property, and that is his right. When I wrote to him yesterday, I asked him for the deed, and I asked him to give you time. What more would you like me to do?"

"I want you to leave," she said simply, cutting him to the quick.

"I'm not leaving this house until you do."

"What if your brother told you to stand down—to leave my uncle and me in peace?"

He blew out a long breath. "I don't give a damn what he does with his great many properties." All Sam wanted was to heal the rift between him and Nigel. To try and span the chasm that had formed when their father died and salvage what was left of their family. "If he has a change of heart and decides you and Alistair may stay, I'll gladly walk out your front door and never look back."

"Pardon me for interrupting." The elderly butler strolled into the dining room waving a few envelopes. "All three of these arrived within the last hour. Lord Travis," he said, handing him the largest envelope, "this is addressed to you. And Miss Juliette"—he shot her an affectionate smile—"these are for you. Perhaps you'll have an update from one of your sisters."

"I do hope so, Mr. Finch—thank you." She waited until the butler left, then turned each envelope over in her hand. "This one's from Meg," she said wistfully.

"And the other?" he asked, even though it clearly wasn't his place.

"I don't know." She made no move to open it, but inclined her head at the envelope he held. "Is that from your brother?"

"I assume so. No one else knows I'm here." He tapped it lightly on the table, then hesitated. "Shall I open it?"

She swallowed soberly—as though she knew what he was really asking. Whether she was ready to hear the truth about the house . . . and accept whatever the consequences may be for her and her uncle.

"I could wait until after you've had a chance to rest," he added.

She sat taller in her chair and shook her head, eyes

flashing with courage. "No. There's no sense in delaying the inevitable. Open it now."

Julie gripped the arms of her chair as Sam slid a finger under the flap and broke the sealing wax.

Deep in her soul, she knew the envelope wouldn't contain good news. And yet, she held out hope. Maybe after seeing her at the ball last night, Nigel had reconsidered his decision to evict Uncle Alistair and her.

Nigel had said that he held her in the highest esteem. That he only required some time to resolve things.

She might have thought his words empty had she not felt the heat of his ardent gaze and heard the hitch of his voice. He still felt something for her—even if he had an odd way of showing it.

But surely, now that Nigel knew she and her uncle occupied the house, he'd tell Sam to leave them in peace. Perhaps there was a message to her as well, telling her that she needn't worry, and that he'd take care of everything.

Her body tense, she watched as Sam unfolded several papers. Watched as his eyes scanned the words scrawled across the pages. "What do they say?" she asked.

"They're tax receipts." He frowned and studied the papers some more. "My father and Nigel have been paying the land assessment taxes for at least three decades."

"But Uncle Alistair has lived here most, if not all, of that time. Isn't it possible he has some sort of lease or tenancy?"

Sam glanced up, sympathy shining in his blue eyes. "Of course, it's possible. But apparently, Nigel has no record of it. Perhaps your uncle does. You should ask him."

Julie's head pounded—she'd never liked being told what to do. "I didn't want to trouble him until I was certain there wasn't a misunderstanding. Even now, I'd prefer to look for a lease or bill of sale myself and turn to him only as a last resort." She scarcely had to add that Uncle Alistair was notoriously disorganized and terribly forgetful.

"Whether or not you involve your uncle is your decision. But unless you can produce proof of a superior title or right to the property, I'm afraid my brother can turn you out of this house. I'm sorry."

Julie's eyes burned at the injustice of it all. "Why didn't he send the deed?"

"Nigel included a note." Sam waved a small piece of paper. "The deed is in a safe in his country house. He can send for it if you wish, but it will likely take a few days. The estate's in the far northern part of Yorkshire."

"Did he write anything else? Did your brother give any indication he'd be amenable to leasing or selling the property to us?"

"No." With frustration mirroring her own, he tossed the papers on the table.

Julie wrung her hands, wishing she knew what game Nigel played. As she watched Sam drumming the table with his fingers, she realized he was equally stymied.

She might as well confide her plans in him, for she desperately needed someone on her side. "I am going to scour the house for the proof that my uncle has a lease, or at least has the right to live out the rest of his life here."

"I'll help you, after I pay my debt." He winked, instantly turning her insides to mush.

"Thank you. But in the event that I cannot prove my

uncle has a superior right to occupy the house, I need to know your brother's selling price."

"There's one way to find out," he said philosophically.

"Yes." She bit her lip. "Will you ask him?"

"I will," he said, thoughtful. "But my involvement ends there. I want to help you, but Nigel is my brother, and I owe him my allegiance. I don't wish to be in the middle of any negotiations."

"Fair enough." Although, in truth, Sam was already in the middle. Julie didn't doubt he was loyal to his brother . . . but he also seemed to care about her.

As more than a potential conquest. For she could not imagine that he routinely befriended the uncles of his paramours or lowered himself to cleaning bookshelves stuffed with nausea-inducing relics.

"Aren't you going to read your letters?" he asked.

Julie had planned to read them in the privacy of her bedchamber, but she supposed it couldn't hurt. "I do hope it's good news from Meg," she said, sighing softly at the comforting sight of her sister's fine, even hand-writing. She unfolded the letter and read it quickly, her heart sinking with each paragraph.

"What's wrong?" he asked, his voice laced with concern. "Is your sister unwell?"

Julie nodded. "The midwife is concerned the baby will come too early, and she's advised Meg to remain in bed for the next two months."

"Should you go to her?" Before she could respond, he added, "I could keep an eye on your uncle for you."

Sam's offer, given so sincerely and naturally, warmed her to the core. "That's generous of you, but Meg wouldn't want me to leave him, and she cannot know that you're here. Besides, she says she is well cared for. Her husband, Will, dotes on her constantly—bringing her books, sweet treats . . . tokens of his affection." She sighed, wistful.

"Would you like me to spoil you, vixen? I cannot afford expensive gifts, but there are other ways I could indulge you."

"And I'm certain they are all improper." She arched a brow and ignored the delicious shiver that ran through her limbs.

He chuckled. "Absolutely. The sweetest things in life are necessarily improper. Running barefoot through the fields . . . swimming naked in the river . . . lounging on the grass as the sun kisses your skin . . ."

"You are the undisputed expert of improper pleasures," she conceded. She could easily imagine him doing all those things. And it wasn't difficult to imagine herself doing those things *with* him.

He grinned, clearly pleased. "I might have to add that title to my calling card."

Julie's face heated, but she pressed on. "Meg also writes that Beth, my other sister, has decided to extend her honeymoon for a few weeks . . . and Meg doesn't want to worry her with the news about the baby. So she forbids me to tell anyone else, lest Beth find out."

"I promise not to breathe a word of it," Sam said solemnly . . . but then he cracked a smile.

"What is so funny?" Julie demanded.

"For sisters as close as you three are, you certainly keep a lot of secrets from each other."

"With good reason," she said, her hackles up. But blast it all, he was correct.

"Perhaps the other letter will contain better news." He pointed at the unopened envelope next to her plate.

"Let us hope so," she said, pulling out a card. But as she scanned the details, her fingers tingled and went numb. "It's an invitation to a dinner party."

"From whom?" he said, wary.

"Your brother. He's hosting a small gathering tomorrow night. He regrets that the numbers don't allow him to extend the invitation to Uncle Alistair, but he'd be delighted if I would attend."

Sam scowled. "He expects you to attend his little dinner party unchaperoned?"

"What's this? All of the sudden you're concerned about my reputation?" she asked, incredulous.

"I find the circumstances odd. Suspicious."

Tamping down her own niggling sense of unease, Julie smiled brightly. "I'm certain your brother's dinner party will be perfectly respectable."

"And boring," he added pointedly.

"You were the one who encouraged me to speak to the marquess directly," she reminded him. "Tomorrow night could present the ideal opportunity for me to discuss the house with him. I'm going to accept his invitation."

"By all means, go." Sam stood, rounded the table, and leaned close to her ear. "Go to your fancy balls and elegant dinners, temptress. Dance with dukes and mingle with the finest ladies. But when you grow weary of their endless rules and insipid chatter, remember I'll be here at home . . . waiting for you."

Chapter TWENTY-TWO

Sam decided to clean Alistair's bookcase the next afternoon. He'd hoped the task would prove absorbing enough that he'd forget about Nigel's dinner party and the fact that Juliette would be spending the entire evening with his brother.

But as he moved about the study, dusting jars, organizing books, and sorting years' worth of notes, he could think of little else.

He shook his head—as if it were just that easy to erase the image of Nigel and Juliette, together, from his mind—and turned his attention to the bookcase. "These shelves are much deeper than they look." Sam removed two more jars of water from the top shelf, hopped off the stool, and set them on the desk in front of Alistair.

The old man examined the label on one with a magnifying glass. "August, 1798." He checked the other label. "And this one is January, 1801."

Sam scooped both jars off the desk and placed them

in the long line of jars along the floor beneath the window, which he'd arranged in chronological order. "It's a wonder there's any water left in the Thames," he teased. "Surely boats are running aground and fish are flapping on the dry riverbed."

"'Tis merely a thimbleful out of a bathtub," Alistair replied. "But I do wonder what moved me to collect samples month after month for twenty years. Habit, I suppose."

Habit . . . madness . . . it was a rather thin line as far as Sam was concerned. He'd convinced Alistair to dispose of several of the jars he'd pulled off the shelves. After some negotiation, they'd agreed that if a jar was cracked or its contents unidentifiable, it had little scientific value.

But Alistair did seem inexplicably attached to the jars of river water, and Sam had to give him credit for collecting them so meticulously, over such a long period.

"There are only two months missing." Sam stood with his hands on hips, surveying the line of jars winding around the room. "And those jars may be hidden toward the back of that top shelf."

"They're somewhere in here," Alistair said confidently. "I never skipped a month. Even in the winter of 1814 when the river froze over, I took my jar to the Frost Fair and filled it with ice."

"Your dedication is commendable," Sam said. "All I did at the Frost Fair was stuff myself with gingerbread and sip gin."

"Oh, I might have partaken of gingerbread and gin too." Alistair chuckled softly. "One must balance work and pleasure, you know. Without a bit of fun, life is far too tedious."

Sam grinned in agreement. "Wise words. I may have them engraved on my headstone." But it occurred to him that the reverse was also true—that without work or a commitment to anything worthwhile, the most decadent pleasures could seem . . . empty.

In short, it had been too long since he'd given a damn. About anything.

"I heard someone mention a headstone." Juliette breezed into the study, a breath of fresh air in her yellow dress. "Should I be alarmed?"

"Not at all, my dear. We were only speaking in matadors." Alistair waved an arm around the room. "Look at all the progress Samuel has made."

"I didn't manage it alone," Sam said. "Your uncle and I make a good team."

Juliette beamed at him like he'd just slayed a dragon. "I am impressed." Turning to Alistair, she said, "Once all your findings are catalogued, you'll think of something brilliant to present to the Royal Society—I'm certain of it."

"Yes, well, I've accomplished more than enough cataloguing for today, I fear. But as you can see, I am adhering to my end of our bargain. Do not forget that you promised me something in return." Alistair waggled his bushy eyebrows.

Juliette busied herself with a stack of papers, pretending to be thoroughly engrossed with the task. "I haven't forgotten, Uncle. You do look rather weary. Would you like to rest in the parlor? Perhaps take a nap in your favorite chair?"

Sam recognized a dodging question when he heard one. He'd perfected it to an art form himself. And he wasn't letting Juliette sidestep Alistair so easily. "What did you promise your uncle?" he interjected.

"It's a personal matter," she replied, not meeting his gaze.

"Nonsense." Alistair pushed himself out of his desk chair and ambled toward Juliette. "Samuel is family. We needn't keep secrets from him. He might even be able to help."

"I'd be delighted to," Sam said.

"No." Juliette rolled her eyes, appalled at the very idea. "The last thing I require is your assistance."

"She promised to devote herself to finding a husband," Alistair explained. "But she spends far too much time here, with me."

"That's not true. Have you forgotten that I went to a ball two nights ago and am attending a dinner party tonight?"

"Nay, I've not forgotten." Alistair patted her shoulder the way one might soothe a wild pony. "It is possible you are making as much progress toward your goal as I am toward mine. The difference is that *my* progress is evident on the shelves and tables around this room . . . while your progress is in here." He tapped his chest, over his heart.

Guilt sliced through Sam. While Juliette had been trying to make a decent match, he'd been trying to seduce her—and he'd come damned close to succeeding.

"I will do my best to uphold my end of our bargain, Uncle." She laid her hand over his, pressing it to his chest. "And I am working on it."

As Sam stepped onto the stool and removed a box full of envelopes, notes, and God-knew-what-else from the top shelf, he wondered if Juliette spoke the truth.

Perhaps she'd her sights set on Nigel and would use tonight's dinner party to advance her cause.

Maybe tomorrow, Nigel would arrive on her doorstep and ask Alistair for her hand in marriage.

And then Sam's life could return to normal.

He should have been inordinately pleased at the prospect. But the thought of Juliette with Nigel—with *anyone*, actually—made him want to punch something.

"I trust you, Juliette," Alistair said warmly. "Now, I think I will take your fine suggestion and rest in my favorite chair with my wool blanket. Meanwhile, don't exert yourself unruly in here. We've accomplished enough for one day. You and Samuel should play a game of chess."

Sam snorted to himself. In some ways, they already were. He was the pawn to her queen.

Alistair shuffled toward the parlor, and Juliette perused stacks of paper with renewed vigor.

When the old man was out of earshot, Sam said, "Maybe we *should* play chess."

She glanced up at him like he'd sprouted horns. "I've no time for games. I need to search the study while my uncle is resting."

"I've been looking for anything resembling a lease or bill of sale all morning, but I've yet to find anything."

"Have you searched his desk?" She sat in Alistair's desk chair and yanked open a drawer with more force than necessary.

"No," he said cautiously, "but I'll be happy to help you."

She shot him a grateful smile as she heaped a huge stack of documents on the desktop. "This could take a while."

Julie and Sam spent the next two hours painstakingly leafing through the pile, paper by paper—and found no documents related to the house.

Every so often, however, Sam had set a letter or note aside. Julie inclined her head at the small stack. "What is in that pile?"

He shrugged as he stroked his jaw thoughtfully. "Some notes about the Thames. I wondered if they might be related to your uncle's jars. They're probably nothing, but some are fascinating."

"How so?"

Sam picked the top paper off the stack and scanned it. "This letter from a fisherman is over thirty years old. He and his crew caught a shark near Poplar Island."

Julie blinked. "A shark in the Thames?"

"A rare thing, to be sure. It was sickly, and when they cut it open they discovered a silver watch and chain in its stomach . . . but no trace of its owner."

"That's awful." Julie suppressed a shudder. "I trust the other papers are less tragic in nature?"

Sam shuffled through them. "Some contain reports of whales. Others refer to the dwindling populations of plants and water creatures. A few simply contain moving descriptions of the beauty of the river at sunset. Perhaps none of this is worth saving, but your uncle is clearly passionate about the Thames—which makes it a fine subject on which to focus his research."

For several moments, Julie said nothing. Each time she'd thought she knew and understood Sam, he managed to somehow surprise her again. "That's quite insightful," she said at last. "Thank you."

He placed the papers on a shelf and looked away, as though embarrassed. "I wish we'd found something related to the house."

"As do I." Julie sat back and rolled the tightness out of her shoulders. As Sam stood and stretched his arms, she endeavored not to stare at his broad shoulders. Or hard chest. Or taut abdomen.

She straightened the desk pad, ink blotter, and ink well, sighing softly. "I'm going to have to ask my uncle whether he, in fact, owns this house—and hope that my questions don't distress him."

"You should allow me to ask him," Sam said. "I could inquire about it in the normal course of conversation, and it wouldn't seem as odd."

"That's an excellent idea," she said, wishing she'd thought of it first.

"I do have them, occasionally," he quipped. "I'll speak with him tonight, while you're at the dinner party."

"That would be wonder—" She paused and shook her head. "On second thought, let's wait. One more day of uncertainty won't hurt, and perhaps I'll learn the details myself, if I've the opportunity to broach the subject with your brother tonight."

"Suit yourself." Sam shrugged as though he were indifferent, but Julie detected a trace of irritation in his tone. He walked to the sideboard and lifted the stopper off a decanter of sherry. "Join me in a glass?"

She shouldn't. It was almost time to dress for dinner, and tonight more than ever, she needed to keep her wits about her. "Just one."

He filled two glasses and handed her the one without the chipped rim, joining her where she half-stood, half-sat on the front edge of her uncle's desk. Clinking his goblet against hers, he said, "May your evening hold the answers you seek."

She sipped thoughtfully, staring at his handsome face and noting the jaded look in his eyes. "May I ask you something?"

"Anything, spitfire."

"Why didn't your brother invite you to his dinner party? Are you not close to him? That is, I realize you are very different, but I wouldn't dream of having a dinner party and excluding my sisters."

"You mustn't blame Nigel for our strained relationship. I'm a source of constant disappointment to him. He's given me second chances. Hell, he's given me third, fourth, and fifth chances. I always promise to do better—to refrain from gambling and womanizing—and I do. For a fortnight or so. And then, despite my best intentions, I manage to end up in the gossip papers again."

"Your brother wants you to be more respectable. Like him."

"Yes." He slid closer, brushing his hard shoulder against hers. "Tell me something, Juliette."

"Of course." She'd tried to sound breezy, but his nearness made her breathy. His thigh bumped lightly against her hip, awakening every inch of her skin.

"If I were more like my brother—more decent and honorable—would I have a chance to win your heart?"

Julie swallowed. She wanted to say that she couldn't imagine Sam any other way than the way he was. And that his naughtiness and rough edges appealed to her wild side, her passionate nature. But he wasn't husband material. What miss in her right mind would bind herself to a man who couldn't stay out of the gossip pages?

"My heart is not a prize to be won. Love isn't a competition."

"You didn't answer my question," he countered.

She shrugged. "It's a moot point. You said yourself that though you've tried many times to change, you cannot."

"True." He set his wine glass behind him on the desk and searched her face. "But I think the reason I never succeeded in changing was I never cared enough. About anything or anyone. And maybe . . ." Deliberately, he smoothed a tendril behind her ear and traced the shell with his fingertip. "Maybe that's changing."

Her knees went a little weak. Perhaps it was due to his husky voice or his earnest expression or the slight tremor in his hand. "Everyone needs to care about something or someone," she said. "But the change starts inside *you*."

He took her glass, set it down, and lightly ran his fingers down her arms, from her shoulders all the way to her wrists. Pulling her closer, he said, "So you're saying there's hope for me."

"Absolutely," she whispered. Lord help her, she shouldn't encourage him like this, not when he was so utterly wrong for her.

He rubbed his thumb back and forth across her palm, heating her blood. "But my odds are not good?"

"No," she breathed. "Far less than ninety percent."

"I'd be happy with ten, Juliette." He leaned in and brushed his lips over hers. "Just give me a chance."

She melted into him, his strength, his vulnerability, *him*. But just as she parted her lips to taste his, the grandfather clock down the hall chimed, and she jumped.

Gads. The coach Nigel was sending for her would arrive in a half hour. "I must go and dress," she said regretfully. But it was no doubt for the best.

A roguish Sam was hard enough to resist.

But this tender, genuine version of him? Nigh impossible.

Chapter TWENTY-THREE

Julie took extra care in dressing for the dinner party. Her blue satin gown was fashionable, but not ostentatious. The lustrous pearls at her throat were elegant, but not garish. The loose curls around her face were pretty, but not overdone.

No one—not even Nigel, the noble Marquess of Currington—could find fault with her appearance.

And if she didn't turn as many heads as she had in the daring red silk a couple of days ago, she didn't mind.

No one would mistake her for a wallflower tonight.

Uncle Alistair had kissed her cheek in the parlor before she left and reminded her of her promise to find a husband.

Sam was conspicuously absent.

She told herself she wasn't disappointed, that she only wanted to wish him a good night after their heartfelt conversation that afternoon.

But it was just as well that he didn't show, because

she tended to lose her head around him, and tonight of all nights, she needed to keep her wits about her.

Now, she sank against the plush velvet squabs of Nigel's coach, admiring the gleaming woodwork of the cab and fine curtains adorning the windows. Never had she ridden in such a luxurious conveyance, and she felt rather like a princess being whisked away to a royal ball.

She wished she knew who the other guests would be and hoped Charlotte might attend so that there would be at least one friendly face at the table. But the truth was, she wasn't attending Nigel's dinner party to mingle with important people or exchange the latest on-dit.

Her primary goal of the evening was to speak to Nigel about her uncle's house—and convince the marquess to allow her uncle to stay there. Julie was not above begging, although she'd prefer it if Nigel were to meet her half way.

And she saw no reason why he shouldn't.

Which reminded her of her secondary goal of the evening—to determine the nature of their relationship, once and for all.

First, at the masquerade ball, he'd kissed her, then failed to call in the days and weeks that followed.

He'd sent his brother to evict her and her uncle, and then sought her out at the Breckinridge Ball, insulted her family, and promised to see what he could do about her uncle's house—whatever that meant.

And now, he'd invited her to a dinner party, which certainly reflected some level of interest . . . and perhaps an inclination to make their association public or even woo her.

But she couldn't be sure.

More important, she wasn't entirely certain she *wanted* Nigel to court her. After their kiss, she'd been desperate to see him, or at least receive some small token of his affection—a poem, flowers, a note.

But that was before Sam had shown up on her doorstep, confusing her with his heat-filled glances and knee-weakening kisses. Everything about him was dangerous. Deliciously so.

What sort of woman was she, to kiss two brothers? Meg and Beth would be appalled at her wantonness. Gads, she was appalled herself.

But the tentative kiss she'd shared with Nigel was nothing compared to her all-body-consuming kiss with Sam. It was like comparing burlap to silk. Water to champagne.

Not that the kiss with Nigel had been *bad*, precisely.

But it had not set her blood on fire or made her hunger for something she couldn't even name.

To be fair, Nigel had no doubt restrained himself during their kiss. Out of respect for her. He'd probably flogged himself mercilessly for taking the liberty of chastely touching his lips to hers.

And in spite of that minor transgression, he was ten times the gentleman Sam was. If she truly had a choice between the two brothers, it *should* be no contest. Nigel was handsome, wealthy, titled, respected.

But Julie didn't burn for him the way she did for Sam.

As the coach rolled to a stop in front of Nigel's stately townhouse, her belly twisted in knots.

Tonight was important. She must behave properly throughout the evening and make polite conversation with the esteemed guests. Her manners must be flawless.

She alighted from the coach, and glided up the walkway just as she and her sister had practiced as girls, balancing a book on their heads—but without fail, Julie's book had ended up bruising someone's toe.

The marquess's butler admitted her, quickly ushering her into the foyer, as if he'd been expecting her. "Welcome, Miss Lacey," he said stiffly. "I'll see you to the drawing room."

"Am I late?" Julie asked.

He remained stony-faced. "Not that I am aware, miss."

Why, then, was the house so still? She wrapped her shawl more tightly around her shoulders and strained her ears, listening for the buzz of guests greeting one another, enjoying pre-dinner drinks. But the only sound she heard was the click of her heels on the polished marble floors.

The house was cool, sober, and refined—not unlike Nigel.

She followed the servant down a corridor, past muted landscapes and genteel portraits. At last, the butler swung open a door and waved her through. "Lord Currington awaits you inside."

Julie frowned. "And the other guests?" she asked— but the stodgy butler had already turned and left.

So, she took a deep breath and walked into the marquess's drawing room, her head held high.

He stood alone, his back to her, staring out a window at the moonless sky. The resemblance to Sam was so striking that, for a moment, she felt her heart flutter.

"Good evening, Miss Lacey." Nigel faced her, his cool gaze flitting over her appreciatively.

She waited till he approached, and curtsied. "Lord Currington."

He bowed over the hand she offered in a perfectly gentlemanly fashion. "It is good to see you, Juliette."

She arched a brow. "Where are the rest of your guests?"

He had the good grace to look chagrined. "Forgive my bit of subterfuge. There are no other guests."

A chill slithered down her spine. "You deceived me."

"Not exactly. This *is* a dinner party." He paused. "For two."

Rage bubbled and seethed beneath her skin. His good looks, title, and wealth did not give him the right to manipulate her. "I must go." She headed toward the door as fast as she dared, invisible books be damned.

"I had thought tonight would be an opportune time to discuss your uncle's house," he said casually, as if he were commenting on the lack of rain.

She froze, her slippers glued to the floor.

"You are certainly welcome to leave if you wish," he continued smoothly. "My coach and driver are at your disposal. But I was under the impression that you wanted to talk about your uncle's situation. A subject that is best addressed privately."

Steaming, she spun to face him. "Do not pretend that you arranged this evening out of consideration for me. You lured me here under false pretenses. It is beneath you."

He dropped his chin, contrite. "Perhaps I am not the saint everyone imagines me to be. I am only a man, Juliette. And if I've erred in bringing you here tonight, I beg your forgiveness . . . but I do hope you'll stay."

She hesitated. "I want to see the deed to the house. In the unlikely event that my uncle cannot locate his bill of sale or lease, I wish to know your selling price."

He shot her an amused, superior smile—the sort her palm itched to slap off his face. "We may discuss all of those details . . . in due time. But dinner is already served, and I think we shall both need sustenance before we launch into such matters. Will you do me the honor of accompanying me to the dining room?"

Meg and Beth would tell her she was a fool to even consider dining alone with the marquess. But she was already in his home, and she desperately needed answers. Besides, she knew he would never physically hurt her. Whatever his faults, he'd never threatened her in that manner. "I will dine with you," she said slowly. "But you must understand this. I will not tolerate any more lies, any more deception. If you fail to be truthful with me, I'll walk out your door and never speak to you again."

"That would wound me greatly," he said, placing a hand over his heart. Julie searched his face but couldn't detect a trace of sarcasm.

"Then I suggest you do not test me," she said.

"Fair enough." He offered his arm, and she allowed him to escort her through to the most elegantly set table she'd ever seen. Three softly glowing candelabra lined the center of the long table, casting light that danced off every crystal glass, every porcelain plate. The silver cutlery sparkled and the soft green wallpaper shimmered. Two rows of gold-framed landscapes surrounded them like windows to luxurious, exotic worlds.

Julie refrained from gaping as she sank onto her silk-covered chair seat and spread her crisp napkin across her lap. It was a far cry from their cozy dining room at home. Uncle Alistair's table invited shared confidences and genuine laughter. The marquess's table, by contrast, invited careful conversation and controlled smiles.

Though Julie preferred the former, it was impossible not to be impressed with the opulence that surrounded her. And for the briefest of moments, she recalled what it had felt like to be a wallflower. Plain and unfashionable in the midst of a sea of beauty and grace; small and powerless in an ocean of wealth and aristocracy.

She didn't ever want to feel that way again.

Chapter TWENTY-FOUR

During the first several courses, Nigel watched Julie out of the corner of his eye, studying her like she was one of Uncle Alistair's rare specimens. From time to time, he inquired politely about her sisters and solicitously asked whether the meal was to her liking.

Of course it was—every dish was a delicacy, from the poached salmon to the sliced ham to the glazed carrots—but Julie tasted little of it, for she was too nervous to eat more than a few bites of anything.

As she nibbled on her strawberry trifle, she wondered why someone with such extravagant tastes would want to own her uncle's ramshackle townhouse. And since the marquess did not seem inclined to broach the topic, she did.

"Why do you want my uncle's house"—she spread her hands in front of her—"when you have all of this?"

Nigel set his napkin on the table and leaned back in

his chair. "I don't mean to be impertinent, but it is *my* house. Your uncle merely occupies it."

"So do I," she reminded him.

"Let us repair to the garden," he suggested.

Alarms sounded in her head. "I would prefer the drawing room."

"Very well," he said in a placating tone.

This time, she didn't take the arm he offered. She had tried to be civil, truly she had. But her patience had been stretched to the thinnest of threads. She marched ahead of him into the drawing room and paced before the dormant fireplace.

He regarded her thoughtfully, his forehead creased. "You are very agitated. I shall pour you a glass of claret."

"I do not care for anything to drink. What I would like is for you to answer one simple question."

"I shall try." He stepped closer, all attentiveness and concern.

"*If* the house does indeed belong to you, at what price would you be willing to sell it?"

He rubbed the back of his neck as though pained. "That question is more difficult to answer than you think."

"I don't see why. You needn't tell me down to the sixpence, after all—I only want to know approximately how many thousands of pounds you believe the house and property are worth."

"They are worth a great deal to me, Juliette."

Her knees trembled slightly, but she kept the quaver out of her voice. She had very little money of her own, and Nigel surely knew it. "How much?"

"I am not certain I can name my price in pounds." His gaze swept over her face, her breasts, and her hips—so briefly she might have imagined it. "There is something I value more."

"I don't understand what you're saying." Although she had an inkling—enough to make her dig her nails into her palms.

He cupped her elbows lightly. "Above all else, I value . . . our friendship."

"Our friendship," she repeated, incredulous.

"Yes, I've missed you. Your sparkling wit and your zeal for life." He blinked, the picture of innocence. "Is that so hard to believe?"

"It is. If you valued our friendship so greatly you would have called on me after the masquerade ball."

"I wanted to," he said earnestly. "I started to visit you half a dozen times . . . but I didn't want to mislead you."

She recalled his stinging words on the last occasion they'd spoken. "Because you could never court someone like me."

"You are not naïve, Juliette. It's one of a great many things I admire about you. I thought you would appreciate my honesty." He squeezed her elbows affectionately, coaxingly. "I have worked hard to establish myself as a gentleman of the highest honor and cannot simply walk away from that. I'm afraid my good reputation is a cross that I must bear."

She sniffed. "My brothers-in-law—an earl and a duke—were not above linking themselves to my family. But perhaps they are more courageous than you."

"Perhaps. But allow me to remind you that neither of their reputations was pristine to begin with—far from it. I cannot afford to thumb my nose at society's rules. Not if I wish to succeed in becoming one of the most powerful lords in England. And I do."

A chill stole over her skin. "You say you value my friendship, but that duty prevents you from associating with me. I see no way to reconcile those two things."

"We can maintain our bond and, indeed, nurture it further . . . but we must do so privately."

A potent mixture of disbelief and anger pulsed through her, and she pulled away. "I thought you were honorable, but I was terribly wrong. A true gentleman wouldn't suggest something so untoward."

"I am not asking you to do anything that makes you uneasy or that you deem improper. I will savor your friendship—no matter what form it takes."

She arched a brow, highly skeptical. "Even if it is entirely platonic?"

Nigel rubbed his chin, a gesture that instantly reminded her of Sam. "I will not insult your intelligence by pretending I would not wish for more. I would wish for as much of you as you are willing to give. I want to take care of you—and your uncle. I want to spend time with you and grow closer to you." He raked a hand through his hair—perhaps the first time she'd ever seen his control slip. "But I will not pressure you to give more than you wish."

"If you sincerely meant that, you would not try to force my uncle and me out of our house."

"Please, Juliette. Don't try to paint me as some sort of demon. The only thing I ask of you is your friendship . . . and time."

Gooseflesh covered her arms. "Time?"

"Time to be with you," he clarified. "Like we are to-night."

"You mean privately."

He frowned, his face full of regret. "That is of necessity. I wish it were not so. But please do not doubt the depth of my feelings for you. I know that I have yet to earn your trust. Tell me you'll give me a chance."

It seemed to her that the air had been sucked from the room. She could hear the ticking of the clock on the mantel and feel the weight of his gaze on her.

"I shall require time to think about your offer," she managed.

"I understand." But his jaw twitched, belying his patience. He was a man used to getting what he wanted, when he wanted it. "But I implore you to have mercy. Do not deprive me of the pleasure of your company for too long."

Though he didn't explicitly state what the consequences might be if she were to delay longer than he deemed appropriate, the threat was there, hanging over her—a tangible, horrible thing.

He not only had the power to evict her and her uncle . . . he had the power to ruin her. To leave her reputation in tatters and destroy any chance she might have of making a good match.

"I need to go," she said. "But I must ask you something first."

"Of course." His pale blue eyes softened. "Anything."

"Why did you send your brother to our house? Why would you involve him at all?"

"I hoped it would keep him out of trouble for a while.

Besides," he continued, "it was time for Samuel to do something useful. I'm sure you're anxious to be rid of him, and the sooner we reach an agreement, the sooner he will be out from under your feet."

"And in the meantime, I assume he keeps you apprised of my comings and goings?"

Nigel shrugged. "He's been surprisingly helpful."

Julie's heart sank. She'd thought something real was growing between her and Sam, but perhaps he was little more than a spy for his brother.

And a source of blackmail. Nigel was well aware of Sam's roguish reputation, and she'd been a shockingly easy conquest.

"I will give you an answer within the week," she said. That should give her sufficient time to search Uncle Alistair's house for a lease or bill of sale. And in the event she couldn't find one, she'd have time to make a decision.

His eyes narrowed as though he'd object, but then he nodded. "No longer, Juliette. I must have your answer then." She inclined her head, and he offered her his arm. "I'll see you out."

When they reached the elegant foyer, she turned to him. "Good evening, Nigel."

He bowed over her hand and brushed the lightest of kisses across the back of it. "Sleep well, dear Juliette. And know that I shall be haunted by dreams of you."

She walked down his pavement to his carriage on wobbly knees and climbed inside, relieved when the door shut behind her. As the coach slowly rolled away, she took a deep breath and sank into the soft velvet—and felt something on the seat beside her.

It was a small box, wrapped in pretty red paper and tied with string.

And underneath the string was a folded note—with her name carefully written on the outside.

Her mouth went dry. It appeared to be a present. From Nigel.

She removed the note and pushed the curtain aside so she could read by the light of the lantern that hung on the outside of the carriage.

My dearest Juliette,
Please accept this small token of my affection, and know that even when I am not with you, I think of you and live for the day when next we meet.
                                        Faithfully yours,
                                        Nigel

With trembling fingers, she turned the package over in her hands. If she accepted the gift, Nigel might erroneously assume that she was agreeing to the terms of his offer. And though he hadn't explicitly stated those terms, they could not have been clearer.

Nigel would allow her uncle to remain in his home if she would further her acquaintance with the marquess . . . in private. And though he claimed he would be satisfied with a platonic relationship, he would subtly—and sometimes not so subtly—pressure her for more.

Which meant he wanted her to be his mistress.

She slipped the string off the box and unwrapped it, revealing a pink velvet case. Slowly, she opened the hinged lid, revealing a jewel encrusted, crescent-shaped pendant suspended from a gold chain. Another, smaller note was tucked inside the lid.

I adore the way your eyes sparkle in moonlight. —N.

The necklace was beautiful, and the note was the romantic sort she had desperately wished for after their kiss at the masquerade ball.

But she no longer harbored illusions about Nigel. His impeccable manners and extravagant gifts couldn't hide the ruthless man who lurked beneath the polished veneer.

As the carriage slowed, Julie tucked both notes into her reticule and steeled her resolve.

Let Nigel do his worst.

He could threaten to throw her and her uncle out of their home.

He could even attempt to blackmail her by revealing that his brother Sam—an unrepentant rogue—was living under the same roof as she.

She may be the youngest of the Wilting Wallflowers, but she would be no man's mistress.

When a footman opened the cab door, she alighted the coach with her head held high, and glided up the walkway to her uncle's townhouse. She didn't mind the crooked shutter or the chipped paint. It was home.

"Forgive me, miss," the footman called out. She turned to see him holding the pink velvet box in an outstretched hand. "You left this on the seat."

"Yes," she said in the most regal tone she could muster. "I did."

With that, she climbed the cracked front steps and went inside.

Chapter TWENTY-FIVE

Sam woke with a start and blinked at the cozy, dimly lit bedchamber. Jesus, he'd fallen asleep in an armchair after his second brandy, apparently exhausted after his tame evening of playing chess and—after Alistair had retired for the night—searching the study.

Sam had hoped that by the time Juliette returned home, he'd be able to surprise her with good news—like a bill of sale or lease proving her uncle had the right to remain in his home.

But all he'd found were more letters from Alistair's friends and acquaintances—many pertaining to his study of the Thames. There were notes from ship captains about the depth of the water at various points and letters from fishermen about their catches of the day. Sam had tossed them all into a box, in case they proved useful at some point . . . though it seemed distinctly unlikely.

So he'd retreated to his guest bedchamber, closed his

eyes for a few moments, and let thoughts of Juliette fill his head. The memory of the night on the settee haunted him—in the best of ways. Her soft sighs of pleasure, the satin feel of her skin beneath his palms, the glow of her eyes, dark with desire. He'd committed every perfect detail to memory.

A knock, soft but insistent, sounded at the door.

A glance at the clock revealed it was past midnight.

Juliette must have come home . . . and come for him.

Instantly alert, he pushed himself out of the chair, opened the door, and drank in the sight of her. God, she was beautiful. Curls framed her face as she looked up at him from beneath sooty lashes.

He leaned a shoulder on the doorjamb and crossed his arms. "So, you missed me after all?"

"How dare you." She jabbed a finger at his chest as she angled through the doorway into his room. Her clenched hands and rosy cheeks told him her anger was about more than his quip.

"What have I done now?" Searching his mind, he closed the door behind her so they wouldn't wake Alistair.

She planted her hands on her hips. "You came here to *spy* on me. I confided in you—told you my hopes and fears regarding my uncle—and you have reported everything back to your brother."

He blinked. "I don't know what Nigel told you, but my only communication with him has been at your behest. I asked him to provide the deed and to give you time. I thought that was what you wanted me to do."

She snorted. "Do not pretend that you are here to help me. You have no regard for my wishes."

Clearly, Nigel had made Sam out to be the villain . . . which was not exactly a stretch. "That's not true," he said earnestly. "I want you to be happy."

"Forgive me," she said dryly, "but your actions belie your words."

"How have I betrayed you, Juliette? Tell me."

She spun on him. "You bullied your way into this house. You insisted on staying here, when what I wanted you to do was leave."

"I didn't know you then."

"But you do now."

"Do you want me to leave?"

She sank into the armchair he'd recently occupied and pressed her fingertips to her forehead. "Yes. No. I don't know."

He sat on a footstool opposite her and propped his elbows on his knees. "I take it the dinner party was a disappointment?"

She hesitated, just long enough to make the embers of jealousy spark to life inside him. Nigel was everything Sam wasn't—and he was clearly smitten with Juliette.

"The evening didn't unfold as I expected, but I did receive some answers."

Sam searched her face. "Will my brother sell the house to you?"

"He named his price," she said evenly.

"Whatever it is, I'm sure your brothers-in-law will pay it. I would gladly buy it for you myself if I could."

Her gaze flicked to his, grateful. Then the box of Alistair's letters he'd collected earlier caught her eye. "What is that?"

"More of your uncle's letters and notes that may relate to river-water samples. I planned to peruse them here but fell asleep."

She looked at him with an odd combination of surprise, amusement, and . . . affection? "You don't actually have to become my uncle's research assistant, you know," she said. "You're simply playing a part to explain your presence here."

"True. But as long as I'm playing the part, I may as well make myself useful." Besides, he wasn't entirely certain he was playing a part any longer. He liked Alistair. Not in spite of his poignant stories, peculiar foibles, and devotion to his late wife . . . but *because* of all those things. The old man might be mad as a hatter, but he was also wise—and kind.

"I think my uncle is growing quite fond of you," she said. "I must remind myself not to be jealous of the quick bond you've forged."

Sam chuckled. "If he's fond of me it's because we sneak cigars when you're out. But never fear, you hold the highest place in his heart—and I'm certain you always will."

She gave him a wobbly smile that made his chest squeeze. "How did we land in such a mess?" she asked. "And how will we ever manage to crawl out?"

"Together." He took her hand, uncurled her fingers, and placed a kiss on her palm. "We will crawl out of this mess together."

"I don't see how," she said bleakly. "My reputation will soon be in tatters, casting a pall over my sisters' newfound happiness. My uncle shall be forced to leave his beloved home, and I'm no closer to improving his standing in the scientific community, much less gaining his acceptance in the highest social circles."

It gutted him to see her so forlorn. He'd come here at Nigel's request in an attempt to heal the rift between them. But he couldn't hurt Juliette in the process. He'd have to find another way to reconcile with his brother.

"When I arrived on your doorstep, you were a stranger. Someone who stood in my brother's path—and mine. But then I witnessed how fiercely you protect your uncle and how he beams with pride each time you walk into the room. I realized how much this house means to you both and witnessed how loyal you are to the people you love. Sometime in the last few days—after I hid behind your settee and before I first kissed you—I began to care for you. A hell of a lot more than I have a right to. The last thing I want to do is hurt you, so . . ."

She tilted her head, touched and confused. "What are you saying, Sam?"

"I'll leave tomorrow. The only one who knows I'm here is Nigel, and he would never breathe a word of it. Your reputation will remain intact. As for the house, I will do what I can to convince my brother to allow you and your uncle to remain here . . . or at least sell it to you for a pittance."

She stared at him for the space of several heartbeats, her beautiful eyes shining with unshed tears. "You would do that for me? What of your promise to your brother?"

Sam had asked himself the same thing. "He's the only family I have left. My father always hoped Nigel and I would be brothers in the truest sense, supporting one another through life's trials and sharing in each other's joys and successes. He wanted our future children—his grandchildren—to grow up together, understanding what it means to be a family. A genuine family, like the one you, your sisters, and your uncle have. That's what I wanted too."

She swallowed. "But you would turn away from your duty to Nigel . . . for me?"

"Damn it, Juliette. If pleasing Nigel means hurting you, it's no contest. If I must choose between him and you . . . I choose you."

Julie let Sam's words seep into her skin and warm her. He chose *her*.

He'd answered his bedroom door wearing only a shirt and trousers, and the shirt . . . well, it was more off than on. It hung loosely from his shoulders, untied and untucked, revealing tantalizing glimpses of muscled chest and flat abdomen. His hair looked as though he'd run hands through it, and the hint of a beard darkened his square jaw.

She was very aware of his thumb brushing her palm, his knees straddling hers, his strength surrounding them like a cocoon.

And knew she was on the brink of something reckless and foolhardy . . . thrilling and wonderful.

"It's unsettling," she began slowly, "to realize that everything you thought you knew about a person is wrong."

He brought her knuckles to his lips and murmured against them. "How so?"

Savoring the hot pressure of his mouth, she said, "I thought Nigel's character was beyond reproach and that he'd defend my honor at any cost. But he proved to be less than a gentleman, while you . . ." He flicked his tongue over the inside of her wrist, and her nipples tightened deliciously in response. "Your scandalous escapades and rakish behavior are well documented—"

"And only ninety percent true." His heavy-lidded blue eyes crinkled at the corners.

"Yes," she breathed. "So you say. But the other ten percent of you—the part that is generous and noble and kind—is hidden beneath your roguish exterior. And that unexpected combination of sinner and saint . . . well, I find it rather irresistible."

He slid a hand beneath the hem of her gown and traced a path up the back of her leg, his fingertips teasing her sensitive skin and stoking her desire. "How so, temptress?"

Her cheeks flamed, but she needed him to know. Suspected he'd understand. "I fear that I'm rather wanton at heart. I've tried to follow the rules of propriety—to rein in my passionate side and suppress my improper desires. I've done rather well . . . until recently. When I'm with you, my body doesn't seem to want to obey my head."

He went still and looked at her, his gaze unexpectedly vulnerable. "Only when you're with me?"

Wrapping her arms around his neck, she said, "You make me hunger for things I've never wanted before. When you touch me, I feel as though you—*only* you— have the power to heal the ache inside me."

He growled as his warm palm skimmed over her thigh and squeezed her flesh, sending waves of pleasure through her limbs. "I want nothing more than to please you."

"It's not that simple. We cannot go on like this—with

both of us living under the same roof." Not when a wicked look or a covert brush of his hand melted her knees. It was only a matter of time before the staff or Uncle Alistair noticed how the air crackled between them. "The risk is too great, and I would rather enter a convent than bring shame upon my family—though I hope it doesn't come to that."

"I wholeheartedly agree," he said.

"Given the circumstances," she said softly, "I think you must leave tomorrow."

He deflated slightly, but smiled. "First my brother tossed me out on my ear . . . now you."

"Where will you go?"

"Don't worry about me," he scoffed. "I shall be fine." But Julie noticed he hadn't answered her question.

"I may have to find a new residence soon too. Your brother has given me one week to prove my uncle has a right to occupy the house."

He shook his head, confounded. "I'm sorry. I don't understand why my brother is so adamant. I searched your uncle's study for much of the night but found no bill of sale or lease," Sam said soberly. "What will you do if you cannot produce the documentation in a week's time?"

"I suppose I must consider paying your brother's price." She tried to keep her tone light, but a hint of bitterness came through.

A shadow flicked across his face. "How much does he want?"

"We are still in negotiations," she said vaguely, which wasn't entirely true, but it wasn't as though she could admit to Sam that the brother he idolized wished to make her his mistress. "I will delay as long as possible and hope that Beth and Alex return from their honeymoon before Uncle Alistair and I are evicted."

Sam's palm slid to the outside of her thigh, all the way to her hip, and her breath hitched in her throat. "It seems we both face an uncertain future," he said.

"Yes. But tonight . . . tonight is ours," she breathed. "And to waste it would be a sin."

Chapter TWENTY-SIX

Sam's eyes turned dark. Hungry. He cradled Julie's cheek in his hand and brushed his thumb over her lower lip. "Will you stay with me, until dawn?"

She swallowed as she mentally cataloged everything she had to lose. Her innocence, her virginity, her heart. But she wanted this night with him. Needed it.

He'd unlocked a part of her she'd denied for too long. He'd reminded her that she was more than a dutiful sister and niece. She was sensuous and bold and free.

And Sam didn't think less of her for it. Rather, he respected her.

"I will stay with you," she whispered. And she would have this small part of him, forever.

He reached behind her, pulled the pins from her hair, and tossed them on the floor. Heavy curls cascaded around her shoulders, and Sam wound a thick lock around his finger, staring as though mesmerized. "This is how I will remember you," he said, tilting her chin so that her gaze met his. "Passionate. Beautiful. Mine."

His words thrummed through her body and echoed in her head, obliterating any stubborn trace of self-doubt that remained from her wallflower days. All she had to do was look at Sam, for the proof was in his eyes.

He burned for her.

With a tortured groan, he stood, pulled her to her feet, and hauled her against him. "Here are the rules we shall play by."

"This isn't a game to me, Sam."

"Nor to me," he said, serious. "The rules are to protect you."

She bristled slightly. "I don't need protecting."

"I understand. But the rules are still useful." He swept her hair over her shoulder, bent his head, and kissed a scorching path from her neck to her ear. "Rule number one," he murmured. "If you want me to stop, you simply say the word."

"I know. I trust you." She sighed blissfully.

"Rule number two. No hiding."

Distracted by the heavenly feel of his hips pressed to hers, she murmured, "What does that mean?"

"Don't hide any part of you. Your body, your mind, your desires . . . they're all beautiful to me."

"And I assume the same applies to you?" she countered. "You will not hide from me?"

"Never." As if to demonstrate, he hauled his shirt over his head. Tossed it to the floor.

God, he was gorgeous. The muscles in his chest and abdomen flexed as he reached for her, and his skin glistened in the dim light of the lamp.

"Have you any more rules?" she teased.

"Just one. Tonight is only about us."

She frowned. "What else would it be about?"

"Your family, my family, the gossip rags . . . the future. But not tonight. There's no world beyond that door. No one else on earth save you and I." His fingers drifted from her nape to the base of her spine, and back again. "Understand?"

"I don't anticipate you'll have any trouble keeping my attention." She could scarcely think of anything but the brush of his fingers over her skin.

With panther-like grace, he stalked to the door, locked it, and turned the lamp lower. Lean but powerful, he moved with the ease of an athlete. Julie couldn't take her eyes off him.

He approached her with a promising, predatory stare and walked behind her, lightly bumping his bare torso to her shoulders. "One of us has too many clothes on," he grumbled.

Making short work of the laces at her back, he loosened her gown and pushed the delicate puffed sleeves off her shoulders. Her dress fell to her waist, and then—with a little help from Sam—skimmed past her hips and billowed around her feet like frothy blue waves.

Before she could step out of the satin, he placed his hands on her shoulders and gently kneaded them. "No rushing."

She leaned into him as his warm fingers eased the tension from her body, moaned as he kissed the column of her neck. Either her corset was growing tighter, or her breasts had swollen, for it seemed she couldn't catch her breath.

With a tortured groan, he spun her to face him and

traced the dipping neckline of her shift with a fingertip . . . then followed the same path with his mouth. As the light stubble on his chin grazed her skin, her legs turned to jelly.

When at last he unlaced her corset, she wriggled it over her head and delighted in tossing it aside. Wearing only her fine, thin shift and silk stockings, she smiled shyly at Sam—and resisted the instinct to cross her arms. He'd said no hiding, and she didn't *want* to hide from him.

"Come." He led her by the hand to the armchair, sat, and pulled her onto his lap. "I can't believe you're truly here with me."

Julie wound her arms around his neck and touched her forehead to his. "There's no place I'd rather be."

Slowly, deliberately, he pushed the hem of her shift above her knees and tugged one stocking down. Inch by inch, the silk slid lower, until one leg was bared . . . and the other followed suit.

"I must see you," he rasped. "All of you."

Beneath the transparent fabric of her shift, her nipples puckered. She nodded, sat back, and pulled off the garment, leaving her completely naked. She felt no shame or regret—only desire.

"Juliette." He uttered her name reverently. Humbly. As though she'd given him a gift so great he could barely comprehend it. He dipped his head to her breast and took the tip in his mouth. His hand stroked the inside of her thigh, teasing the supple flesh there and sliding higher, closer to the center of her desire.

She splayed her palm over the hard wall of his chest, letting her palm graze his flat nipple. He moaned in response, and the vibrations pulsed through her body. Her head fell back as he laved attention on one breast . . . and then the other. All the while, his wicked fingers drifted closer to her entrance. Circling. Stroking. Awakening.

When he touched her, she whimpered, unsure. The ache spiraling inside her was sweet and fierce, dizzying in its intensity.

"Do you like this, temptress?" he murmured, his voice throaty.

"Yes, but . . ." It wasn't enough. She was wound tight as a spring. Her back arched, her skin tingled, her core pulsed.

He slid a finger inside her, and she clutched his shoulders, breathless with need. "Oh, Sam."

"You're perfect—do you know that?" The words drifted over her skin like a thousand kisses. His finger thrust in a rhythm that made her hips buck. "I will ease the ache. All you have to do is trust me."

"I do." Her body was his—as was her heart.

His thumb circled the center of her pleasure, winding her tighter, taking her higher.

She was on the brink of something glorious, she could feel it. And just when she might have soared over the edge, he uttered a curse and withdrew his hand. "Not yet. Not here," he said.

He scooped her in his arms, strode to the bed, and laid her across the soft counterpane. Bracing himself above her, he said, "It's your first time. I want to make it special."

She swallowed, touched. He might be London's greatest rogue, but tonight he was hers—thoughtful, considerate, and utterly determined to give her pleasure. "How do you propose to do that?" she asked, amazed her lips could form the words.

"One kiss at a time," he said.

With knee-melting tenderness, he kissed the tip of her nose, her cheeks, her lips.

He traced the shell of her ear with his tongue, then trailed more kisses along her collarbone and in the hollow at the base of her throat. He nuzzled the soft undersides of her breasts and the valley between them. When she thought she'd die of pleasure, he blazed a trail south, lingering near her navel and cruising around her hip bones.

Positioning his shoulders between her legs, he nudged her thighs apart . . . and flicked his tongue . . . there. Her body bucked. His assault was exquisite and relentless, giving her no quarter. His fingers spread her flesh and entered her, his mouth sucked and moaned.

She fisted the counterpane and cried out softly as she hurtled over the edge . . . and time stopped.

She was floating, shimmering from within, awed by the intensity of her release. The world outside the bedchamber door had ceased to exist. All that mattered was here and now.

Julie and Sam.

When the delicious tremors subsided and her body turned limp, he crawled beside her, propped himself on an elbow, and gazed at her with something akin to adoration. "You are amazing," he whispered.

"Me?" She'd simply lain there while he'd worked magic. "This is all your doing."

"Is it, vixen?" He arched a wicked brow. "Because I've only just begun."

Chapter TWENTY-SEVEN

The sight of Juliette lying naked beside him, her expression dreamy and sated, was the most beautiful, awe-inspiring thing Sam had ever seen. No spectacular sunset could compare. No scenic ocean view could come close to moving him the way she did.

Her beauty transcended the physical. She was unapologetically loyal and fiercely protective of the people she loved. She was passionate and funny and courageous.

And damn it all if he wasn't falling in love with her.

He shouldn't. He knew it without a doubt.

He could give her pleasure and amuse her for a while, but she was destined for bigger things . . . and for a better man than he. Her sisters had married well—an earl and a duke who each possessed vast fortunes. Before long, Juliette would have scores of men vying for her hand in marriage too, not the least of which could be his brother.

But dwelling on that would be a clear violation of his

third rule—the mandate that tonight was to be about *them,* to the exclusion of everything and everyone else.

If Sam only had one evening with Juliette, he refused to spoil it with thoughts of her other suitors or her promising future—which held no room for the likes of him.

As she snuggled into the crook of his arm, he savored the feel of her soft breasts pressed against his chest, her warm skin touching his. His arousal strained against his trousers, but he would not rush this, would not pressure her to give him more than she wished.

As he kissed her temple and smoothed a strand of hair away from her face, his hand trembled.

Good God. He couldn't be nervous—the very idea was ridiculous. He hadn't even been nervous *his* first time.

It was as if his body knew what his head didn't want to admit. He wasn't just *bedding* Juliette. This was more. *She* was more.

More than he deserved.

She blinked up at him and lazily swirled a fingertip over his chest and down his arm. "You say you've only just begun," she said shyly. "I can't wait to see what the rest of the evening holds."

"I can't either," he said honestly.

She rolled her eyes and swatted him playfully. "Surely, you already know."

"No." He laced his fingers through hers and brought the back of her hand to his lips. "That is, I have some idea. But it's all different with you. It feels new . . . special."

Her eyes softened and pleaded with his. "Make me yours, Sam," she breathed. "I want to lay with you. I want us to be as close as two people possibly can."

Her words were a torch, setting fire to his blood. He closed his eyes for a moment—a valiant but probably futile attempt to remind himself to go slowly.

And then he crushed his mouth to hers.

Jesus, she tasted sweet—like ripe berries and cream. She bowed her body toward him, her hips pressing against his, and he murmured a curse. Damn if he could resist her another moment.

He sat up, stripped off his boots and trousers, and returned to the bed. He wanted to pounce on her, fill her, and pleasure her until neither of them knew their own name. But she was sitting up now, letting her gaze rake over him from head to toe, her unabashed curiosity making him even harder.

"May I touch you?" she asked.

Holy hell. "You may do anything you like, Juliette. Anything."

Smiling like a satisfied cat, she skimmed her fingers over the ridges of his abdomen, down the hard length of him. Jesus.

"You like that," she said.

"You have no idea."

Emboldened, she explored further, curling her fingers around him and stroking in a rhythm that drove him mad. On the brink of exploding, he let out a groan and pushed her back on the bed, positioning himself between her legs.

Poised to bury himself in her, he cupped her cheek in his hand and searched her face. Saw a flicker of fear in her eyes. "Are you frightened? We don't need to do this." But heaven help him, he wanted to. More than anything.

"I'm a little nervous I suppose. Now that I've seen you—all of you, that is. But I don't want to stop now."

"It might hurt at first," he admitted. He'd had no experience with virgins, so he couldn't say for certain. "But I swear I'll make it good for you." Or God help him, he'd die trying.

"I know you will. You already have." She tilted her hips upward, eliciting another groan from him. "I think it will help if you kiss me."

"Damn it, Juliette." He slanted his mouth across hers and slowly entered her, inch by inch, filling her until he was slick with perspiration and trembling with restraint.

Mewling sounds in her throat—that could have come from pain or pleasure—made him freeze. But she speared her fingers through his hair and wound her legs around his hips, urging him on.

God, she was hot, tight, and perfect. So perfect. He rocked into her, searching for a rhythm she liked. Felt her body contract around him.

He wanted her to come with him. No, he *needed* her to. And just when he thought he couldn't wait a moment longer—she did.

And he was gone. The world went black for two seconds before a hundred stars streaked across his vision. His head buried in her neck, he moaned her name.

Expending his last shred of self-control, he rolled off her and spilled his seed onto the bed. Christ. Heart pounding and breathing ragged, he slung an arm over her and pulled her body flush with his. They fit perfectly together—as though they'd been made for each other.

Her limbs were limp, her eyes closed. Her lips curled

into a satisfied smile. "That was heavenly," she whispered. "I'm suddenly very tired."

After covering her with a corner of the counterpane, he massaged her scalp lightly and kissed the top of her head. "Sleep for a while."

"Will you do the same?" She wriggled closer, tugging at the darkest corners of his heart.

"Yes," he replied—because he sensed that was what she wished.

But he had no intention of sleeping this night.

The hours with her were far too precious to waste. Instead, he stared at the thick lashes fanned across her cheeks. He wondered at the luminescence of her skin and the comforting weight of her leg flung over his. He lost himself in the citrusy fragrance of her hair.

He committed every detail to memory so that in the cold and lonely days to come he'd remember how it felt to be one with her—to bask in the glow of her light and goodness.

So he'd remember what it felt like to love.

As she slipped into a sweet, sound sleep, he shook his head at the irony of it all.

He'd barged into her house, upended her life, and taken her innocence—and yet, *he* was the one who'd changed. Deeply, irrevocably.

Because after spending a few days with Juliette, his heart was hers.

And he'd never be the same again.

When Julie woke, the candle was out and the bedchamber was dark, but Sam was all around her. His chest was pressed to her back, his knees were bent behind hers, and his hand rested on her hip.

"Are you awake?" she whispered.

He responded with a low chuckle that vibrated through her in the most delicious way. "Yes, vixen."

"This feels lovely." Sighing, she shimmied closer to his warm, solid body—and felt the evidence of his desire pressing against her leg. She delighted in the knowledge that she did that to him. That he wanted her. "I wish we could stay like this."

"So do I," he murmured against her neck. He skimmed his palm over the curve of her hip and playfully squeezed her bottom, instantly igniting her blood. A steady, insistent pulsing began at her core, and now she knew precisely what would satisfy her hunger. Moaning, she started to turn toward him, but he slipped his arm around her waist, halting her. "Relax," he ordered. "Let me pleasure you."

Her nipples tightened at the promise of his words. As if he knew, he reached for one bud, lightly pinching it while he planted hot kisses at the base of her neck. Heaven help her, he turned her body to liquid. She arched her back and pressed her bottom against his erection, pleased to hear him groan in response.

But if they were engaged in a game where the goal was to arouse each other, Sam had the distinct advantage. He nibbled on the lobe of her ear while he slipped his hand between her legs and stroked the folds at her entrance. "Are you sore?"

"No," she breathed. Though her flesh was tender, she couldn't bear it if he stopped.

She saw nothing in the darkness of the bedchamber,

but her other senses were heightened. His masculine, musky scent surrounded her. The hair on his chest tickled her back. The sound of his raspy breathing filled her head.

He slid a finger inside her and nipped at her shoulder, making her whimper with need. "Sam."

As though he were hers to command, his wicked fingertips moved to the center of her pleasure, circled it, and stroked. "How's this?"

Her head lolled back. Oh God. But she wanted him inside her. Wanted that intimacy again. Now. "I need you."

"I need you too, love." For some reason, the endearment—clearly spoken in the heat of passion—brought tears to her eyes, and she was grateful that he couldn't see. He entered her from behind, filling her as he had before, but deeper.

He whispered her name like a prayer—soft, sacred, and true. There was no room for doubt or loneliness or fear when she was with Sam, no time for worry. All she could feel was the joining of their bodies and souls. His hand on her breast, his breath in her ear, his heart pounding in time with hers.

When, at last, her release blossomed, it was slow, full, and impossibly sweet. Tendrils of pleasure unfurled inside her, radiating from her core all the way through her fingers and toes.

She clung to him as bliss overtook them both in waves that lasted forever.

But not nearly long enough.

Chapter TWENTY-EIGHT

The soft glow behind the faded velvet curtains told Julie dawn had broken.

The cool, empty mattress beside her told her Sam wasn't there.

She blinked, expecting to look up and find him stuffing the few things his valet had brought him into a valise, preparing to leave her uncle's house.

But she wasn't in Sam's room. Rather, she was in her own familiar bedchamber, in her bed—still naked but covered with a soft quilt.

She bolted upright, wondering momentarily if the whole night had been a dream. But the tenderness between her legs and soreness of her muscles were evidence enough that her night with Sam had been real. Indeed, she vaguely remembered him carrying her to her bed and kissing her lips sometime in the wee hours of the morning.

Scanning the room, she found her gown and underclothes were folded and hung over the back of a chair;

her slippers were tucked neatly beneath it. A small envelope rested on the chair's threadbare seat. Her belly lurched at the sight.

Sam couldn't be gone already.

Heart pounding, she tossed back the coverlet, sprang out of bed, and shoved her arms into her dressing gown. She cinched the sash as she dashed out of her room and headed for Sam's.

At the threshold, she halted.

The door was ajar.

But Sam was gone—and so were his things.

His shaving kit had disappeared from the top of the bureau; his boots no longer stood guard at the foot of the bed.

Her gaze lingered on the empty armchair where he'd removed her stockings and shift, where he'd worshipped her body with his hands and his mouth. She stared at the neatly made bed where they'd become one, where he'd given her bone-melting pleasure.

His faint scent was the only trace of him that remained.

She reminded herself that she'd asked him to leave—and that it was surely for the best. Why, then, did she have a painful lump in her throat?

Remembering the envelope he'd left, she hurried back to her room, lifted it from the chair, and opened it.

Juliette,
If you should ever need me, send word and I will be there in a heartbeat. I would gladly move mountains for you, but I will also step aside, since that is what you wish.

I regret any pain I have caused you or your uncle
and wish you both every happiness.

Sam

Julie pressed the note to her chest, willing her pulse
to slow. Her heart pleaded for her to run after Sam right
now—but her head knew she should not.

The problems she had to face—possible eviction, her
uncle's faltering mental state, and Nigel's indecent
proposal—were all best dealt with on her own. As long
as Sam had been living under her roof, she'd been unable to think clearly, and the risk to her reputation hung
over her, a constant threat.

She believed that Sam wanted to help her, but how
could she ask him to, when his own brother was the
source of her distress?

Last night, Sam had said that if he had to choose
between her and Nigel, he would choose her . . . but it
wasn't fair of her to demand that of him. No one
should have to forsake a sibling for someone else. Julie
could scarcely imagine it, for she'd never betray her
sisters.

And so, it was up to her to fix things, to make things
right.

She would begin by washing her face. Then she'd ask
Lucy to comb out her wildly tangled hair and help her
dress in a no-nonsense gown.

And once she was presentable, she would join Uncle
Alistair for breakfast and talk to him about the house—
something she should have done days ago.

But before she could accomplish any of that, she intended to take a quarter of an hour for herself.

So that she could bury her face in her pillow and have a good, hard cry.

Julie joined Uncle Alistair at the dining room table, her stomach tied in knots. She pushed away the poached egg on her plate and sipped her tea, hoping it would calm her. How could she tell her uncle that his new research assistant—and fellow cigar connoisseur—had abandoned him already, without even saying good-bye?

Earlier, while Lucy had coaxed her hair into a tidy twist, Julie debated what explanation to give for Sam's sudden departure. She could say that a family crisis requiring his attention had arisen, but her uncle would then worry unnecessarily. Perhaps she'd say that Sam had been invited to join an expedition to Egypt, or some other exotic place, and that he had to prepare to leave at once.

Now that the time had come to inform her uncle that Sam had left, she wasn't at all sure what explanation would come out of her mouth. She only knew that she was very weary of lying. Pasting a smile on her face, she said, "Uncle Alistair, you may have noticed that Cousin Samuel isn't here this morning."

"Well of course I noticed, my dear." He chuckled good-naturedly. "His chair is quite empty."

"Yes." Heavens, this was harder than she'd thought it would be. "I'm sorry to have to tell you this, but he won't be staying with us any longer."

Her uncle blinked several times, his bushy white eyebrows knit in concern. "Didn't Samuel say good-bye to you?"

Blast it all. "He did. And he regrets that he had to leave so suddenly, but—"

Uncle Alistair waved a hand dismissively. "He told me all about it."

Julie gaped. "He did?"

"Well, he explained in the letter he left on my desk." Her uncle speared a hunk of ham with his fork and devoured it with gusto. "I shall miss him."

"I shall too." She brushed at her eyes nonchalantly, pretending they didn't sting. Leaving a note for both her and her uncle was distinctly un-roguish of Sam, but she had neither the time nor inclination to examine what that might mean—at least, not at the moment. Intensely curious about what he'd written to her uncle, she asked, "Did he mention his plans?"

"Not prolifically. Only that after spending time in my company he realized he needed to find his own passion—work that motivated him as much as my research does me."

Her chest squeezed, but she reminded herself that Sam's note was probably a lie—a well-intentioned one designed to spare her uncle's feelings—but a lie nevertheless. She leaned across the table and squeezed her uncle's hand. "You are serving as an inspiration," she said. "And I'm not surprised."

"Pshaw. Samuel doesn't need an old codger like me to mentor him. He's savvy and charismatic—he'll succeed in whatever he chooses."

Julie pondered this. "You may be right."

Uncle Alistair froze, butter knife in one hand and toast in the other. "Of course I am, my dear. Our cousin will inform of us of his address once he's mettled. He asked that I keep him apprised of my presentation for the Royal Society."

"Excellent," she said approvingly. "We will have to keep up our efforts on that front so we don't disappoint him."

Relieved that her uncle had received the news of Sam's departure so well, Julie prepared to broach the next sensitive subject.

"Samuel asked me a question yesterday, and I didn't know the answer," she said casually.

Her uncle nibbled on a triangle of toast. "Oh? What did he wish to know?"

"He wondered how long you'd lived in this house."

"Let's see now." Frowning, he murmured, "How long has it been, Elspeth?"

Julie's heart lurched, and she immediately sought to bring him back to her. "Perhaps two decades?"

He cocked an ear as if he was listening to an invisible guest at the table. "Twenty-two years, you say? Yes, we moved in shortly after your mother passed, God rest her soul."

A chill slithered down her spine. Uncle Alistair was not talking about Julie's mother, but Elspeth's.

"Twenty-two years is a long time." Julie tilted her head until her uncle's gaze finally met hers. And for a moment, he looked surprised to see her sitting at the breakfast table. Good heavens—he was deteriorating before her eyes. One moment, he'd seemed jovial and robust; the next he was a ghost of himself.

Her throat constricted painfully, and she was tempted to delay the rest of the conversation until this spell, this odd state of mind, had passed. But the truth was that the time would *never* be optimal for discussing the house.

She had to inquire about it now.

Taking a fortifying breath, she asked, "I'm curious to know how you came to live here. Did the house once belong to Aunt Elspeth's family?"

"I do believe so," he said vaguely. "Now where is my newspaper? I must have left it in my study."

He started to stand, but she was not going to let him escape so easily. If she was going to fight Nigel on her uncle's behalf, she needed to be armed with facts. "Wait," she pleaded. "Before you go, would you please tell me a little more? Was the house a gift to you from Aunt Elspeth's family? Or did you lease it?"

Sinking back into his chair, he swallowed. "I can't recall exactly. Elspeth never shared the details with me. Why do you wish to know?"

"No reason in particular." Julie tried to keep her voice light. "It's only that while we're going through the process of organizing your study, it would make sense for us to gather any important legal documents for safe-keeping."

"Legal documents?" His voice quavered.

Julie looked on, horrified, as her uncle spooned strawberry jam into his tea and stirred, his hand trembling. "Yes, documents related to the house—perhaps a lease or bill of sale for the property?"

His shoulders slumped, and he suddenly looked smaller. More feeble. "I imagine we have some record, don't we?" He looked past Julie, scratched his head, and brightened. "There are at least half a dozen trunks in the attic. One of them might hold the documents you seek."

"That's a wonderful idea," she said encouragingly.

"Oh, I can't take the credit. Elspeth suggested—" He snapped his mouth shut as though he'd belatedly realized how mad his words might sound to another's ears. Perhaps the dismay welling up inside Julie showed on her face. "In any prevent," he continued, "the attic would be a capital place to begin your search."

"Thank you," she said. "I think I shall venture up there later this afternoon."

He reached for his teacup, sipped, and made a face. "Strange tasting tea leaves—I can't say I care for them. But maybe it is I . . . I've been a bit off of late. I think I shall rest in my armchair for a while."

"Come, I'll make sure you're settled." She walked him into the parlor, helped ease him into his worn chair, and laid a blanket over his lap. "I'll draw the curtains so you may sleep if you wish. You'll feel more like yourself when you wake."

Julie desperately hoped so.

She was partially to blame for his decline. He'd been cooped up in the house too long. No wonder he'd resorted to talking to Aunt Elspeth.

Now that Sam had left and her sisters were away, Julie was the only person he could converse with. His mind required more stimulation. He needed the opportunity to employ his social skills occasionally so he wouldn't forget them altogether.

As she patted his shoulder and kissed the smooth top of his head, she resolved to peruse the stack of invitations on the escritoire and choose at least one social event to attend with her uncle in the next few days.

An outing would be good for both of them, she

reasoned. He would mingle with real live people, and she'd have something to take her mind off the ultimatum that Nigel had given her.

She didn't even fool herself into thinking she'd be able to forget Sam or the glorious way he'd made her feel—beautiful, respected, and loved.

And if she never felt those things again, well, she supposed she was lucky to have had them for a short time.

Chapter TWENTY-NINE

Sam had known he couldn't go home.

There was no telling what sort of reception he might have received if he'd tried. Nigel's temper could have cooled sufficiently that he'd have grudgingly allowed Sam to move back in. On the other hand, his brother might have slammed the door in Sam's face and ordered the trio of dockworkers to drag him away again.

But Nigel's willingness to grant him another chance wasn't the only issue any more . . . because Sam had changed.

He had Juliette to blame—and thank—for that.

After spending a few days with her, he'd realized he wanted more than an endless cycle of drunken nights, hungover mornings, and lonely days. He needed a purpose and a plan and *work*. Most of all, he needed to be worthy of someone like her.

And if he was never good enough for her, then at least

he'd be able to look at himself in the mirror and know he'd tried like hell—starting today.

The first task facing him after leaving Juliette's was finding a place to live, at least temporarily. He still hoped to mend the rift with Nigel, because their father would have wanted that. Deep down, Sam did too. But it wasn't going to be easy.

Especially now that it appeared Nigel and he were in love with the same woman.

The possibility of reconciling with his brother while they both competed for Juliette's heart was distinctly remote. All Sam knew was he had to try.

Outside of Juliette's house, he'd hailed a hackney cab and ridden to Oxford Street where his friend, Jonathan Griffith—Griff for short—ran an extremely profitable mercantile business.

Griff was precisely the sort of friend that Nigel disapproved of. Born to an innkeeper and raised in a taproom, his manners were coarse—but then, so were Sam's.

When his father died, Griff sold the inn and traveled to India where he amassed a fortune that rivaled Nigel's. Griff could have afforded to buy a seat in Parliament; he could have married the daughter of an impoverished duke. But he had no interest in trying to finagle his way into the uppermost echelons of society. His only goal was to make money—a great deal of it.

As Sam approached his friend's offices, he admired the gold-plated, engraved sign next to the door: *Griffith Mercantile*. He'd never been inside—wasn't even sure that Griff would be there—but he entered, valise in hand.

"Good morning, sir. How may I help you?" A young

bespectacled man looked up at Sam from behind his tidy desk, his cleanly shaven face and crisply folded cravat making Sam feel distinctly unkempt.

"My name's Samuel Travis. Is Griff—er, Mr. Griffith—in his office? I'd like to see him."

The secretary looked down and ran a finger across a page of the book in front of him. "He's finishing up with a client right now, but I can see if he's available afterward. May I tell him the nature of your visit?"

Sam glanced around the small anteroom. The thick Turkish carpet, rich curtains, and polished wood chairs managed to walk the line between sumptuous and businesslike. A closed door behind the secretary's desk presumably led to Griff's office. "I'm a friend," Sam explained. "I don't mind waiting."

If the young man thought it odd that Sam had brought a valise with him, he didn't let on. Instead he smiled warmly. "Please, make yourself comfortable, Mr. Travis. My name is Timothy McFarren. Would you care for some coffee?"

Sam's stomach growled. "That would be wonder—"

A crash on the other side of the office door made Sam stop mid-sentence. He cast a questioning look at Timothy, but the secretary's face remained impassive. "You were saying?"

Sam blinked. "Should we see what's going on in there?"

"Mr. Griffith doesn't like to be disturbed," Timothy said. Angry shouts sounded from the office behind him, but he carried on as though he didn't hear a thing. "I'll ask Alice to prepare coffee and a tray of scones. Would you like to read the newspaper while you're waiting?"

"Thank you." Sam chuckled as he took the newspaper and sat in a chair next to the wall. He wasn't worried about his friend—much. Griff had seen his share of pub fights and tended to inflict more damage than he sustained.

Timothy went through a side exit into a corridor, leaving Sam alone in the antechamber. He couldn't make out the conversation on the other side of the office door, but Griff and another man were clearly at odds and arguing vehemently.

Sam opened to the gossip column, pleased that, for once, his name would not be in it. He was reading the latest scandal involving an earl and an opera singer when the door behind the desk burst open and slammed against the wall.

A beefy man with a mottled, tomato red face stumbled through the doorway and shouted over his shoulder. "I'll be damned before I pay that price. It's cotton, not spun gold."

Griff strolled out behind him, his hands shoved deep in the pockets of his expensive trousers. "And I'll let five hundred bolts rot in my warehouse before I sell them to you any cheaper." He spotted Sam in the antechamber and arched a sardonic brow.

The large man—a shopkeeper or tailor, if Sam had to guess—sputtered in frustration and turned to Sam. "He wants to charge me twice as much per bolt this shipment than he did for the last. I'm making gentlemen's shirts. Do you know what would happen if I doubled the cost of my shirts? My customers would buy their shirts at the shop five doors down from mine."

Sam tilted his head sympathetically. "I don't know—I'd be willing to pay more for a fine shirt."

"My point exactly." Griff waved an arm demonstratively.

"Maybe *you* can afford to squander your money," the tailor said, obviously unaware that Sam couldn't afford much at all. "My clients are thriftier—out of necessity."

Sam stroked his chin, thoughtful. "Fair enough. I still think you should use the finest cloth . . . but perhaps instead of raising the price, you could sell *more*. Make them faster."

The tailor snorted as if affronted. "And sacrifice quality? I think not."

Griff planted his hands on his hips. "If you were as concerned about quality as you pretend to be, you wouldn't balk at paying a fair price for superior fabric."

Sam stood and walked between the men. To the tailor he said, "You could make two different lines of shirts. One tailor-made—and more expensive; the other cheaper—but produced in a factory."

"Why in God's name would I wish to drive my own tailors out of business?"

Griff shook his head as though Sam had just sabotaged any chance at striking a deal.

But Sam wasn't finished. "Factories will be making most men's shirts before long, whether we like it or not," he predicted. "You should use your expertise at constructing shirts to open a small factory. Retrain some of your tailors and employ them as supervisors. They could oversee the work to ensure that the shirts are worthy of the label you put on them."

The tailor ran a hand through his hair, incredulous. "I have no investment capital. I can barely afford to pay my shop's rent month to month."

"What if I fronted you some of the money?" Griff asked.

"This business has been in my family for three generations. You're bloody mad if you think I'd turn over the reins to you."

"Wait." Sam paced, thinking. "The business would still be yours. In exchange for Griff's investment in the factory side, he'd get a share of the profits."

"Seventy-five percent," Griff announced.

"Forty," the tailor countered.

"The exact split can be negotiated later," Sam said. "But at least we know that we can use your cotton"— he pointed at Griff—"and your expertise"—he gestured to the tailor—"to expand the business and make everyone significantly richer."

The tailor dragged a hand down his face. "I'll need some time to think it over . . . but the proposal has merit," he added grudgingly. "And I wouldn't mind being richer."

Griff barked a laugh. "Mr. Warren Blake, meet Lord Samuel Travis; Sam, meet Blake."

As they shook hands, the secretary scurried into the room carrying a tray of steaming coffee and scones. Flicking his gaze from Griff to Blake, he said, "Shall I bring more coffee, Mr. Griffith?"

"No. Brandy, I think."

Timothy set the tray on a low table and quickly fetched another from Griff's office. After pouring a healthy splash into three snifters, he handed one to each man.

Sam raised his glass. "To the finest gentlemen's shirts

in London." The brandy burned a path down his throat and warmed his empty belly.

"I propose that the three of us meet again tomorrow to work through the details," Griff said. "I'll have my solicitor join us as well."

They arranged a time and finished their drinks before Blake stuffed his hat on his head and left, his sour mood vastly improved.

The moment the door closed behind the tailor, Sam scooped a scone off the platter and popped it into his mouth.

"I was about to lose that deal," Griff admitted. He sank into the chair beside Sam and blew out a long breath. "You stepped in, and I'm now oddly enthused at the prospect of owning a share in a bloody shirt factory. I owe you drinks, dinner, whatever the hell you want."

Sam looked at his friend earnestly. "I'd like a job."

Griff choked, then blinked. "You want to work?"

"I do." He *needed* to work. And not just for the money, but for the satisfaction. "I'll do whatever you need me to. I haven't much experience in the business world, but—"

"It's not much different from the gaming tables. You try to figure out the other fellow's hand and place your bet accordingly."

Arching a brow, Sam smiled. "I'm sure there's more to it than that, but I'm willing to learn, and I'm a quick study."

Griff leaned his elbows on his knees. "Is that why you came here this morning?"

Sam nodded, then said, "I also need a place to stay."

"You're welcome to stay with me. But beware, my mother lives with me as well. She's almost given up on trying to marry me off. She may take you on as her next project."

Snorting, Sam said, "And the job?"

"You're savvy, shrewd, and so affable that few realize the extent of your business acumen—that's an asset. With a minimum of guidance, I could easily see you running half my company within a few years. Here's the hard cold truth, Sam. You don't need to sell me on your raw abilities. You need to sell me on your dedication."

"I will." Sam extended a hand and shook Griff's. "Just give me the chance, and I'll prove my commitment to you and your company. One day, week, and month at a time."

"As it happens, I may soon have a shirt factory to manage. But there are countless other projects in the works too."

The more work, the better, as far as Sam was concerned. Anything to keep his mind off Juliette and the ache in his chest from missing her. "When can we start?"

Chapter THIRTY

Julie emerged from the attic for the third straight day. After hours of meticulously sorting through brittle papers, moth-eaten clothes, and precious mementos, she had nothing to show for her efforts—except a thick coating of dust on her dress and hair.

She'd found no documents related to Uncle Alistair's house, and she was acutely aware that time was ticking by. In just three days she would have to face Nigel and reply to his ultimatum.

And she still didn't know what she'd say to him.

Her heart belonged to Sam, but it wasn't as though he'd offered marriage. Even if he did wish to propose, he was a second son, dependent on his brother's generosity, and Nigel was unlikely to welcome Sam and her under his roof.

Julie had tried to keep busy in the days since Sam left, and yet she still found herself looking for him when she walked into her uncle's study. Still half-expected to see him sitting in his chair across from her at the dining room table.

She'd thought perhaps he'd send another note. Or that their paths would cross during her walks in the park or on her outings to Bond Street. But it was as though he'd vanished into thin air.

At least there was always a chance—however remote—that she'd see him tonight. She and Uncle Alistair were attending a soiree hosted by Lord Torrington, Charlotte's employer, and her governess friend was sure to be there. Buoyed by the thought, she dashed to the kitchen to request hot water for a bath, then stopped by Uncle Alistair's study to remind him of their plans.

He sat at his desk and stared out the window, forlorn. She almost wished he was standing on his chair again, swinging his cane like a mad cricket player. Sam had wrought a change in him, but now that he was gone, her uncle seemed to have aged a couple of decades.

"It's a beautiful day outside," she said brightly in a valiant effort to convince both Uncle Alistair and herself.

"Indeed it is, my dear." Facing her, he offered a weak smile. "Did you discover anything of interest in the attic?" he asked, hopeful.

"Not yet. But I'm sure I shall," she added quickly. "I'm going to wash off the dust and dress for this evening's outing. You haven't forgotten about the soiree, have you?"

"Pshaw. When I have the honor of escorting the loveliest girl in all of London? Never."

"Will you rest before we go? I don't want you to overtax yourself."

"I feel as though I've done little but rest since Samuel

left. I am glad that he's perusing his own passions, but I must admit that I miss him."

Julie swallowed the lump in her throat. "I do too."

"I received a brief note from him today." Her uncle held up a small folded paper, and Julie barely resisted the urge to snatch it from his hands. "He gave the address where he's staying, in St. James Square."

Julie pretended she was only mildly interested. "Who is he staying with?"

"He only mentioned it was a friend."

"Did Sam have anything else to say?" About missing her or calling on her soon . . .

"Just that I should send word if we need anything." Her uncle's gaze swept across the long line of jars beneath the window.

Julie tamped down her own acute disappointment. "I'm sorry that I've left you to your own devices for the last few days. Tomorrow we shall devote some time to working together on your research, if you like."

"I suppose we should," he said, unenthused.

"And if you're not inclined to work, we can play chess instead. Of course, I shall win resoundingly," she teased.

He grinned. "I wouldn't be so sure. Samuel taught me some new moves."

"Then perhaps I've reason to worry after all." Winking, she added, "I shall see you at dinner. Be sure to wear your best coat."

A half hour later, Julie drew the curtains in her bed-chamber, lit a lamp, and sank into a steaming tub. Once she'd scrubbed her skin, washed her hair, and rinsed it well, she laid back and closed her eyes, letting the warm water lap around her and ease the tension from her body.

Her sisters had only left town a few weeks ago, and Julie had already managed to make a royal mess of things. Admittedly, she'd had help from Sam.

She shouldn't have made love with him. And she certainly shouldn't have fallen in love with him.

If her sisters learned of her recklessness, they'd be beyond furious.

And yet, Julie couldn't quite regret anything with Sam—except letting him go.

The hollowness was keenest at night. She imagined his strong arms around her or the comforting weight of his leg resting on hers . . . but it was the cruelest form of torture, for it only made her ache for him more.

She lingered in the bath until the water grew tepid and the sky outside turned dark. When she could delay no longer, she climbed out of the tub and wrapped herself in a large, soft towel. While she was rubbing her hair dry, a knock sounded.

From the other side of the door, Lucy called, "Forgive the interruption, Miss Julie, but a package just arrived for you."

"Come in."

The maid entered, holding a small, neatly wrapped box.

"Who is it from?" Julie asked.

"A messenger delivered it, miss. He didn't say who it was from. Shall I leave it on the bed?"

Hope warmed Julie's chest. She should have known Sam hadn't forgotten her. He'd written to her uncle, and now he'd sent her something too. "Yes, please."

"Would you like me to finish drying your hair?"

"No thank you, Lucy. But would you please return in a quarter of an hour to help me dress?"

"Certainly," the maid said demurely, but her eyes gleamed as though she was already planning an elaborate coiffure for Julie's evening out.

As soon as Lucy left, Julie sat on the edge of the bed and examined the package. About the size of her fist, it was wrapped in indigo-colored paper and tied with twine.

She didn't give a fig what was inside, as long as it was from Sam. It could be a pretty pebble or a simple ribbon or a silly sketch—any sign that he missed her as much as she missed him. That he still thought of her.

That he still cared.

Tingling with anticipation, she slid off the twine, removed the paper, and lifted the lid off the box.

Nestled inside was a pair of earrings so extravagant, they took her breath away. Round aquamarines surrounded by smaller diamonds dangled from tiny studs. Even in the dim light of her bedchamber, the gemstones twinkled and shined.

They were more ostentatious than she preferred, but all that mattered was they were from Sam.

She rushed to her dressing table, clipped them on, and sat before the mirror, admiring the way they sparkled when she moved. If only Sam were with her now, to brush aside her hair and kiss her neck . . .

But surely he'd sent a note with the gift. She retrieved the discarded wrapping and discovered a small note tucked inside the lid of the box. Jubilant, she unfolded it.

*You did not care for the moon. Perhaps the
stars are more to your liking. —N.*

No. They should have been from Sam.

Moaning, she crumpled the paper in her fist and flopped back onto the bed, all of her earlier joy gone. Sam had penned a note to her uncle. Could he not have spared a moment to write to her as well?

And Nigel surely knew that the gift was highly improper. She'd rejected the necklace he'd offered; he must have known she would refuse the earrings. True, she'd loved them when she'd thought they were from Sam, but that was different.

She and Sam . . . they cared for each other. And while he hadn't made her any promises about the future, she had faith in him. At least, she was trying to believe in him.

The bedchamber door opened, and Lucy angled her way through. "I've brought extra pins," she announced. "I thought we would sweep all your hair to one side and let the curls cascade over your—" The maid paused and narrowed her eyes at Julie. "Those earrings," she said, almost reverent. "They're magnificent. They were in the package?"

Julie fingered one of the dangling stars. "Yes."

"What a precious gift. Who are they from?"

Good heavens. Julie couldn't very well admit the truth, so she said the first lie that popped into her head. "Meg and Will. I was just about to take them off."

"Don't you dare," Lucy protested. She'd never been the meek sort. "They'll complement your sapphire ball gown perfectly. The gentlemen won't be able to take their eyes off you."

"Very well." It was no use arguing with Lucy once she'd made up her mind. Besides, the earrings were lovely, and if they were truly from Meg, Julie would have been thrilled to wear them. She'd simply sneak them off later, before she left or even after she was in the coach.

The maid tapped her foot impatiently. "We haven't time to spare. Come, let's put on your shift and corset."

Julie dutifully submitted to Lucy's ministrations, and after nearly an hour of brushing, pinning, lacing, and powdering, she was ready for the evening.

Lucy looked over Julie's shoulder at her reflection in the mirror. "You look beautiful, Miss Julie."

"If I do, it's all thanks to you." She plucked the shawl from the back of her chair and draped it over her arm. "Now I'd better be off before Uncle Alistair falls asleep in his chair."

But she found him downstairs, looking dapper and alert. Lucy and Mr. Finch helped bustle them out the door and into the carriage, and soon they were on their way to Lord Torrington's soiree.

She sat across from her uncle as the coach rumbled down the street. "You look quite dashing, Uncle."

"As long as you are in the ballroom, I can assure you no one will be looking at me." His eyes crinkled affectionately.

"Nonsense. You have plenty of admirers—not the least of which is the Dowager Duchess of Blackshire. I've heard the way she laughs at your wit. I'd wager she's more than a little charmed by you." Nothing would make Julie happier than if her uncle found another love. He deserved to spend the rest of his years with someone who was as kind and big-hearted as he. Julie's sister Beth had once been the duchess's companion, but now she was the duchess's daughter-in-law. Fortunately, they adored each other.

"The duchess and I are old friends. Nothing more." His words held a note of wistfulness, and Julie quickly sought to change the subject.

"Charlotte tells me that the earl invited Lord Vane to the soiree, and he happens to be a member of the Royal Society. I'll make certain the two of you are introduced. You'll have plenty to discuss, no doubt." Julie hoped that the gentleman would offer some guidance to her uncle, and perhaps even smooth the way for him to join the society. The more connections he established, the better. Julie resolutely believed in her uncle and his scientific mind, but he didn't always make the best first impression.

She hoped he wouldn't make too many social blunders this evening—and if he did, that the earl's guests would not judge him harshly. The coach lurched to a stop, and her uncle's white hair waved wildly. She checked the urge to smooth the wayward tufts like a mother hen.

"You spend far too much time worrying about me when you should be thinking about which gentlemen you wish to dance with. You shall surely have your pick, my dear. Do not forget—you made me a promise."

"I like worrying about you. It keeps me out of mischief." Most of the time. "And I haven't forgotten my promise. I'm working on it."

A footman opened the door of the cab and helped them alight. She took Uncle Alistair's arm as they strolled up the pavement. "Does that mean that you have set your sights on someone?" he prodded. "If so, I expect the gentleman will call on me and ask for your hand any day now."

If only it were so. "When I find the right gentleman, you will be the first to know, I assure you."

"Excellent." He paused halfway to the earl's front door and tilted his head as he looked at her. "I've never seen those earrings before—they're stunning."

Drat—she'd been so preoccupied, she'd forgotten to take them off. Feeling the need to explain, she said, "Meg sent them as a gift."

His eyes shone and he blinked away tears. "All those years that you girls had to go without fashionable gowns and pretty slippers, much less jewels. I wish I could have taken better care of you."

"Don't say that." Her own eyes burned. "You treated us like princesses. And we've always known we were loved."

"Never doubt that, my dear." He clasped her hand over his arm. "Your beauty—yours and your sisters'— always shone through. And now, Margaret is married to an earl and Elizabeth to a duke. It's difficult to believe, isn't it?"

Julie sighed. "Yes. Like a fairytale—except it's true."

"And when I see the evidence before me—like your pretty new earrings—I'm reminded just how much our family's changed."

"We *have* changed in some ways, but not in the most important," Julie said. "We're no longer wearing cast-off gowns or all living under the same roof, but we're still as close as ever." Julie wasn't sure if she was trying to convince him or herself. Patting his hand, she said, "Meg, Beth, and I would do anything for each other . . . *and* for you."

"All that I want is for you—the apple of my eye—to

find the same happiness your sisters have found." He tilted his head back and gazed up at the inky sky.

"What are you doing, Uncle?" she asked, bemused.

"Looking for a comet or a falling star, so that I might wish on it."

Julie chuckled and pulled him along the pavement. "More carriages are pulling up, and we've stood out here long enough. We wouldn't want to miss the entire soiree."

But as they ambled into Lord Torrington's elegant townhouse, Julie looked for a shooting star herself. It couldn't hurt, and she'd need at least a dozen or so wishes if she were to have any hope of receiving her own happy ever after, for she'd botched things horribly.

She'd willingly—nay, eagerly—given herself to London's greatest rogue.

To make matters worse, she now wore earrings his brother had given her in order to coax her into some sort of clandestine arrangement that seemed very much like an affair. And if she refused Nigel, he would toss Uncle Alistair out of his beloved home.

Given the circumstances, her chances of making a good match were remote. And even if there *was* an honorable gentleman left somewhere in London who'd have her . . .

Julie didn't want him.

She wanted the rogue.

Chapter THIRTY-ONE

When Julie and Uncle Alistair entered the magnificent ballroom, Lord Torrington greeted them warmly. "I'm so pleased you could join us this evening," he said. "And I'm sure Charlotte, er, Miss Winters, will be delighted as well." To Julie, he said, "She is so fond of you and your sisters."

Julie attempted a demure smile but struggled to hide her amusement. The earl and his governess seemed to be rather cozy. Julie only hoped that her friend was more fortunate in love than she.

Charlotte found Julie and her uncle near the entrance and drew them in, introducing them to other guests along the way. The governess's pretty green gown matched her eyes, and her cheeks were pink with excitement. "Lord Torrington has arranged for a variety of diversions," she explained. "Everyone is welcome to dance, of course,"—she waved a gloved hand at the four-piece orchestra in one corner of the room—"but there are whist tables in the adjoining tea room, charades and other parlor games in the drawing room, and a garden walk past the terrace lit with lanterns."

"Did you say charades?" A boyish grin lit Uncle Alistair's face.

"He adores the game," Julie said with a mock groan. "Once he begins playing, it will be nigh impossible to lure him away."

"Nonsense. I shall not ignore my duties as your chaperone, my dear." To Charlotte, he said, "I profess I'm curious, however. Are there a fair number of people playing? And do they seem to be adhering to the traditional rules of the game?"

At Charlotte's questioning glance, Julie said, "My uncle cannot abide sloppy play. He is a purist when it comes to charades."

The governess smiled and raised a brow. "I'm impressed. We must take you to the parlor without delay so that you may join the next round."

"It's no rush," Uncle Alistair protested weakly. "However, it is rather bad form to enter in the middle of a round."

"Let us go. I insist." Charlotte managed to keep a straight face as she graciously led the way to the elegant parlor. A multitude of chairs, sofas, and settees formed a semicircle, providing an optimal arrangement for viewing the miming. Even Uncle Alistair nodded in approval. Julie and Charlotte settled him with the small group of ardent charade enthusiasts, which was an odd mix of guests who considered themselves too old for dancing and several younger men and women who thrived on any sort of competition.

But Uncle Alistair seemed to fit right in, and Julie breathed a sigh of relief. As long as the game continued, he would be in his glory—and out of trouble. Julie would be free to spend time with Charlotte and perhaps even dance a set or two without worrying that he was wandering aimlessly or inadvertently making a scene.

He sat in an overstuffed armchair with an excellent vantage point, staring intently at the young man miming.

"Will you be all right here if Charlotte and I go and mingle?" she asked.

He nodded enthusiastically but continued to study the man who had dropped to the floor and crawled on all fours in a valiant attempt to mimic some sort of jungle animal. "Of course. Enjoy yourself."

Julie planted a kiss on the top of his smooth head. "I shall return to see how you're faring in a bit. Do not forget that we must speak with Lord Vane about the Royal Society."

"I won't forget." But the lines of concentration on his forehead said he was only half-listening—and that his attention was devoted to the game.

"Have fun, and try to let the others win once in a while," she whispered.

"Must I?" he asked, arching a fuzzy white brow.

She glared in a mockingly stern manner. "Play nicely."

As she and Charlotte left the parlor, Julie shot her friend a grateful smile. "He'll never want to leave. Lord Torrington shall have to summon footmen to carry us to our carriage in the wee hours of the morning."

"You are welcome to stay all night if you wish," Charlotte said. "I'm just delighted that you'll be free to dance and converse with your many admirers this evening."

Julie linked an arm through her friend's. "Ever optimistic, are you?"

Nodding confidently, Charlotte said, "With your classical features, your ethereal gown, and the cascade of curls over your shoulder, you could pass as a Greek goddess. Trust me—you shall not want for attention tonight."

"Neither shall you, my friend."

They returned to a ballroom that was three times as crowded as it had been before.

"Goodness!" Charlotte exclaimed. "This has turned into quite the crush. I wish your sisters—"

"Good evening, Miss Winters," a sour-faced matron interrupted.

"Lady Gotham," Charlotte said smoothly. "What a pleasure. I believe you've met my dear friend, Miss La—"

"I'm in need of a chair." Lady Gotham didn't spare a glance at Julie. "And some champagne, if you please. I'm positively parched."

Gracious as ever, Charlotte smiled at the older woman. "You'll find plenty of seating near the refreshment table." She motioned across the dance floor where lines of dancers surged toward one another and retreated in time to the music.

Lady Gotham nervously fingered her lace fichu and stared at Charlotte as though she'd suggested crossing the Pyrenees or swimming the Nile.

"Please, allow me to escort you there," Charlotte offered.

"If you insist." Lady Gotham sucked in her cheeks and clung to Charlotte's arm.

The governess gave Julie an apologetic look.

"Do not worry about me," Julie said brightly. "I see a friend of my uncle's and should pay my respects." Which was not quite true, but she didn't want Charlotte to fret over her, and she could certainly survive a quarter of an hour on her own.

Indeed, for a one-time wallflower, the perimeter of the dance floor was familiar territory. Not in the least bit daunting.

She watched as Charlotte and Lady Gotham weaved their way through the crowd and was debating whether to peek in on her uncle when—

"Miss Lacey." The deep, familiar voice at her ear made her shiver.

"Good evening, Lord Currington," she said, keeping her tone chilly. Reluctantly, she faced him. "I was just headed to the parlor to see my uncle."

Nigel stepped in front of her, the wall of his chest a blockade. "I cannot tell you how pleased I am to see you wearing the earrings. You liked my gift?"

Blast. "They are lovely. However, I shall be returning them to you in the morning."

"Nonsense. You look like a princess in them. They were *meant* for you, Juliette."

"You misunderstand. I'm only wearing them because I didn't have the opportunity to—"

"No need to explain." He surreptitiously placed a hand at the small of her back. "We need to speak about the house. Privately."

She snorted. "I have nothing to say to you."

"What of your decision?" he said more sharply. "Time is running out."

"I still have three days." She was hoping for a miracle. Divine intervention. But there was no cavalry charging over the horizon to save her and Uncle Alistair. "I am close to procuring the necessary documentation," she bluffed.

"Are you?" He smiled smugly, apparently unperturbed. "I don't know why you would concern yourself with legal papers and such when all you have to do is say the word." In a whisper, he added, "Let me take care of everything. The only thing I ask for in return is your friendship."

Damn him. For trapping her in a crowded ball room.

For pretending to be a gentleman when he was the worst sort of scoundrel.

For making her consider his rotten proposal for even one second.

Frustration welled up inside her. "I really must go," she said. "My uncle will be looking for me."

Subtly, Nigel grasped her elbow and pulled her back, toward the wall. "You can't dismiss me so easily, Juliette."

Chills skittered over her skin, but she boldly met his gaze. "No? Watch me."

She yanked her arm free and took one step away before he called after her, "I understand my brother is no longer staying with you."

Halting in her tracks, she feigned nonchalance. "What of it?"

He shrugged. "Samuel can be exceedingly charming, can he not?"

"I don't pretend to know what you mean," she choked out.

"You mustn't blame yourself for succumbing to his dashing good looks and infamous wickedness," Nigel said. "You aren't the first innocent miss he's seduced, and you certainly won't be the last."

"You are mistaken. He did not seduce me." He'd made her fall in love with him, which was entirely different. Wasn't it? She glanced over both her shoulders to make sure no one was within earshot. "In any event, my relationship with Sam is none of your concern."

"I hope he hasn't broken your heart, Juliette—as he has so many others." Frowning, he crossed his arms and leaned against the wall. "He led you to believe he cared for you, didn't he?"

She swallowed the lump in her throat. "Why are you asking me this?"

"I hate to see you hurting," he said, his voice laced with sympathy. "I'm all too familiar with the way my brother operates. He seduces with passion, pretty words, and promises. And then he leaves. It's not your fault that you fell under his spell—*I* know that. The rest of London, however, will likely judge you more harshly."

Heaven help her. "I know precisely what you're implying, and I do not care for it." She'd attempted to sound outraged, but the skin on the back of her neck tingled ominously.

"It's hardly fair," he continued, undaunted. "Samuel will continue on his merry way, debauching other naïve young ladies. Meanwhile, your reputation will soon be soiled beyond repair."

Dear Jesus. A low buzzing sounded in Julie's ears. "Is that a threat, Nigel?"

He placed a palm on his fine brocade waistcoat as though the mere suggestion offended him deeply. "On the contrary. I am offering you my *protection*. The last thing I would want is to see your family's name sullied."

Julie closed her eyes briefly. Nigel knew her family was her Achilles' heel. Just the mention of the shame she might bring upon them was like the twist of a knife in her chest. "If you were half as concerned for my reputation as you claim to be, you would never have sent your brother to stay with us in the first place—and you certainly wouldn't be making such an indecent proposal to me now."

His icy blue eyes gleamed, and his thin lips curled into a snide smile. How had she ever thought he resembled Sam? Sam was warm, true, and charming. Nigel was cold. Devious. Calculating.

"You make me sound like a villain, Juliette. But the truth is that the Duke of Grimby has offered me a prime piece of land next to my country estate—in return for marrying his daughter. It is an offer that I simply cannot refuse. Perhaps in a storybook world, I could ignore my obligations. I would offer you marriage, and you would bear me a houseful of children."

"My, what an enchanting tale," she said dryly.

"But we cannot ignore our responsibilities. I have a duty to my title, just as you have a duty to your family. That doesn't mean we should be denied each other's company."

Of all the—"I do not *wish* for your company, Nigel.

Not in a storybook world, nor in the real one. Not now, nor ever." She brushed past him, intent on finding Charlotte.

"Samuel hasn't called on you, has he?" Nigel drawled.

Julie froze but did not turn to face him, loath to dignify his rude question with a response. Perhaps because it hurt too much to admit the truth—that she'd had no word from Sam since their passionate night together. No visit, no chance encounter, no note.

"My brother has always been the charismatic one— the one adored by ladies, admired by men . . . even favored by our father. But Samuel, as you may have noticed, is fickle and cares for naught but his own pleasure. He cannot give you and your uncle the stability and protection you crave." Nigel approached her from behind and dipped his head so that his breath blew hot on her neck, turning her skin clammy. "You still have three days in which to come to your senses, darling, and I am confident you shall. Do not worry—I shan't hold this little episode, this slight lapse in judgment, against you. In fact, the cat and mouse game that you're playing only heightens my desire—and makes me want you more."

With that, he strode away, leaving his awful words echoing in her ears and a violent shudder wracking her body.

Chapter THIRTY-TWO

Sam had left a mountain of work piled on his new desk, which was temporarily situated against a wall in Griff's office. Sam's friend had assured him he'd have his own office as soon as it could be arranged, but Sam didn't mind. He watched everything Griff did—and learned.

He'd planned to stay late into the evening looking over the contract Griff's solicitor had drafted. But as dusk fell, one of Griff's footmen brought Sam a message that had been delivered to the house, to Sam's attention.

Dear Cousin Samuel,
I'm gratified to know you are well and committed to pursuing your own passions, whatever they may be. I do hope that you will keep me disguised of your progress and visit Juliette and me on occasion. In the event that you plan on attending Lord

Torrington's soiree this evening, we shall see you
there. I know Juliette would be delighted.

Alistair

Sam had barely read the last word before he'd extin-
guished the lamps and locked up the office. He couldn't
forgo the chance to see Juliette. He'd thought of her constantly, and the mere prospect of being near her made
his heart hammer in his chest.

He quickly changed into an evening jacket and walked
the three blocks to Torrington's brightly lit townhouse,
where a line of coaches wound around the corner. The
soiree was obviously well underway.

As he entered the bustling ballroom, he searched the
crowd for Juliette's familiar form—the long line of her
neck, the sprightly curls at her nape, and her willowy
limbs. But he didn't find her twirling on the dance floor
or chatting in one of the clusters of guests along the
edges. He'd overheard someone mention charades and
cards, so he headed toward the parlor in hopes of finding her there. Just as he was about to exit the ballroom,
a hand clamped his shoulder.

"If it isn't the prodigal son—or brother, as the case
may be."

A chill slithered down Sam's spine. "Nigel." He shook
the hand his brother offered. "It is good to see you."

"Is it?" Nigel arched a sardonic brow. "I haven't heard
from you in days. I'd begun to suspect you'd met your
demise in a ditch on the side of the road."

"It's a wonder you've been able to sleep at night,"
Sam quipped, but he was grateful—and somewhat

surprised—that Nigel and he were at least on speaking terms.

"Come. Let's nick a drink from Torrington's study." Nigel rotated his shoulder in invitation.

"Give me a half hour to greet some friends and acquaintances, and I shall meet you there."

Nigel rolled his eyes. He must know Juliette was there—and had no doubt sought her out as well. "What's happened to us, Sam? What would our father think if he could see us now?"

Guilt niggled at Sam's gut. "He'd tell us we were acting like idiots and make us muck out the stable together until we forgot why we were ever at odds."

"Right," Nigel said. "Let's skip the stables and have a brandy instead."

Sam hesitated. Now that he was so close to Juliette, the need to see her was a real, physical thing. But part of his new approach to life was putting duty before his own selfish desires. And if Nigel was willing to extend an olive branch, the least Sam could do was meet him halfway.

He'd be honest about his feelings for Juliette, and his intentions. Both he and Nigel had to accept that in the end, she would decide whom she chose to be with.

Sam swallowed past the knot in his throat. He prayed Juliette would choose him. But if she didn't, he hoped that one day—in the very distant future—he'd be man enough to wish her and his brother every happiness. And mean it.

"I suppose a quick drink couldn't hurt." Sam had been curious about Nigel's true motivation for taking back the house on Hart Street. Maybe he'd learn something that would be useful to Juliette. Sweeping a hand in front of him, he said, "Lead the way."

As they slipped inside Torrington's darkened study, Nigel sniffed the air. "Mmm, cigars. Maybe we should nick a couple of those, too."

Sam snorted and lit a lamp on the earl's desk. "It's bad enough that we're sneaking his brandy." As he poured, Sam added, "Don't think the irony of this conversation has escaped me. You're the one suggesting less-than-gentlemanly behavior, and I'm keeping you in check." He handed Nigel a snifter, and they sat in a pair of chairs that flanked the dormant fireplace.

"You're looking well," Nigel said, swirling the brandy in his glass. "Your jacket and cravat are immaculate, your hair has been cut, and the dark circles beneath your eyes have vanished. I scarcely recognize you."

"I've been staying with Griff—er, Jonathan Griffith."

"The wealthy merchant?" Nigel asked, with just a hint of disdain.

"And my friend. I've begun working for him," Sam said, unapologetically. "As soon as I'm able, I shall pay off my debts."

"You'd rather work for a living than accomplish the single task I gave you?" Nigel shook his head, incredulous.

"I wouldn't be able to live with myself if I forced Juliette and her uncle out of that house." Sam stared into his drink. "But let us be honest with each other. You're not really interested in the house, are you? You knew she lived there from the start. This was all an attempt to manipulate her—and me."

Nigel sniffed, hesitated a beat. "Yes. As you've probably already deduced, I am enamored of Juliette."

"Then why the hell would you try to toss her out of her house?" Sam sputtered. "She thinks you're a cold-hearted cad."

"No, she thinks *you're* the cad. After all, you're the one who first tried to evict her and then seduced her. *I'm* the gentleman who's allowing her to stay in her beloved home. *I'm* the one who's salvaging her reputation."

Sam's blood simmered. "I had no idea you were so morally corrupt."

"Few people do." Nigel smiled smugly. "I believe our father knew, deep down. That's why he preferred you."

"Father *loved* you. Did you know he always counseled me to be more like you? It would break his heart to know what you've done."

"Then I guess I should be glad he's not here to witness it."

Sam slammed down his glass and stalked across the room so that he wouldn't throttle his brother with his own neckcloth. "You underestimate Juliette's intelligence. Once she learns how you've deceived her, she'll want nothing to do with you. She deserves to know who you truly are."

"Who I really *am* is of little consequence, brother. What matters is who people *think* I am, and they think I'm the honorable, steadfast, dutiful Marquess of Currington."

Sam spoke through gritted teeth. "Juliette won't be so easily fooled. I won't let you take advantage of her."

"What's this?" Nigel asked, amused. He stood, rounded

his chair, and stood toe to toe with Sam. "Never say *you've* developed a *tendre* for the wallflower."

Shit. Sam grabbed Nigel by the collar of his jacket, yanked him forward, and looked straight into his cold blue eyes. "She's no more a wallflower than I am a saint. And my feelings for her"—Sam shoved his brother backward and released him—"are *none* of your damned concern."

Chuckling, Nigel smoothed his collar. Regained his composure. "You fancy yourself the hero, do you? I suppose you'll come charging to her rescue upon your white steed?"

"Maybe." Sam was breathing hard from the Herculean effort it took to resist throwing Nigel against the wall and wreaking havoc right there in Torrington's study.

"You're no prince, Sam. You don't even have a god-forsaken cottage to live in," Nigel said coolly. "Do you honestly think you could give her what she needs? What she wants?"

"That will be up to her to decide."

Nigel picked up his snifter and threw back the rest of his brandy. "She's already decided. She's chosen me."

"What are you talking about?"

"Juliette and I have a past. I tasted those sweet lips long before you knew her name."

Sam gripped the back of his chair. "I don't care."

"She's a passionate creature, as you well know. But she's also a practical sort. She wants what's best for her uncle and her family." Nigel rubbed the back of his neck as though it would pain him to say the next bit. "Even if you were capable of providing for her, your reputation as London's greatest rogue would do naught but damage her standing in society. She and her sisters have been struggling to crawl out of the hole they were in, through no fault of their own. If this town were to discover that you lived with her—even for a brief time—you'd essentially be kicking the whole family back into a pit of disgrace."

"You're despicable," Sam spat. "If you cared for Juliette, you wouldn't threaten to expose her."

Nigel shrugged. "In any case, she has agreed to let me take care of her."

Bile rose in Sam's throat, but he had to ask. "You are engaged?"

"Not precisely . . . but under my protection, she'll want for nothing."

Sam blinked, unbelieving. "I don't understand. You intend to make Juliette your *mistress*?"

Leaning an elbow on the fireplace mantel, Nigel said, "If circumstances were different, I might have offered her marriage. As it is, her devotion to her lunatic uncle is a serious liability. So I intend to take Lady Clementine—the Duke of Grimby's eldest chit—as my wife. She's pitifully plain, but her dowry more than makes up for her looks. The duke intends to gift me several hundred acres adjacent to my estate in Yorkshire." Nigel's blue eyes gleamed with greed. "I set my sights on that land years ago, and now it shall be mine."

Sam gaped, incredulous. "Juliette would never agree to be anyone's mistress."

"She is headstrong, no doubt. That's why some . . . persuasion was required on my part. Perhaps it is not the life she envisioned for herself. However, her choices are limited now that . . ." Nigel let his words trail off.

"Now that *what*?" Sam demanded.

Nigel snorted. "You've defiled her."

Sam stalked toward Nigel, his thoughts lethal. "You don't know what you're talking about."

"Oh, I do," Nigel replied nonchalantly. "Juliette admitted as much tonight. I don't mind though. You're merely the stable boy who's broken my wild pony. *I* shall be the one to ride her."

Sam tackled his brother before Nigel knew what hit him. The snifter flew out of his hand and shattered on the hearth. Nigel bucked beneath him, but Sam pinned his shoulders to the floor and spoke in a low, lethal tone. "*Don't* speak of her that way."

"Why not?" Nigel spat, his face purple with rage. "It's the bloody truth."

Sam cocked his fist. "Keep talking. See what happens."

"Maybe if you'd controlled your baser urges . . ."

Damn it. Nigel was right—Sam *was* partially to blame for Juliette's predicament. He let his fist drop and shoved himself off his brother. "I don't believe a damned word that comes out of your mouth."

Nigel sat up and coughed. "Fine. Ask her yourself."

Sam was already heading for the study door. "It would be an insult to even ask her the question. But I will seek her out." One look into her beautiful eyes would tell him everything he needed to know.

"Fool yourself if you like, brother." Nigel barked a hollow laugh, stood, and dusted off his trousers. "If you think of it, inquire about the earrings she's wearing."

"We've more important matters to discuss than jewelry. If you're even one tenth of the gentleman I thought you were, you'll allow her and her uncle to remain in their house—without any remuneration."

"And if I don't?"

Sam paused at the doorway. "Then you're ten times the scoundrel I ever was."

Having delivered that parting shot with considerably more confidence than he felt, he went in search of Juliette.

Chapter THIRTY-THREE

Julie had considered telling her uncle that she'd developed a headache and asking him if they could return home. But when she found him in the parlor, he was miming in front of a small but enthusiastic crowd of onlookers. He held his forefingers at his temples like horns.

"Antelope!" one bespectacled matron cried.

"Demon!" slurred a man well into his cups.

"Viking!" a young woman guessed.

Julie smiled to herself. Uncle Alistair was a satyr—one of his favorite creatures to act out during charades—but she wouldn't dream of spoiling his fun. She watched him for a while, but when he spotted her, he grinned and waved her back into the ballroom.

Relieved to know he was enjoying himself but still shaken by her conversation with Nigel, she decided to seek out Charlotte. She'd barely ventured into the corridor before she ran smack into a rock hard, unyielding torso. She bounced lightly off the elegant but understated burgundy brocade waistcoat, barely managing to keep her balance.

Large warm hands cupped her elbows. "Juliette. I've been looking everywhere for you."

Sam. She looked up at him, and her heart tripped in her chest as she drank in the sight of his familiar, heart-breakingly handsome face. Dear God, it *was* him.

She opened her mouth to speak. She wanted to tell him that she'd been looking for him too, hoping to see him around every corner. That she'd missed him and wished he hadn't stayed away. But all the emotion of the last few days bubbled up, threatening to erupt like a volcano.

"Forgive me for startling you," he said. "Are you all right?"

She nodded, glad that no one else happened to be in the corridor. "It's good to see you," she managed. "I'd hoped . . . that is, I . . ."

He glanced up and down the hallway. "Would you like to go somewhere we can talk privately—the garden perhaps?"

She shook her head. The garden path was bound to be teeming with other couples, and she desperately wanted Sam to herself. "I'd rather find a spot where we won't be disturbed."

The wicked grin that lit his face made her knees go weak. Pulling her by the hand, he whispered, "Secluded spots happen to be my specialty. Come."

He led her past the parlor into an unlit part of the house. Several yards down the hallway, he paused and pressed an ear to a closed door. After waiting a moment, he opened it a few inches and peered inside the room.

"It's the library," he said. "No one's here."

Feeling deliciously naughty, she tiptoed in and waited as Sam closed the door behind them. The moment the lock clicked, they crashed together.

No candles or lamps illuminated the interior, but they didn't require light to find each other. His hands encircled her waist, and he tipped his forehead to hers. She pressed her palms to his chest, savoring his strength and the solid feel of him—irrefutable proof that he was truly there, with her.

God, she'd missed him.

As though privy to her thoughts, he said, "I wanted to come to you. You have no idea how difficult it was for me to stay away."

Warmth and desire mingled in her chest, then unfurled through her limbs. "Then why did you?"

He held her cheek in his hand and brushed a thumb over her lips. "You needed time to think, and I didn't want to take the chance of jeopardizing your reputation, as I did before. I was wrong to blindly follow my brother's orders without regard for you or your uncle. I hope you'll be able to forgive me."

Soft moonlight streamed through the library's towering windows, and now that her eyes had adjusted to the dark, she could see his sober expression. Tracing a fingertip over the swirling pattern stitched onto his waistcoat, she said, "If you hadn't done Nigel's bidding, we never would have had the opportunity to know each other."

"About Nigel," he began. "I just spoke with—"

"Did you mean what you said earlier? That it was difficult for you to stay away?"

"The last three days felt like three years. I thought of you every waking moment—and most of the non-waking ones as well." He tilted his head and looked at her curiously. "You don't truly doubt my feelings for you, do you?"

"No." She sighed. "But you might have written a note."

He hung his head, chastened. "I'll write you a note every damned day, if that's what you wish."

"If you're granting wishes," she murmured, "what I'd like is for you to kiss me."

He easily scooped her in his arms and stalked to a long leather sofa in front of the windows, where he sat and held her on his lap. Smoothing a curl behind her ear, he said, "You should know that you may have as many wishes as you like. I would give you the world if I could."

"For now, I will be content with a kiss," she whispered.

Smiling, he steadied her face in his hands and crushed his mouth to hers.

Sweet heaven above. He's said he'd give her the world if he could . . . and it felt as though he had. His tongue traced the seam of her lips, demanded entry, and plundered her mouth. He swept his hands down her sides and cupped her breasts, tweaking the aching tips with his thumbs.

All the fear she'd felt while talking with Nigel in the ballroom slipped away, for as long as Sam loved her, nothing truly awful could happen. He hadn't *said* that he loved her, hadn't actually spoken the words, but he proved it with every passionate moan and every gentle caress. And their connection transcended the physical.

She felt Sam in her heart, knew he'd always take her side and support her. He was her partner in the truest sense.

He kissed her as though she was at the center of his universe—which was precisely where she wanted to be. She savored this precious intimacy—a few stolen moments where they could draw strength, comfort, and peace from each other.

"Juliette," he whispered. "We cannot remain here for long. Your uncle and friends will be looking for you."

She peppered kisses along the hard line of his jaw and trailed more down his neck, delighting in the slightly abrasive shadow of his beard beneath her lips. "Then we should not waste this time."

"I agree," he said softly. "But we have much to discuss."

"We can talk later—in the garden or ballroom. But we can only be together here. Now." She looked up at his blue eyes and felt as though she were drowning in their depths. "Please . . . I need you."

He frowned and swallowed. She could almost see the battle raging inside him. "I am powerless to deny you, Juliette—as you well know."

"I don't know when I'll see you again," she said, memorizing the crinkles at the corners of his eyes and fine scar above one brow. "But I do know that no one else can make me feel the way you do."

"That's because you're mine. No matter what happens to us, in my heart, you always will be." He tightened his hold on her and ravaged her mouth, his kisses almost bruising in their intensity.

She felt his arousal beneath her bottom and wriggled

against him until he groaned. "And you are mine," she countered.

He brushed his lips over the sensitive swells of her breasts and slid a hand beneath her skirts. With wicked fingers, he traced a path up the back of her calf, alternately kneading and stroking till he reached her thigh. His warm palm skimmed the inside of her leg, higher and higher, teasing her with feather-light caresses.

She already ached for him. A steady pulsing had begun at her core, and her legs parted of their own accord.

"If we had all the time in the world," he breathed, "I would do this properly. Your hair would be down. Your gown would be on the floor. You'd be gloriously naked, and I'd kiss every inch of your body. Every. Single. Inch."

She looked into his eyes, too dazed to speak.

"As it is, you will have to employ a little imagination."

She blinked up at his handsome face, confused—for this seemed very real to her. "How so?"

"Close your eyes," he ordered, even as his hand traced circles on the inside of her thigh. Smiling, she let her eyes flutter shut.

"Imagine we're alone in a beautiful field of heather. It's warm, but we find a shady spot beneath a tree and spread a soft quilt on the ground."

"Mmm, that's nice."

"Not *nice*. Sensual. Delightfully wicked."

"Very well." She melted a little more. "I stand corrected."

"I strip off every article of your clothing and pull every pin from your hair. A mild breeze kisses your skin and rustles your curls. I lay you back on the blanket and place wildflowers on your belly."

Julie could almost smell the heather and feel the dappled sunshine on her bare limbs. "Why would you do that?" she asked.

"Because I want that picture in my head—forever." He kissed her neck as his palm continued to stroke the supple flesh of her thigh. "And after I've showered you with flowers, I pick out the prettiest blossom, brush it over your lips, and follow its path with my mouth."

Her lips tingled as if he'd actually done it. "Oh," she said, swallowing.

"Next, I swirl the flower lower, around your breasts, between them, and over their taut peaks . . . before I capture one in my mouth. Do you remember how that feels?" he asked huskily.

Her nipples tightened into hard buds. "Yes." As if she could forget.

"Good," he said, approving. "I drag the flower lower still. It's here"—he caressed the tops of her thighs—"and here"—he stroked the sensitive spot between her legs, making her whimper with pleasure. "My mouth follows," he reminded her. "And I stay here until you are certain you cannot bear another second of pleasure. I stay here until you come apart."

She opened her eyes and found his dark, heavy-lidded gaze trained upon her face, as though he were gauging her reaction to every word and touch. "I wish we were back in your bedchamber at Hart Street," she said, "and that we had all the time in the world."

"But we're in a field of heather," he said, mildly offended. "Your eyes are supposed to be shut."

"I don't need to imagine fields and flowers. I only want you, Sam."

"Say that again."

Bemused, she said, "I don't need to ima—"

"Not that part. The next."

Oh. "I only want—" He slid a finger into her, and she groaned with a potent mix of pleasure and need. "You. Sam."

He crushed his mouth to hers and kissed her hungrily. Beneath her gown, his fingers stroked her inside and out until she arched her back, breathless and on the brink. But it wasn't enough. She wanted all of him. That raw, primal connection. That deep, abiding intimacy.

She shifted on his lap, trying to straddle him, but her legs tangled with yards of silk.

"Easy, temptress. I wouldn't want to tear your gown. Well, I *would*, but it wouldn't be at all prudent."

Running her fingertips over the edge of his jaw, she looked earnestly into his eyes. "I don't feel like being prudent. I want you, Sam. And I know you want me too."

Chapter THIRTY-FOUR

Sweet Lucifer. Sam wanted Juliette more than his next breath.

In five seconds flat he could free his cock from his trousers, grasp her hips, and bury himself deep inside her. She could wrap her lithe legs around his waist, throw her head back, and ride him until they both cried out in ecstasy.

But, damn it all, he had to say no.

One of them had to stay on guard and be alert—and even with his trousers still on he was having the devil of a time maintaining a shred of control.

"I can't make love to you here, in Torrington's library." He cupped her dismayed face in his hands. "It's too risky. Someone could come looking for you. Or we could ruin your gown or muss your hair."

"You act as though you've never had a tryst in a library before." He detected the hint of a pout in her gorgeous lips. "Why must you be so honorable all of the sudden? You're supposed to be a rogue."

"What if I'm not any longer?"

She looked at him warily. "What do you mean?"

"I mean there's only one woman I want." Given everything Nigel had just told him, he must be mad to admit it, but the words tumbled out. "In case it's not glaringly obvious . . . it's you, Juliette. I only want you."

As he awaited her response, his heart hammered in his chest, so loudly she must hear it. She seemed to return his feelings . . . but passion and love could be difficult to distinguish. And it was hard to be certain of anything when Nigel's words still echoed in his head.

Juliette and I have a past.

Under my protection, she'll want for nothing.

She's chosen me.

"Why?" she whispered. "*Why* have you changed?"

"You and your uncle made me realize I need to be part of something bigger than myself. A profession . . . a cause . . . a family." He wanted to drop to his knees and beg her to marry him, but he needed to make something of himself first. He needed to be worthy of her.

"Oh, Sam." She kissed him tenderly, and his doubts evaporated like a morning fog.

He kissed her back, stoking the flames of her desire once more. Though he couldn't make love to her, he could give her pleasure—or die trying.

She bit her bottom lip as he turned her on his lap so that she faced him, her knees straddling his. Slowly, deliberately, he slid a hand beneath her skirts once more. "Shall I close my eyes again?" she asked coyly.

"No, Juliette." He stroked the slick folds at her entrance and slid a finger into her. "Look right at me."

A strawberry stain colored her chest and crept up her neck as he set up a rhythm she liked. She clung to his shoulders, moaning each time he stroked the most sensitive spot, and her eyes took on a dazed, faraway look.

God, she felt good. Hot, tight, and ready. "Next time," he promised, "I will make love to you properly. Or improperly if that's what you wish. I can promise you there will be no clothes, no interruptions, and no limits."

"I . . . I like the sound of that," she said breathlessly.

"But now, vixen, I need you to come for me."

Her head lolled back and her breasts thrust forward, her nipples visible even through her corset and bodice. Gorgeous. His.

"Move against me," he said. "Take your pleasure."

She leaned forward and rocked her hips, meeting him thrust for thrust. "Yes," she breathed. "Faster."

He obliged and watched in wonder as she crested. Every muscle in her body was tight as a drum when the first wave took her. He marveled at the power of her release, feeling it in her core and watching in wonder as it rippled through her body.

Slowly, she drifted down from the clouds. Her face softened, and she sagged against him, sated. He smoothed her skirts and kissed her sweet mouth, humbled beyond measure that she'd trusted him.

More than ever, he was determined to make her his. For always.

He savored the weight of her head on his shoulder and the way she fit perfectly in his arms. Though he was loath to rush her, they simply couldn't linger in the library. Not if they wished for their rendezvous to go unnoticed.

He rubbed her spine and nuzzled her neck. "We must go," he said regretfully.

She sat up and blinked as though disoriented, then said, "Yes, of course." She slid off him and stood, smoothing her hair and slowly regaining her composure. Already she was looking at the door, as though trying to figure out how to cross the bridge from this magical world back into the real one.

But he couldn't let her go just yet. "Before we part, there's something I must ask you."

"What is it?"

"I spoke with Nigel earlier this evening." She frowned, instantly wary. "He said that you and he . . . that you've agreed to an arrangement."

"That's not true," she sputtered. She crossed her arms, adamant. "I've agreed to nothing."

Thank God. But Sam's relief was tempered by her shuttered expression, and he sensed there was more to the story. Filled with foreboding, he asked, "So you haven't agreed to the arrangement he proposed . . . but you haven't refused him either?"

For several beats, she didn't answer—and her silence told him everything.

"I didn't refuse him outright, but only because I need more time," she said hoarsely. "I realize how awful that must sound to your ears, but it's terribly complicated. This isn't solely about me. I must think about Uncle Alistair and my family."

Jesus. It sounded like she was actually considering Nigel's proposal. "Juliette, I understand all that. But you

deserve more than . . . than . . . what my brother is offering. You deserve . . ."

Her eyes widened expectantly. But Sam was in no
position to make promises—at least not yet. "You deserve better," he said resolutely.

"I agree. But we don't always get what we deserve."
She gazed at him, wistful. "There's no one I'd rather be
with than you."

Her words gave him hope, but something else his
brother had said still niggled at him. "You and Nigel
were involved before we met?"

"I kissed him," she replied, unapologetic. "Just as, I
presume, you have kissed other women."

"I don't judge you for kissing him," he said, even
though the thought made his stomach roil. "Hell, I'd
be the worst sort of hypocrite if I did. But we're talking about my *brother*—and both of you hid the truth
from me."

She gazed at the toes of her slippers. "At first I thought
it was none of your concern. And I was embarrassed
because . . ." Her cheeks flushed. "It's so difficult to
talk about this with you, but I fancied myself in . . . love
with him."

Her words hit Sam like a kick in the gut, and he sank
onto the sofa to keep from doubling over. "And now?"

"I don't love him, if that's what you're asking." She
lifted her chin, and the jewels at her ears sparkled in a
shaft of moonlight—and a chill slithered down his spine.

"The earrings you're wearing," Sam said evenly. "Are
they from him?"

He desperately wanted her to say *no*. Let the damned
earrings be a gift from her parents or her uncle or one

of her brothers-in-law. Hell, let them be from her first true love. Anyone but Nigel.

She fingered a lobe guiltily but didn't reply.

No. "Please, Juliette," he begged, his voice raspy. "You know the significance of such a gift. For the love of God, tell me they're not from him."

Tears shone in her eyes, and she blinked for a heartbeat before meeting his gaze. "They're from him," she choked out. "But you should know I—"

Voices sounded in the hall. A woman giggled. A man shushed her. Their conversation grew louder then faded as they staggered past the door and down the corridor, but they'd soon reach a dead end and circle back. Bloody hell.

Instinct kicked in despite the hollow, sick feeling in the pit of his stomach. He pressed a finger to his lips in a silent warning and quickly guided Juliette toward the exit of the library.

And maybe that was for the best.

Juliette claimed she hadn't agreed to be Nigel's mistress, and maybe she hadn't—in so many words.

But she'd kept the expensive baubles Nigel had given her *and* worn them in public.

Her actions told the true story. The woman Sam loved beyond reason had tied herself to his brother.

Chapter THIRTY-FIVE

Sam pulled Julie across the dark library, cracked open the door, and peeked into the hallway. Her body still shimmered from the pleasure he'd given her, but he wasn't whispering tender words in her ear. He wasn't pulling her close for a lingering good-bye kiss or promising to call on her tomorrow.

Instead, he was stiff and stilted, his words clipped and cold. "Go. Find Charlotte or your uncle. I'll wait here a while before I leave."

Dear God. How had she botched things so terribly? She needed to convince him he was the only one she wanted—the only one she loved.

"Sam," she said, placing her palm over his heart. He flinched as though her hand had scorched him. "Allow me to explain."

"The couple who passed by earlier will return any moment. You need to go."

He nudged her toward the corridor, but she kept her

slippers rooted to the floor. "Listen to me. I realize how it must look, but *you* are the one I care about . . . and the only one I want to be with."

"Then why haven't you refused my brother's offer?" he asked, the question tinged with accusation and hurt.

She swallowed, keenly aware that every second she remained increased the risk of a monumental scandal. "Nigel said I had a week before I had to provide my answer."

"You require a *week* to deliberate?" he asked, incredulous.

His sharp tone cut her, but she pressed on, determined to make him understand. "Of course not. I have no intention of accepting his ridiculous offer, but I thought the extra time might be useful. I'm still looking for the deed, and—"

"If you plan to refuse him, why are you wearing the earrings he gave you?"

Blast. She wished she'd never laid eyes on the stupid things. "I'm wearing them because I thought . . ." She couldn't quite bring herself to admit that she'd believed they were a gift from Sam. It presumed too much. "I only meant to try them on. I was going to remove them before I left the house . . . and then I forgot." Heaven above, the excuse sounded lame to her own ears. "I'm going to return them," she added firmly.

He arched a brow, clearly skeptical.

Her hands shook with frustration. "Do you believe me?"

"I don't doubt that in this moment you are sincere . . . and yet, your actions belie your words. My brother and

I have placed you in difficult circumstances. I don't fault you for being confused about your feelings."

"I'm *not* confused," she said, a bit too loudly. "I know my mind, Sam. I love you."

Sweet Jesus. It wasn't the most romantic of declarations and certainly not how she'd intended to reveal her heart. But now that the words hung in the air between them, she longed for him to return the sentiment—even if all he could manage was a simple kiss, gesture, or smile.

Something.

But his face was devoid of expression. She'd bared her body and soul to him, and the only sign that he'd heard her was a tiny tic in his jaw.

"You said you once loved Nigel."

"I said I once *fancied* myself in love. I love you," she repeated, her voice cracking. "Not him."

"I'm not certain that matters." Ironically, laughter sounded from down the hall as Sam stared at her, impassive.

"How can you say that?" she demanded, her heart breaking.

"You needn't love someone to be his mistress." He angled his broad shoulders through the crack in the door and looked back at her, regret in his eyes. "Good-bye, Juliette."

Julie started to go after him, but the drunken couple stumbled toward her, so she slipped back into the library and sagged against the wall, debating her options.

Perhaps she should chase after Sam and create a scene worthy of being featured in next week's gossip rags. She could cause a scandal so great that he'd be forced to marry her. Her brothers-in-law would be livid with him, and her sisters would be gravely disappointed in her. But it was a small price to pay if she could have Sam.

More tempted than she cared to admit, she stayed put in the library until the other couple was out of sight. She wanted Sam to marry her, but not because she was the alternative to a duel at dawn.

No, she wanted the grand passion, the utter devotion. The romantic, if unconventional, courtships that her sisters had. And though this evening's soiree had gone spectacularly wrong, she wasn't about to give up on her chance at the fairytale.

She wasn't about to give up on Sam.

He was understandably shaken after hearing Nigel's lies and seeing her wearing the earrings, but she'd begin to heal the rift tomorrow. Somehow.

She wished it were as simple as returning the earrings to Nigel along with a note saying she wanted nothing to do with him, now or at any time in the future.

But she feared he'd immediately retaliate, not only by removing her and her uncle from their home, but also by spreading salacious rumors about her and Sam.

Rumors that happened to be true and easy to verify, if anyone should be inclined to do so.

So she had to bide her time. Refuse to give in to the panic that threatened.

Taking a fortifying breath, she checked the corridor, found it clear, and glided through the door.

No one seemed to be about, and if she did encounter anyone, she'd simply say she'd taken a wrong turn on the way to the parlor.

She retraced her steps, wondering if Sam had already

left the soiree, for that was what she intended to do. Much as she hated to cut short Uncle Alistair's enjoyment, they couldn't stay—not when Nigel might attempt to corner her again.

So she would simply collect her uncle, say a quick farewell to Charlotte, and head for the safety of their carriage and home.

She rounded the corner undetected and was only a few yards away from the parlor's doorway when she heard the shouts. Men's voices, highly agitated, peppered with jeers, laughter, and scuffling.

Dear God. Please don't let Uncle Alistair be involved in a fracas. Let the commotion be part of the game or a minor disagreement between other guests.

But she already knew the truth in her gut.

Steeling her nerves, she rushed into the parlor to find a chaotic scene. Uncle Alistair stood nose to nose with another bespectacled gentleman who appeared to be— good heavens, don't let it be—Lord Vane. The gentleman from the Royal Society, whom she'd hoped would ease her uncle's way into the esteemed group.

Julie weaved her way through the circle of chairs, ignoring the whispers of onlookers who were far more riveted by the warring gentlemen than they'd been by the game of charades.

"The very idea," Lord Vane sputtered with disgust. "It's preposterous."

"On the secretary," Uncle Alistair countered, the white tufts atop his head waving wildly. "It's scientific fact, and I have the correspondence which proves it."

"Is that so?" Lord Vane's face was an unnatural shade of red. "And *I* have a letter from a drunken pirate saying mermaids are real creatures. That doesn't make it so, Wiltshire."

Uncle Alistair's wiry brows shot halfway up his forehead. "How *dare* you compare Mr. Shaw—a respected zoologist—to an inebriated primate? Of all the—"

Oh no. Julie laid a hand on her uncle's shoulder, and he turned to face her, startled. "My dear, I didn't know you'd returned," he said conversationally—as if he hadn't been shouting at Lord Vane one second earlier.

"I came to see how you were faring," she responded. "It certainly appears as though it's a . . . er . . . spirited game of charades." She attempted a charming laugh, as if uncivil shouting matches were part and parcel of silly parlor games. To Lord Vane she said, "Please, forgive my uncle. He is a devotee of the game and a rather fierce competitor. I'm afraid his enthusiasm may have gotten the best of him."

"I'll say." Lord Vane yanked on his lapels, but nodded, slightly mollified. "I've never heard such an absurd claim. And as a respected member of the scientific community, I feel obliged to point out fallacies."

Checking the urge to defend her uncle, she pasted on a smile and through gritted teeth, said, "Yes, of course." Though she had no idea what had spawned the argument between the men, she was certain nothing was to be gained from revisiting it.

Lord Vane sniffed pompously and droned on. "I simply cannot allow such outrageous myths to be perpetuated. It would be irresponsible of me."

Julie bit her tongue—but only for her uncle's sake. She could not afford to alienate a member of the Royal Society. Even if he was a puffed-up, self-important ass.

Uncle Alistair shook his head in frustration. "It's a pity, Vane, that you are unable to open your mind sufficiently to accept the existence of nature's beauty and plunder."

Lord Vane snickered and smiled smugly at her uncle's gaffe.

Julie felt the eyes of at least two dozen guests trained on her and Uncle Alistair. She could hear his breaths coming in shallow, strained puffs. Curling her fingers around his creaky elbow, she said breezily, "I'm sure you must have tired of the game by now, Uncle. Shall we take a stroll to the ballroom and find some refreshment?"

"Platypus anatinus," he replied proudly.

The crowd of onlookers burst into raucous laughter, and Julie tugged on his arm, desperate to whisk him away and spare him further humiliation. "Let us go," she whispered urgently.

"In just a moment, my dear." To the room in general, he said, "The animal whose name escaped me earlier is the platypus. It possesses the flat bill of a duck and the body of a quadruped."

After a second of stunned silence, the guests erupted into a fresh fit of laughter. A young man wearing a peacock blue waistcoat roared and slapped his knee. A gray-haired woman wiped tears of mirth from her eyes. Julie wanted to melt into the floor.

But Uncle Alistair smiled sagely, unperturbed. Shouting above the din, he said, "It *is* an odd-looking creature, no doubt—that's what makes it such a marvel." He turned to Julie. "*Now* we may leave."

"Let's make our way directly to the carriage," she suggested.

"Of course—if that is what you wish."

They couldn't escape the room—nay, the house—fast enough for her liking, but Uncle Alistair refused to be rushed. He covered her trembling hand with his own and proceeded toward the door at a stately pace. "Hold your head high, Juliette. We have nothing to be ashamed of."

Julie swallowed. Perhaps *he* had nothing to be ashamed of. Her conscience wasn't quite as clear.

Nevertheless, she raised her chin and blinked back tears, incensed on her uncle's behalf. A man as sweet, learned, and generous as he deserved the ton's recognition, not their scorn.

But Julie's anger was not directed solely at Lord Vane and the insensitive onlookers—she was furious with herself as well. *She* was the one who'd dragged her uncle to the soiree and then left him to his own devices while she'd slipped off to the library with Sam.

Blast. In the space of a few short hours, she'd managed to expose her uncle to ridicule, provide ample leverage to the man who would employ blackmail to make her his mistress, and irreparably wound the man she loved.

In retrospect, it would have been an excellent evening to remain in bed with a good book. Or even a bad one.

When at last she and Uncle Alistair were settled in the carriage, she stared out the fogged window and sighed.

"Don't be so forsworn, my dear," he said kindly. "I regret any embarrassment I caused you, but confess I have little tolerance for the small-mindedness Vane and the others displayed. I shall never understand why people are predisposed to disbelieving when the world is full of wondrous things."

"Is there really a creature that is part duck and part . . . ?"

"Mole," he provided. "There truly is." He smiled to himself, bolstered by the thought.

But she was still mulling over something else her uncle had said. Though his displeasure hadn't been directed at her, she wondered if perhaps *she'd* been one of the small-minded people. She hadn't believed that her uncle could really speak to Aunt Elspeth. Or that she herself deserved a husband who was devoted to her and her happiness. Or that a rogue could change his ways.

Perhaps . . . it was time for her to take a leap of faith.

Chapter THIRTY-SIX

Two days after the soiree, Sam moved out of Griff's house and into the Albany. Though his friend claimed Sam was most welcome to remain there indefinitely, Sam needed his own place—and distance from Griff's well-intentioned but ruthlessly matchmaking mama.

Sam knew several other gentlemen who let apartments in the grand townhouse, and he slept soundly the first night in his new bed. The chambers were the perfect living quarters for a bachelor, and if they didn't feel quite like home, the stark furnishings weren't to blame.

The most luxurious of palaces wouldn't have felt like home without Juliette.

Even home didn't feel like home any longer, now that he and his brother were at such odds. After past rows, Sam had always gone crawling back to Nigel, seeking absolution.

But Sam wasn't the prodigal son any longer. He was determined to make something of himself—on his own.

Sam had spent most of his time at Griff's offices, working and learning. And yet, he managed to think about Juliette constantly. She'd said that she had to give Nigel an answer within three days . . . which meant she would inform him of her answer tomorrow.

Sam knew that his brother was trying to force her hand—but he also knew Juliette was sufficiently strong-willed that she wouldn't enter into an arrangement unless she wished to.

The choice was hers.

And as much as Sam wished to protect her and make her his, she deserved the freedom to make her decision without his interference. So he'd resolved to wait in the wings until she'd made up her mind and refrain from meddling—at least openly. He couldn't help taking a few measures behind the scenes.

The truth was that even if she didn't choose Nigel, she might not choose Sam. But he would fight for her—and a future with her.

In the end, no matter what happened, he needed to know she was happy.

The next morning, Julie headed to breakfast with trepidation. The grains of sand had relentlessly slipped through her metaphorical hourglass, and she owed Nigel a decision that very evening. Though she'd been working without respite since the soiree, she still had much left to accomplish before speaking with him.

The first order of business, however, was breakfast. And tea.

She hustled toward the dining room but slid to a stop in front of the study door and blinked at the sight of her uncle toiling at his desk. The tip of his tongue poked out of the corner of his mouth as he read a letter with one hand and scribed with the other. Ink stained his fingers, and a smudge marred his cheek as well.

"My, but you're up early this morning," she said.

He looked up at her, his eyes brighter and clearer than she'd seen them in ages. "I'm analyzing some new information which supports my case for safeguarding the Thames from further contamination."

Julie wrinkled her nose. "Do people truly need convincing? The water's the color of mud and smells . . . horrid."

"Quite right, and yet, Parliament's done nothing about it." He held up his pen, heedless of the ink droplets that leaked from the nib and plunked onto his desk. "My hope is that when they're faced with empirical malevolence as to the dreadful effects of dumping human waste and animal carcasses in the river, they'll take steps to curtail it."

Julie placed a palm on her belly, thinking perhaps she'd forgo breakfast after all.

"A very worthy cause," she said, her chest squeezing with pride. "And you were able to find the evidence you require among your papers?"

"Some." Uncle Alistair's gaze drifted back to his scribblings. "Cousin Samuel found scores of relevant letters while helping me organize this room." He dipped the tip of his pen in the ink pot, and his tongue poked at the corner of his mouth once more.

"That's wonderful." Julie hoped her voice didn't betray the sadness and longing wrought within her at the mere mention of Sam's name. "You see, the information you needed was here all along."

"Much of it was," he said distractedly. "But a few key pieces were delivered yesterday. From Samuel."

Julie's breath caught in her throat. "Samuel?"

Her uncle glanced up at her, beaming. "Yes, he was good enough to query several of the barge captains whom he's met in his new line of work. Some fishermen as well. I wouldn't have dreamed of asking him to do such a thing, but he said that he thought the information might prove useful—and it is."

"Did you speak to him?" She felt an unseemly pang of jealousy in her belly.

"No, I just had a brief note from him yesterday evening. Apparently he's extremely busy with his new responsibilities."

"Did he have any other news of import?" she asked, keeping her tone light.

Uncle Alistair frowned slightly. "Only that he's moved into the Albany. That should suit him nicely."

She had no doubt the sumptuous quarters would suit him. The Albany was a bachelor's natural habitat as surely as New South Wales was the platypus's.

And Julie was happy that he'd moved on with his life so swiftly and surely.

Yes, she was still floundering a bit, but at least she now knew what she wanted. All that was left was figuring out how to achieve it.

"Would you care to join me for breakfast?" she asked her uncle.

"Thank you, my dear, but I think I shall finish another page or two beforehand. Everything is right here"—he tapped his temple emphatically—"and I want to write it down before it flees."

"I don't think your knowledge is going anywhere," she said with a wink, "but enjoy yourself."

As she made her way to the dining room and poured her tea, she wondered at Sam's thoughtful gesture. Perhaps it had been a simple thing for him, but it meant the world to her uncle—and to her.

It was kind and selfless. Not rogue-like in the least.

And it made her miss him all the more.

She filled a plate from the sideboard, and as she took her first bite of egg, Mr. Finch entered the dining room waving a note. "This just arrived for you, Miss Juliette." He placed it on the table beside her plate with a flourish and said, "I've the newspaper for your uncle as well. I shall deliver it to his study."

"Thank you," Julie said, even as cold dread filled her veins. The note must be from Nigel. She'd expected some sort of summons, but she'd foolishly hoped the marquess might grant her at least a short grace period.

She should have learned by now that Nigel was too ruthless to show the slightest mercy.

Drawing a tremulous breath, she unfolded the note.

My Dearest Juliette,
The past week has lasted a year, but now the waiting ends. Arrive at Gunter's this afternoon at a quarter past three o'clock, and, for the sake of discretion, act as though our meeting there is coincidental.

　　I look forward to discussing our future, for it begins today.

　　　　　　　　　　　　　　　　　　　Yours, N.

Julie pushed her plate away. She wished she could reply with a note, informing him in no uncertain terms that she found his offer abhorrent, but while penning such a response would be satisfying, it would not be prudent. Not when she still hoped to persuade him to sell the house to her uncle or at least allow him to rent it.

She had to firmly but gently refuse Nigel, and, at the same time, appeal to his sense of compassion. If that tack failed—as she suspected it would—she had one final ace to play.

Over the past few days she'd concluded that perhaps the best way to deal with a bully was to give him a taste of his own medicine. She wasn't proud of stooping to his level, but if her plan helped her keep Uncle Alistair in his house and spared her sisters humiliation, it would be worth it.

The thought of her sisters made her belly churn with guilt. Meg and Beth would be aghast if they knew Julie intended to meet with Nigel, especially since he'd proven to be less than a gentleman in his past dealings with her.

Julie was fully aware that any face-to-face contact with the scoundrel was ill-advised at best, but she would take the precaution of bringing Lucy along with her. Besides, what harm could come to her in front of a renowned confectionery shop in the broad light of day?

Chapter THIRTY-SEVEN

At the appointed time, Julie and Lucy strolled toward Gunter's in Berkeley Square. Sunlight reflected off the shiny storefront windows, making the street seem doubly bright and warm. Julie was grateful for her parasol, which not only protected her from the sun, but also provided some semblance of anonymity. Or at least the illusion of it.

They'd stopped in a milliner's shop on the way and purchased a smart hat for Uncle Alistair. He was in need of a new one, but the routine errand also served to calm Julie's frayed nerves.

As she and Lucy approached Gunter's, Julie paused and pretended to look at a pair of slippers in the window of a neighboring shop. She wasn't certain whether she should go inside the confectionery to wait for Nigel or linger outside, but her maid would be curious if Julie dallied too long on the pavement.

Turning to Lucy, she said, "Let's pay a visit to Gunter's and treat ourselves to a pastry."

The maid beamed. "That sounds lovely."

They started to walk toward the shop door when a long shadow slanted over them, instantly cooling the air by several degrees. A midnight blue coach with no markings rolled to a stop along the curb. Dark curtains hung at every window of the elegant cab, concealing the interior and any passengers.

But Julie knew who was inside.

She hesitated briefly but remembered what Nigel's note had said about pretending that the meeting was unexpected. Forcing a smile at Lucy, she decided to enter the shop and let Nigel follow.

She'd only taken a couple of steps when a liveried footman rudely blocked her path. She opened her mouth to admonish him, but he merely pointed at the coach, his expression apologetic.

"Good heavens," Julie murmured—mostly for Lucy's sake. "What could this be about?"

She walked back toward the coach but hung several feet back from the open door.

"Good afternoon, Miss Juliette." Nigel peered out of the darkened cab. "What an unexpected pleasure."

"Quite," she said through her teeth.

His gaze flicked to her maid then back to her. "It's a lovely day for a ride. Would you care to join me?"

Behind her, Lucy gasped.

"Don't be alarmed," she said to the maid. "He's Cousin Samuel's brother and a friend of the family's." To Nigel she said, "I would vastly prefer to take tea inside the shop like two civilized persons."

His face hardened, sending a chill down Julie's spine. "I'm afraid I haven't the time for tea," he said politely.

"Surely you could spare half an hour for a family friend. I thought we might take a brief ride through the park and enjoy the sights."

Alarms sounded in Julie's head. "Perhaps we could take a *walk* through the park," she suggested. That way, Lucy could follow at a distance that allowed them to talk while still serving as a proper chaperone.

"I'm afraid that's impossible. You see, I injured my leg while boxing yesterday and neglected to bring my cane with me. Why doesn't your maid enjoy a treat at Gunter's while we take a short ride?" To Lucy, he said, "I promise I shall deliver Miss Lacey safely back to you before you've finished your water ice."

The maid grasped Julie's elbow protectively and whispered in her ear. "I don't like this, Miss Juliette."

Julie didn't either, but she did want the opportunity to make her feelings abundantly clear to him.

"Do not worry." Julie handed Lucy her parasol, then reached into her reticule and gave her a few coins as well. "Enjoy yourself and wait here for my return. If I am not back in precisely half an hour, please go to my uncle and ask him to send for Cousin Samuel at once."

The maid frowned. "Are you certain, miss?"

"Absolutely. No harm will come to me." Julie pasted on a bright smile, but her ankles wobbled as she climbed into the coach. "I shall see you soon."

She caught one last look at Lucy's troubled face before the cab's door shut and clicked, as though it had been locked.

Wrapped in a sudden and unnatural darkness, she settled herself on the plush velvet seat opposite Nigel and blinked, waiting for her eyes to adjust.

"At last." He rapped on the ceiling of the cab, and the coach lurched forward.

She ignored the roiling of her stomach and reached for the curtain to admit some light, but he shot out a hand and clasped her wrist. "Leave it. For the sake of your reputation, it's best if no one knows you're with me."

Julie barely refrained from rolling her eyes. "You pretend to be concerned about me, but I've come to realize that you care only for yourself."

"That's not fair," he chided. "And it's no way to begin our conversation." He ran a hand through his hair and drew a deep breath. "Allow me to start over. You are a vision today. You quite take my breath away, Juliette."

"That was not my intention. And I confess I'm surprised you can see anything at all. It's dark as a mausoleum in here."

"That's one of the things I love about you," he said smoothly. "You do not mince words."

"I do not. And I won't prevaricate now." She slipped her reticule off her wrist, reached inside, and pulled out the aquamarine and diamond earrings. "I cannot accept these."

"Of course you can. You've already worn them. They're yours."

In answer, she let them drop onto the seat beside her, where they landed with a satisfying clink. "The reason I'm here is to ensure you understand—I reject your offer. I shall not enter into any sort of arrangement with you."

He sniffed, and although it was too dark in the carriage to read his expression, his shoulders stiffened perceptibly. "I suggest you reconsider. Have you forgotten all that is at stake? The house you and your uncle currently live in, your reputation, your family's good name . . ."

"I know what is at stake. The question is, do you?"

"I do. I know I want you in my life. And I am certain, that given the chance, I could make you happy."

"I appreciate the sentiment, but I'm capable of seeing to my own happiness." The coach slowed and rolled to a stop. There definitely hadn't been enough time for them to ride through the park. "Why have we stopped?" she asked.

"Peek outside." He gestured to the curtain on his right.

She brushed aside the heavy velvet and looked out at an elegant stone-front building—somewhere near Mayfair, if she had to guess. "I do not recognize the address."

"I've rented a suite of rooms here—they're yours. Your private haven from the world. I've hired a maid who will provide anything you need. Only the basic furnishings are there now. I thought you'd enjoy decorating the rooms to suit your taste. You may purchase anything you like—spare no expense."

Sweet Jesus. He didn't seem to understand, and he certainly didn't respect her decision. She reached for the handle of the cab door, intent on jumping out. They hadn't been in the carriage for long—she'd figure out where she was and walk back to Gunter's before Lucy alerted her uncle and Sam.

But the door handle didn't budge. Nigel rapped on the ceiling again, and the carriage moved forward again.

Her fingertips tingled with panic. "I wish to leave. Immediately."

"What do you mean? I said I'd return you to the confectioners shortly, and I will."

Dear God. She must have been mad to climb into the carriage with him. "You're not listening to me. A true gentleman wouldn't ignore a lady's wishes."

"I'm not a monster, Juliette. You've nothing to fear from me. It's my brother you should worry about. Samuel's the one who seduced you and provided fodder for every gossip in London." He pinched his bottom lip, thoughtful. "Of course, the news hasn't circulated. Yet."

Gooseflesh broke out on her arms. "I don't know what news you're referring to," she said blithely. "However, if unsavory rumors began to spread about me, I shall find it necessary to confide in my new friend."

Nigel straightened the cuffs of his jacket, unperturbed. "I should think you'd want to refrain from recounting the humiliating details, but that is your decision."

"It is indeed. And I think my friend would be sympathetic. If I explained my predicament, perhaps she could counsel me."

"Is she a sensible sort?"

"It is hard to say. Perhaps you know her. She is the Duke of Grimby's daughter—Lady Clementine."

"Juliette." He spoke her name like a warning.

"A mutual friend introduced me to Lady Clementine yesterday, and we had tea together. She's charming—but then, I'm sure you're already aware of her many assets. I wonder if she would still be amenable to marrying you if she knew how you'd tried to manipulate me."

"It would be your word against mine." He chuckled cockily.

"True. Although I do have the notes you wrote to me.

The ones that accompanied your gifts. They could prove rather incriminating."

Nigel shifted on his seat. "I understand your jealousy and am incredibly flattered by it, but—"

"I'm not jealous," Julie said evenly. "I pity her, because I think perhaps she was fooled by your reputation—just as I was. Now I know that one need not be featured in the gossip papers to be a true scoundrel."

Nigel barked a laugh. "If I were as noble and honorable as the ton thinks I am, you would find me boring indeed." He leaned across the carriage, so his knees were almost touching hers. "Be honest, Juliette. Beneath your ivory gloves and modest gown lives a wildly passionate creature. You need a man with an edge. Someone who can keep you safe but also make your heart beat faster."

Julie kept her face a mask, giving no sign that his assessment hit rather close to the mark. "You know nothing about me."

Propping his elbows on his thighs, he said, "I know that your lips taste like ripe strawberries and your skin is as soft as down."

Good lord, *why* had she ever permitted him to kiss her? She sat up straighter and looked down her nose at him. "Your words, gifts, gestures—even your threats— have done nothing to persuade me to accept your offer. Your efforts have done naught but lower my opinion of your character. I wish to return to Gunter's. Now."

Nigel heaved a sigh. "We shall be there soon."

They sat in uncomfortable silence as the carriage rolled along. After several seconds, he dragged his hands down his face. "You are a shrewd negotiator, Juliette. You know your worth, and I admire that."

"My only goals are to keep my uncle in his home and to avoid bringing shame upon my family. I want nothing from you, other than to be left alone."

"Fine," he said, as though he'd finally accepted defeat. "I will marry you."

She stared at him, speechless.

"Forgive me. That wasn't the most romantic of proposals, but I am sincere. I desire you too much to let you go. You have forced my hand, but I am willing to sacrifice my standing in society as well as Lady Clementine's sizeable dowry in order to have you."

A month ago, she would have swooned at the prospect of a marriage proposal from Nigel. But that was before she'd met Sam.

Before she'd understood that love wasn't flowery proclamations or precious jewels. Love was in small, meaningful gestures, like playing cricket with her uncle and pretending to look away when her dress slipped. It was knowing precisely how she liked her tea and writing her uncle an encouraging note. It was holding her in his arms all night long and whispering her name like a prayer. Most of all, it was becoming one's truest self.

The ride with Nigel had seemed interminable, but the coach finally slowed. Julie prayed they were outside the confectionery shop.

"I do not wish to marry you," she said firmly.

He flinched as though she'd slapped him.

Her heart hammered as she awaited his response. He'd never behaved violently toward her, but he was a marquess, remarkably stubborn, and used to having his way. Every drop of the bravado she'd shown earlier was used up.

When the vehicle stopped, Nigel lifted the corner of a curtain to glance outside but made no move to disembark. "I am sorry to hear that," he said slowly. The mix of shock and hurt in his voice almost made her feel badly for him. But not quite.

"I do not anticipate our paths will cross often," she said evenly, "but if they should, I trust we're capable of behaving civilly toward each other."

The marquess snorted at that. His jaw clenched and nostrils flared ominously. "You and your uncle will vacate my property by noon tomorrow."

"*What?*" She closed her eyes and swallowed, praying he'd misspoke. "You cannot mean that."

"Oh, but I do," he said, his tone brooking no argument.

Panic clawed at her insides, and she scrambled for an escape route—some path out of this nightmare. "Have you considered how this will look . . . what people will think of a wealthy marquess tossing a feeble old man and his niece out of their home? When the news spreads, it will not cast you in a flattering light."

"I plan to be as shocked and dismayed as anyone." Nigel examined a perfectly manicured nail.

She shook her head, confused. "How?"

"I'll simply explain the unfortunate turn of events. I asked my solicitor to oversee the sale of the property and was completely unaware the house was occupied. After I am briefed on the matter, I shall be outraged at his callousness and lack of sensitivity. I will vow to make things right and allow you to return to the house—but, alas. By then, it will be too late."

"What do you mean?"

"I will have already sold the house."

Her stomach sank like a stone. "By *tomorrow*?"

"We already have two offers. The moment I return home I shall instruct my solicitor to accept one. Which is why you and your uncle must go. It's regrettable," he said mockingly. "And to think, all of this could have been avoided if only you'd—"

"We'll leave," she said firmly, "but we shall require a bit more time to pack our things. Give us a fortnight. Please." She'd have to inform her sister Meg about the terrible mess she'd made. She'd have to explain to Uncle Alistair that the home he loved wasn't truly his home.

"Noon tomorrow," he repeated stiffly. "Anything you leave behind shall be confiscated."

Her neck turned cold and clammy. "And if we are not able to leave by noon?"

"I shall send a few ancillary members of my staff to assist you. I should warn you, however, they are neither patient nor well-mannered. I certainly would not trust them with your fine china." He rapped his cane on the ceiling and waited, his expression stony.

A moment later, the carriage door opened and light flooded the cab. Julie squinted as she scooped up her reticule and moved toward the door.

She didn't dare look back at Nigel as she hastily descended the carriage steps.

But she heard his menacing laugh—a sound that might well haunt her forever.

Chapter THIRTY-EIGHT

Nigel was plotting something devious.

Sam strolled down Charles Street, feeling the same sense of foreboding he'd experienced when he and Nigel were boys.

Sam had been a lad of eight, sitting on a river bank with a fishing pole in his hands, when he suddenly turned wary. He *knew* Nigel was stalking him, and yet, he didn't move. He supposed he was trying to prove something to his older brother—that he wasn't afraid of him, wouldn't be intimidated into putting down his rod.

But his foolish pride had made him a veritable sitting duck. Nigel crept up behind him, hoisted him by the collar, and tossed him into the frigid river. Sam plunged beneath the surface of the icy water, and his heart stopped. Or it felt as though it had. He thrashed frantically, certain he would drown.

He didn't. But he did earn a stern scolding from his father for ruining a perfectly good pair of boots.

Nigel watched as their father administered several painful swats to Sam's backside. He opened his mouth to explain that he hadn't jumped into the river or even slipped, but Nigel's glare made him clamp his lips together. He'd taken the blame.

Just as he had on several occasions after that. Somewhere along the way, he'd been labeled the wicked brother, and he'd started to believe it. Decided he may as well live up to the expectation.

Perhaps he'd gone a bit overboard with the gambling, womanizing, and drinking, but he knew he wasn't truly evil. It only seemed that way.

That day on the riverbank had been the first incident in a long line of misdeeds he'd been accused of—some rightfully, and some unjustly.

But Sam didn't fault his father for disciplining him as a boy of eight. He'd deserved it. Not for being thrown into the river, but for sitting there like a simpleton when he *knew* Nigel was up to no good. He shouldn't have ignored his instincts.

Which was precisely what he was doing now.

Sam suspected Nigel was planning something equally nefarious—worse, if the note Sam had received earlier that morning was any indication. Both cryptic and intriguing, the missive had been delivered to his office. He pulled it out of his pocket and re-read it as he walked.

I've reason to believe Miss Lacey will be at Gunter's this afternoon at approximately a quarter to four. Thought the information might be of interest.

—Nigel

Clearly, Nigel intended to draw Sam to Berkeley Square . . . but to what end?

He was through being a pawn in his brother's maneuverings, damn it all. As much as Sam would have liked to reconcile with Nigel, he would not allow his brother to use him against Juliette, her uncle, or anyone else.

And yet, Sam couldn't stay away from Berkeley Square. Partly because he longed to see her again—even if only from a distance. But also because he suspected Nigel was up to no good, and Sam couldn't let her walk into danger.

Besides, if she truly was at Gunter's this afternoon, maybe he'd have an opportunity to speak with her and see how she fared. Perhaps a look into her beautiful brown eyes would help him discern if she missed him in the slightest.

Because he'd never stopped thinking about her.

It didn't matter that she vacillated between him and his brother or that she'd worn the extravagant earrings Nigel gave her. It didn't even matter that she hadn't refused to be Nigel's mistress on the spot.

Sam needed to know she was safe—and happy. Even if that happiness didn't include him.

He rounded the corner onto Berkeley Street and spied the confectioner's shop in the distance. The mild weather was ideal for a shopping excursion or a jaunt to Gunter's for ice cream. Ladies, gentlemen, and footmen laden with packages ambled down the pavement, occasionally pausing to greet passersby or admire a parasol or snuffbox in a store window.

But Sam saw no sign of Juliette.

Hands stuffed in his pockets, he walked along, feigning interest in a window display at a boot shop. Every so often, however, he glanced sideways and checked the entrance to Gunter's. He considered going inside and taking a seat at the table, but his instincts—the same ones he'd ignored at the riverbank—told him he should remain outside.

He was probably still a little early in any event, he mused, and—

Wait. A petite woman holding a closed parasol paced to and fro outside the pastry shop. There was something familiar about her. She definitely wasn't Juliette. Sam could have spotted her profile, with her smooth brow, pert nose, and elfish chin from a mile away.

And yet, he associated the woman on the pavement with Juliette. She was shorter than her friend Charlotte, and a bit older. Too plainly dressed.

He mentally snapped his fingers. Her lady's maid, Lucy. Which meant Juliette must be nearby.

He remained several yards away, keeping an eye on the maid and the confectioner's shop door. Perhaps Lucy was waiting out front while Juliette said good-bye to a friend inside. The maid glanced up and down the street fretfully as though she were late or . . . worried.

The skin on the back of his neck prickled. What if Juliette was in trouble?

He walked toward Lucy and raised his hand to capture her attention, but she was suddenly fixated on the dark blue carriage that rolled to a stop in front of the shop. There was nothing distinctive about the carriage, no way to see inside, but it looked vaguely like . . . Bloody hell.

Heart hammering in his chest, he waited and watched.

A footman hopped down from his perch behind the carriage, scurried around to the side, and opened the cab door.

Juliette emerged, and his chest ached at the sight of her. A long brown curl at her nape caught in the warm breeze and floated over her shoulder. The skirt of her simple apple green gown billowed around her lithe legs. Her face was pale, her expression unreadable. She clung to Lucy and hurried off in the opposite direction without looking back.

Dear Jesus. Something was wrong. Sam started after her.

The maid hastily opened the parasol, and Juliette ducked underneath as though she were hiding. Not from him, certainly—she was completely unaware he was there. But she seemed almost . . . ashamed.

He didn't want to think about why. Or who might be inside the carriage.

Juliette may have needed time to think through her options where Nigel was concerned, but she would never agree to be his mistress. She would never choose wealth and security over . . . love.

The wheels of the carriage slowly began to roll in the same direction Juliette was walking. As Sam watched, perplexed, the curtain at the back window of the cab shifted. Someone pushed it aside and turned to peer outside.

Shit. A face remarkably like his own stared back at him, sneering. Nigel raised a hand in a mock salute, then drew the curtain closed.

Sam's blood turned cold. He was back in the river, thrashing. Fighting for breath. Drowning.

Nigel had done it again. But this time, he'd ruined more than a pair of boots. He'd obliterated any opportunity of a reconciliation between him and Sam.

Worse, he'd wrecked Sam's one shot at redemption, his one chance at happiness—because neither was possible without Juliette.

Chapter THIRTY-NINE

"But I've lived here for years." Uncle Alistair frowned. "Even if the marquess *does* legally own the property, why would he force us to leave now?"

Julie perched on a stool opposite her uncle's favorite chair and patted his knee. "It's rather complicated." Her voice cracked on the last word, and she paused until she was sure she could speak without crying. "I'd hoped to spare you from this—from having to move. But I fear we must leave tomorrow. I've already written to Meg and Will, informing them that we'll be moving into their house here in town."

"And we're not coming back?" He blinked rapidly and gazed at her with tear-filled, imploring eyes.

She swallowed past the lump in her throat. "I'm afraid not. But I'm going to direct the staff to carefully pack up all your things. I'll make sure you're comfortably settled in our new quarters—at Meg's."

"You'll be staying there too?" he asked, his voice threaded with panic.

"Of course," she assured him. "And when Meg and Will return to town with the twins and the new baby, we'll all be together again. Won't that be lovely?"

"Hmm? Oh, yes," he said, unconvinced. He rose from his chair and shuffled across the parlor toward the fireplace mantel that held an eclectic mix of prized possessions. His gnarled fingers skimmed over the clock with the broken face and the drinking cup with the griffin's claw stem. "But it won't be the same, will it?"

"Not precisely. But you needn't worry—you shall have all your treasured objects, and we'll find a place to display them. In fact, if you should decide you prefer to have your own residence, I'm sure that Meg and Beth will persuade their husbands to procure a new, grander house for you."

"I've never wanted a grander house," he said meekly. "I want *this* one—with all its memories and character and charm."

"I know." She went to him, hugged him, and rested her head on his shoulder, recalling all the times he'd comforted her.

When her older sisters had locked her out of their room so they could share secrets about boys.

When she'd humiliated herself by botching a pianoforte performance at a musicale.

After she'd helped both Meg and Beth pack their things to begin their new lives with their husbands.

Now, it was her turn to remain strong for Uncle Alistair. "I'll miss this house too—more than I can say.

But the memories, character, and charm you speak of aren't contained within its walls. They're in *you* and will go wherever you do." She kissed his wrinkled cheek.

"What shall I do now?" He sounded tired. Lost.

"Try to rest if you can. I've asked Mr. Gibson, Meg and Will's butler, to send over additional staff to help us pack. They should arrive shortly. Shall I have a dinner tray sent to your room?" It would be easier for him if he didn't watch as his entire life was unceremoniously dumped into scores of crates and trunks.

He nodded. "Thank you . . . that is, if you're certain I can't help."

"Mr. Finch intends to personally attend to the packing of your bedchamber," she said with a smile.

"The staff." He pressed a hand to his sunken chest, aghast. "What will become of them?"

Julie's belly twisted as she recalled giving their butler the news, not a half hour earlier. "I told them we'd give them six months' salary and excellent references."

"But they're almost family," Uncle Alistair mumbled. "How can we—"

Julie's heart broke for him. "Come. I'll walk you upstairs."

A knock at the front door sounded, filling Julie with dread. It was already beginning. All the footmen and maids from Meg's house who could be spared for the evening were arriving. Soon they'd be dismantling the life Uncle Alistair and Aunt Elspeth had built. They'd strip the cherished pictures from the walls and leave the bookshelves bare. They'd remove the shabby furniture and roll up the stained carpets.

Someone new would move in, and they'd paint over

the wallpaper that had been the backdrop for countless family tragedies, comedies, and dramas.

And the house would cease to be anything special at all.

Julie woke to the sound of a trunk slamming shut. It took her a moment to recall she was not in her bedchamber, but in the parlor.

"Sorry to disturb you, Miss Juliette." The dark circles beneath Lucy's eyes said her maid had slept even less than she.

"What time is it?"

"Nearly seven in the morning. Would you care for some tea?" The maid placed a hand on her hip and tilted her capped head. "You haven't eaten since luncheon yesterday."

"No tea, thank you—and I'm not hungry. How's the packing progressing?"

"The dining room is nearly done," Lucy said with forced cheerfulness. "We haven't quite begun your uncle's study, but I'm almost finished with the upstairs rooms."

"Thank you," Julie said earnestly. "I'll begin on the study in just a moment." As the maid hurried off, Julie sat up on the settee, rubbed the sleep out of her eyes, and gazed at the towers of crates surrounding her.

The parlor looked nothing like the cozy room where she and her sisters had giggled at stories in the gossip rags, or where they'd cursed at knots in their needlepoint, or where they'd cried over empty dance cards. Without Uncle Alistair's unique trinkets displayed on every surface and wrinkled sheet music piled on the ottoman, without the colorful satin pillows covering the threadbare chairs, the room's imperfections were more pronounced.

The hairline cracks in the plaster ceiling now resembled fissures. Bright robin's-egg blue rectangles marked the spots where paintings had graced the walls, hiding much of the peeling wallpaper. Haphazardly stacked boxes and trunks threatened to topple over with one inadvertent slam of the door.

Along with Lucy and the rest of the servants, Julie had been awake most of the night. They'd run out of crates to pack things in around midnight, so they'd begun transporting trunks to Meg and Will's townhouse. The staff there hastily emptied the contents and sent the trunks back so that they could be filled again.

Still, it seemed as though they'd made frighteningly little headway.

The heartache of moving would have been easier to bear if her sisters were here, but as it was, Julie felt very alone—and she wondered if she always would be. Oh, she and her sisters would be reunited eventually, she had no doubt of that. Uncle Alistair would continue to support her in his own quirky way too.

But Julie wanted someone to share silly, secret jokes with. Someone to hold her hand on walks while whispering deliciously wicked things in her ear. Someone to build a life with—complete with all the joyous, messy, glorious emotions that a real family entailed.

And the only person she could imagine filling that role was Sam.

She knew she was partially to blame for their row—if it could even be called such—on the night of the soiree. But she needed someone who wouldn't run at the first sign of trouble. She needed someone who would remain by her side not only on the sunny days but the challenging days as well. Days like today.

She stood, then gripped the back of the settee as her head swam. Once the dizziness passed, she brushed the dust and dirt off her gown—the very same one she'd worn to meet with Nigel yesterday. That carriage ride seemed an eternity ago, and yet, time was ticking by much too quickly. She'd give her favorite slippers—nay, her entire wardrobe—for an extra day in this house.

She located an empty trunk near the front door and ignored the ache at the base of her spine as she lugged it into Uncle Alistair's study. There was a reason she'd saved his favorite room for last. She looked up at Aunt Elspeth's portrait and sighed. It was going to be the hardest.

The grandfather clock was still chiming twelve o'clock—Nigel's deadline—when the pounding on the front door began, the banging so loud, Julie imagined a band of marauding Vikings stood just outside.

Extremely *punctual* Vikings.

Her heart skipped a beat as she closed the crate lid and gazed at half a dozen of Uncle Alistair's bookshelves that she and Lucy still had left to pack. She stood and wiped her damp palms on her skirt.

"Would you please check on my uncle?" she asked the maid. "He's been resting in his bedchamber, but if he's anxious, he can travel to Castleton House with the next shipment of trunks. I'm going to tell our, er, visitors that we require another couple of hours. I cannot imagine they'll object when they see how much we've already accomplished."

Lucy frowned. "Of course I'll see to Lord Wiltmore. But be careful. Especially if Lord Currington is on our doorstep."

"I will." Julie refrained from mentioning that the doorstep wasn't truly *theirs* any longer—and therein lay the problem.

She met Mr. Finch at the front door just as he was about to open it. He hesitated when he heard the rough voices and coarse language outside. "Allow me to deal with this, Miss Juliette. I shall tell these gentlemen"—the word clearly stuck in his throat—"that we are in the process of vacating the house, as anyone with two eyes in his head could plainly see, and that we would be happy to send word once the task is accomplished."

Julie wanted to hug the butler but settled for squeezing his arm. "Thank you. It's worth a try."

He smiled bravely and shooed her away. "Back to the study with you," he said. "I'll not expose you to such ruffians."

Before the words were out of Mr. Finch's mouth, the banging began anew—only louder and more insistent. Julie stopped several yards from the front door as the butler opened it a crack. "Good morning, sirs," he said dryly. "How may I be of service?"

"Stand aside, old man." A beefy hand reached through the narrow opening and shoved Mr. Finch in the chest, making him stagger backward.

Julie rushed up behind the butler to steady him, but they were both flattened against the wall when three large, barrel-chested men swaggered inside. "Your time is up," one shouted, giving notice to the entire household. You have one minute to leave, and I suggest you take all your personal effects with you. Because once you walk out that door, you won't be coming back."

Dear God. Ignoring the throbbing in her head and the low buzz in her ears, Julie ran ahead of the largest man and stepped in front of him just before he reached the parlor. "I'm afraid there's been a misunderstanding," she said smoothly. "My uncle and I are in the process of packing our things but require a—"

"There's no misunderstanding," he said. "The marquess wants you out. Immediately."

"Juliette?" Uncle Alistair descended the staircase as fast as he dared, an ornate box tucked under one arm. "Is something amiss down here? I thought I heard—" He stopped in his tracks when he saw the three brawny men dressed like dockworkers standing just outside the parlor.

"Why don't you make your way to the carriage," Julie said soberly. "Mr. Finch and I will collect your bags and meet you there."

He nodded courageously but wobbled as he took the next step, so she met him on the staircase and held his elbow the rest of the way.

"This is it," he said wistfully. "This is good-bye, Elspeth."

"For now, but not forever. We'll be back," Julie said, praying it was true.

One of the brutes clucked his tongue, mocking her. "You're squandering your time."

She checked the urge to lash out at him. Nigel was

the one who'd hired him and his cronies. Nigel was the one who deserved her ire. To Uncle Alistair, she said, "Ignore him. As soon as Will learns of this travesty, he'll return to town and sort it all out, mark my words. But for now, it's best if we avoid a confrontation. I'll simply walk you outside and return for the rest of our things."

"The chit doesn't listen very well, does she?" The man with the square jaw jabbed a thick elbow in the leader's side.

The larger man cracked his knuckles and spoke to her slowly, as if she were a simple child. "You won't be returning. Take what you need *now*."

Mr. Finch, the footmen, and Lucy rushed past them, balancing towers of crates and boxes—all they could possibly carry.

A scream started to build in the back of Julie's throat, but she couldn't fall apart—not yet, at any rate—so she swallowed it. "On second thought, Uncle, go outside with Mr. Finch. I'll follow shortly."

He looked at the men and hesitated. "You're sure, Juliette?"

"Positive," she said with forced cheer. "Off with you now. We'll be on our way to Meg and Will's townhouse in a matter of minutes."

"More like seconds," one of the men grunted.

As her uncle hobbled down the pavement, defeated, Julie debated what to bring with her.

The silver, her parent's china, and her best jewelry had been sent to Meg's in one of the midnight shipments, thank God. But so many things remained. How could she choose two or three boxes out of scores?

Julie's first instinct was to run for her clothes and undergarments, but they could be replaced.

The trunks in her uncle's study, on the other hand, held decades of research, notes that could be essential to the paper he was writing for admission to the Royal Society—and critical to gaining the acceptance and respect he deserved.

But his research wasn't the most important thing either.

If she could bring only one thing, she knew exactly what it must be. And though it wouldn't be easy, she simply could not fail.

She dashed past the men to the study, slid a chair in front of the fireplace, and carefully stood on the seat. Staring into the kindly eyes of the large portrait above the fireplace, she announced, "Aunt Elspeth, you're coming with me."

Chapter FORTY

Sam was amazed at how much he was able to accomplish before noon nowadays. It turned out that if one wasn't hungover or laying low after the previous night's excesses, the hours between dawn and luncheon could be surprisingly productive.

This morning, he was eager to tell Griff about a meeting with a merchant who'd claimed he could provide all the tea Griff's company required for half the price he currently paid. Sam had taken care not to let on how anxious he was to negotiate a contract, but he could sense a good deal like a shark smells blood—and this was an excellent deal.

He hustled back to Griff's offices, angled through the door and nodded at the secretary, who was making accounting entries in a ledger that covered half his desk. "Good morning, Timothy. Is Griff available?"

"Good morning, Lord Travis. Mr. Griffith is attending to a personal matter, but I expect him soon." The secretary adjusted his spectacles on his nose. "I hope you'll be pleased to learn that your office upstairs is finally ready for you. It's freshly painted and has a pleasant view of the street."

"Thank you." This was what it was like to be a part of something. To have people expect more of you. "I'll move my things out of Griff's office this afternoon."

"No, no," Timothy protested. "You must allow me to attend to it. I took the liberty of selecting a carpet and a couple of paintings in addition to the standard office furniture. We want the room to be conducive to business, after all."

Sam smiled. "Perfect. Anything else for me?"

Timothy tapped the head of his pencil against his chin as he rifled through the neat stacks of correspondence on his desk. "Ah, yes. Mr. Youngman left this"—the secretary handed a large brown envelope to Sam—"and said he'd return this afternoon to discuss the property on Hart Street."

Hart Street. Juliette's uncle's house. Maybe not legally—but Sam hoped to rectify the matter soon.

Youngman, Griff's solicitor, had submitted an anonymous offer on Sam's behalf to purchase the property from Nigel. Sam turned the envelope over in his hands, encouraged by its weight. Still, his fingers tingled as he opened it and scanned the papers inside.

His brother had accepted the offer.

Sam released the breath he'd been holding. This was his chance to undo some of the damage he'd caused. To make amends.

Warmth flooded his chest—not happiness, precisely. Without Juliette, he doubted he'd ever be truly happy.

No, what he felt was more akin to satisfaction, and that came from knowing that *she* would be happy.

Sam glanced over the contract and frowned at the purchase price, which was considerable, but reasonable. Nigel had never really wanted the house. He simply wanted to bend Juliette to his will. He needed a buyer before her powerful brothers-in-law were able to come to their rescue. He needed a plausible explanation for his cruelty.

Well, Sam may not have possessed a title or a fortune, but, for the first time in his godforsaken life, he had purpose.

With Griff's help, he'd secured a loan—one that would probably take him a decade or more to repay. Not long ago, that sort of responsibility would have crippled him, but now, he welcomed it. It would give him a goddamned reason to wake up and work every day.

In the meantime, he'd have the solicitor transfer the deed to Wiltmore so that he and Juliette could stay in their house without living in fear that Nigel would toss them out.

Youngman would handle it all while keeping Sam's involvement in the deal a secret. He didn't need Juliette's gratitude, and he certainly didn't want her to feel beholden to him.

He'd be content knowing that she and her uncle were safe. Happy.

And if he was careful, Juliette would never know what Sam had done for her.

Or how much he loved her.

She'd be free to lead the life of her choosing—one that maybe, just maybe, had room for him.

He glanced at Timothy. "I'll go have a look upstairs. Would you inform me when Griff returns?"

"Of course," the secretary said. "And if Mr. Youngman—" He paused as the front door opened and a harried young man dressed in livery stumbled into the office. Sam blinked, trying to place the familiar face.

And then it hit him. Bloody hell.

"How may I help you, sir?" Timothy inquired politely.

Before the man could reply, Sam said, "You're a member of Lord Wiltmore's staff."

Nodding vigorously, the servant dug a paper out of his jacket pocket and thrust it at Sam. "Forgive the intrusion, Lord Travis. Lord Wiltmore asked me to deliver this to you at once."

The skin between Sam's shoulder blades prickled as he took the note. "I trust everything is well at the house?"

The footman shifted from foot to foot. "Not exactly, my lord."

Damn. Sam unfolded the paper. The sight of the shaky handwriting took him back to Wiltmore's study—and the hours they spent playing chess, trading stories, and swinging his cane like a cricket bat.

Dear Cousin Samuel,
It seems Juliette and I are moving out of our house today. We shall preside in town with my niece Meg and her husband, the Earl of Castleton. I thought you should know.

Alistair

He met the footman's gaze. "Have Lord Wiltmore and Miss Lacey departed for the earl's house yet?"

"I'm not certain. They were loading up the carriage when I left."

Sam stuffed Wiltmore's note and the contract in his jacket pocket and shot out the door. There wasn't a hackney cab in sight, so he ran, praying he arrived in time to stop the madness.

As his boots slapped against the pavement and his breath rasped in his chest, Sam debated what to tell Juliette and how to explain the sudden reversal of fortune. Maybe he'd say that upon further investigation, he'd discovered the house was Wiltmore's all along. That he'd come to tell her they could stay.

All he knew for sure was that he couldn't wait to see her again . . . and that he'd be gutted all over again when he had to say good-bye.

Sweet Jesus, Aunt Elspeth was heavy. Or rather, her portrait was. The gilt frame measured a little over a yard wide and was nearly twice as tall. Gripping the sides, Julie hefted the picture up and away from the wall, almost toppling backward off the chair she was using as a stepstool. The bottom corner of the frame clipped an old vase on the mantel, sending it crashing to the floor before she was able to rest the portrait on the arms of the chair and catch her breath.

Her heart was still galloping from the near fall when one of the brutes Nigel had sent to evict her filled the doorway and eyed the shattered glass and dirty puddle of water. "Having a tantrum, are we?"

"Much as I'd like to," she huffed, "I haven't the time."

He narrowed his eyes. "What are you doing?"

"Taking this picture. I see no reason you should object, as its value is purely sentimental," she said dryly.

"You've a sharp tongue, haven't you?" he said with a sneer.

"Occasionally." She stepped off the chair, careful to avoid catching the toe of her slipper in her hem. Now all she needed to do was lug the portrait from the study to the front door, which, unfortunately, seemed a continent away.

She briefly considered asking the man to assist her, but even if he were inclined to do so, she didn't trust him in the least. He didn't know how precious the portrait was to Uncle Alistair—and she doubted he'd care.

The man watched her struggle with the picture, his arms crossed, face smug.

She took several deep breaths, then hoisted the portrait off the chair onto the hardwood floor where it landed with a thud, barely missing her toes.

Good heavens, this was going to be tortuous. Wisps of hair clung to her damp neck, and her fingers were already numb from the weight of the frame. She managed to lift the picture and carry it a few steps before it slipped from her hands.

What she needed was a blanket or quilt that she could place beneath the bottom of the frame, allowing her to slide it out of the room and down the corridor to the front door. She scanned the study but saw nothing among the crates or furniture that would be of use.

"Oh, Aunt Elspeth," she sighed in exasperation. "What are we going to do?" She briefly rested her forehead against the top of the frame—

And had an epiphany.

"Stay right here," Julie whispered, leaning the portrait against the wall.

"Where do you think you're going?" the brute demanded. "You've already tested my patience. Do not dally any longer—unless you'd like me to carry you out of here over my shoulder."

"That won't be necessary," Julie said with mock sweetness. She walked to the worn curtains hanging from Uncle Alistair's window, fisted a velvet panel in both hands and yanked with all her might. The rod holding the curtain popped off the wall and banged to the floor. Bits of plaster and paint rained down on her head, but she clutched the curtain in her hands, momentarily victorious.

"You're bloody insane," the man muttered, a hint of awe in his voice.

Perhaps she was. She swiped the chalky dust from her face and slid the velvet off the rod, then balled up the fabric and deposited it on the floor beside the picture. Using all her remaining strength, she lifted the portrait so that the bottom rested on the curtain.

After a brief, fervent prayer, she tried sliding it.

It worked—not precisely like gliding over ice, but infinitely easier than lifting the frame.

Julie couldn't wait to see her uncle's face when she walked out the door holding Aunt Elspeth's picture. This horrid day had been especially difficult for him, but perhaps the portrait would bring a smile to his dear, sweet face.

She ignored the man skulking behind her as she carefully, steadily slid the frame out of the room, trying not to dwell on the finality of it all. She resisted a childish but intense urge to run to the newel post and carve her initials and her sisters' in the wood.

It was just a house, she told herself. Four walls and a roof. Plaster and wood.

She did a fairly good job of convincing herself. But halfway down the corridor she heard shouts from the front of the house. Someone outside was creating a stir.

Good heavens. *Please, don't let it be Uncle Alistair*— not when he'd already been through so much.

The man who'd been hovering over her brushed past in order to investigate the commotion outside, and she craned her neck from the hall, equally curious.

The front door was flung wide open, and she caught a glimpse of impossibly broad shoulders, sandy brown hair, and a rugged profile.

Her heart caught in her throat. But . . . it couldn't be.

The man's jacket was pressed, and his boots were polished to a sheen. He wore a *cravat*, for goodness' sake— and it was as white as downy snow or angel's wings or a newborn sheep.

"Move out of my way," he demanded. The voice was low and lethal, but she'd recognize it anywhere. *Sam*.

Chapter FORTY-ONE

Julie leaned the portrait against the wall and ran to the door. The three men Nigel had sent stood shoulder to shoulder, a barricade of muscle and flesh. Sam bumped chests with the middle one. "Out of my way," he repeated. "Now."

The tallest brute laughed. "We don't answer to you."

"Not unless you've more blunt to spare than your brother," another mocked.

Good heavens. The men were already clenching their fists, eager for a fight. And Sam didn't stand a chance against three of them.

"Sam," she called from behind the men. "What are you doing here? Where's my uncle?"

"Alistair is fine," he said calmly. "I told him to wait in the carriage while I sort out this misunderstanding."

"There's no misunderstanding," one of the men growled. "This house belongs to the marquess."

Sam frowned. "Go back into the parlor, Juliette. I'll come for you once this matter has been resolved.

He was mad if he thought she was going anywhere. "You haven't answered my question, Sam. Why did you come?"

He muttered a curse. "I heard that Nigel was forcing you to leave, but now you don't have to. I'm going to talk with him."

Her throat grew thick with emotion. She was touched by the gesture, but it was far too late for talking. Besides, they'd tried that tack already. "It's all right, Sam." She hated that they were reduced to having a conversation while peering between the necks of the dockworkers. "My uncle and I have resigned ourselves to the fact that we must leave."

"No," he said, emphatic. "You don't have to. Trust me."

"You should listen to the lady," the middle brute said. "She has the right of it. And I'm all out of patience." With that, he turned toward Julie, savagely grabbed her wrist, and hauled her out of the hallway onto the front doorstep.

"Take. Your hand. Off her." Sam yanked the man by his collar and shook him so hard that Julie heard his teeth clatter.

The man released her and flung her toward Sam, who wound an arm around her waist, steadying her. Solid and strong, he held her tightly and murmured in her ear, "Everything is going to be fine."

It wasn't going to be fine. She *knew* it wasn't. But with Sam there, at her side, she felt as though she *might* be able to make it through this ordeal without crumpling into a sobbing heap. For her uncle's sake, she must try.

"I'm taking my uncle to my sister Meg's house," she explained, trying to defuse the powder keg. "I just need to retrieve Aunt Elspeth's portrait, and I'll be ready to go." She raised her chin and prepared to walk past the men, but they made no move to step aside.

"I've had enough." The middle thug stared straight past her. "No one's going back in the house."

"But the portrait . . . it's right in the corridor."

"Go to your carriage," the man said, impassive.

The last remnant of her self-control snapped like a dry twig. "*No.*" She breathed heavily through her nostrils. "I'm not leaving without that portrait."

Sam pulled her back and wrapped a protective arm around her. "Juliette, let me—"

"No, no, *nooo.*" She flung herself at the man, beating his chest with her fists. He chuckled in response and swatted her away.

Sam jumped into the fray, inserting himself between Julie and the brute. "Wait on the pavement," he said to her, his tone brooking no argument. "I will take care of this."

She choked back a sob. Her hair had come loose in the scuffle, and half of it hung over her shoulder. Her dress was soiled. Every muscle in her body ached. She'd barely slept or eaten in two days, and didn't have the energy to fight anymore.

But she couldn't let Sam take on three brawny dockworkers. If something happened to him . . .

"I don't want the portrait," she lied. "Let's go."

"Wait for me by the carriage," he said to her, even as he glared at the men. "I'll join you momentarily."

Too exhausted to protest, she did as he asked. She

waved at Uncle Alistair, who peered through the carriage window at her and attempted an encouraging smile. Then she watched Sam and the men from her vantage near the street, her heart in her throat.

Sam pulled a paper out of his jacket and showed it to the men, who merely laughed and shoved him backward. Incensed, Sam dropped the paper and charged at them. He slammed his fist into the gut of the largest man, threw an elbow at the chin of another. While the third looked on, stunned, Sam ran into the house.

Julie's fingers went numb. What on earth was he doing, picking a fight when he was so outnumbered? The third man chased after him, and she could hear their grunts and moans from outside. The entire house seemed to vibrate from the impact of flesh against plaster.

An eternity later, Sam emerged from the front door, blood trickling from his brow, carrying the portrait over his head. When the biggest man blocked his path, Sam kicked him in the knee and quickly handed off the portrait to a footman, who whisked it away from the mayhem.

But Aunt Elspeth's painting was the least of Julie's worries.

"Be careful, Sam," she pleaded. All three of the dock-workers were back on their feet, circling Sam like grace-less, menacing birds of prey. His feet shoulder-width apart, he sneered at each one in turn, clearly issuing a challenge. *Do your worst.*

And then the fighting began in earnest.

The man with the square jaw lunged at Sam's knees, but he dodged the brute and slammed an elbow into his back as he sailed past.

The largest man locked Sam's arms from behind as the third came at his face with his fist cocked. Sam twisted sideways and kicked him in the groin before he could land a punch. The brute curled into a ball and writhed on the pavement.

But the giantlike man still had Sam's wrists in a vise-hold behind his back. The muscles in his neck strained as he struggled to free himself, and blood dripped from the cut above his eye.

Julie's veins turned to ice. If the men were irritated before, now they were furious.

The man with the square jaw stood and cracked his knuckles, his dull eyes gleaming with anticipation. He walked right up to Sam, pulled back a fist, and buried it in his stomach. He doubled over, coughing and gasping for air.

Dear God. "Stop," she cried, running to him.

"Stay back, Juliette," Sam rasped.

"Let him come with me," she begged the dockworkers. "We'll leave at once if you'll just let him go."

Sam shook his head. "I'm not going anywhere. Those papers"—he inclined his head toward the crumpled papers littering the pavement—"are a contract. I've arranged to purchase the house and give it to you and your uncle. My solicitor made an offer, and Nigel accepted. This has been your home for decades . . . and it shall be your home for decades to come."

In spite of their terrible predicament, a warm glow radiated inside her chest. Not because of the house, but because of the gesture. "You did that . . . for us?"

"Yes," he confirmed. "For you."

A fortnight ago, he'd had no money. Owned nothing of value. "But how?"

"This is all very touching." The dockworker who held Sam prisoner snorted. "Your contract means naught to me, but you can show it directly to the boss." He nodded at the curb where a midnight blue carriage rolled to a stop behind Uncle Alistair's coach. "Here he is, now."

Nigel disembarked from his carriage and surveyed the scene with icy detachment. He walked toward them as though he were out for a casual stroll in Hyde Park.

Sam struggled to free himself, but the brute yanked on his arms till he winced. Julie scrambled to scoop up the papers, then thrust them at Nigel.

"Good afternoon, Miss Lacey." He did not take the contract from her but stared at it like it was a three-day old fish. "What's this?"

"A contract," Sam spat. "I'm buying the house from you so Juliette and her uncle can stay here."

Nigel's eyebrows shot halfway up his forehead. "You?" he asked, incredulous. "You can't even pay your gambling debts."

"Never fear," Sam said, his voice low and lethal. "You'll have your money. Now call off your hired thugs and leave Juliette in peace."

The marquess shook his head. "Your devotion to Miss Lacey would be laughable if it wasn't so pathetic. Do you imagine she'll be so grateful that she'll fall into bed with you—again? Perhaps she already has. Either way, she'll toss you aside once you've ceased to be useful."

Sam lunged toward Nigel before the brute hauled him back. Julie's heart ached for Sam. This was his brother, who he'd been desperate to reconcile with. His only living family member and his last connection to their late father. In his own way, Sam had been fighting to protect his home as surely as she'd been working to protect hers.

"Leave Juliette out of it," Sam snapped. "This is a business transaction, between you and me. Nothing more."

The marquess clucked his tongue and snatched the contract out of Julie's hands. "So you are the mysterious, anonymous buyer," he mused, scanning the pages.

"What does it matter?" Sam countered. "You'll be paid the purchase price, and this house will no longer be your concern."

Nigel sighed dramatically—and ripped the contract to shreds.

Julie gasped and her hand flew to her mouth.

"Don't worry," Sam assured her. "My solicitor has another copy."

"Yes, yes," Nigel said, dismissive. "But all the copies in the world are no good unless the contract has been signed and executed—and this one has not."

"You bastard," Sam growled.

Nigel tossed a handful of paper scraps over his shoulder, smiling as the light breeze made them tumble and scatter across the pavement. "Upon further consideration, I've decided that the house will make an excellent investment property. It will require extensive renovations, of course, and I intend to begin those at once. Which is why, regretfully, I must insist that the house be vacated. Immediately." He tipped his hat mockingly at Juliette and Sam before striding back toward his coach. "Come see me when the job is done," he called to the dockworkers.

And a minute later, the dark blue coach rumbled off. Nigel was gone.

Julie turned to Sam and tenderly pushed his hair away from the cut on his forehead. "Come with me," she pleaded. "I thought nothing was more important than this house, but I was wrong. I don't want it if it means you're hurt or destitute or . . . alone." She placed her palms on his cheeks. "Please?"

His beautiful eyes were haunted. Defeated. But he nodded, resigned.

"That's enough," she said to the man who still grasped Sam's arms from behind. "Let him go."

"I will." A sick, sadistic grin spread across face. "But first, a small parting gift." Before Julie knew what was happening, he twisted Sam's right elbow far behind his back and pulled up—hard.

Crack. Sam groaned and fell to his knees, then collapsed on the ground, his arm dangling awkwardly from his shoulder.

Chapter FORTY-TWO

Holy *hell*.

Sam bit back a curse as he writhed on his back, fighting back the blackness that threatened at the edges of his vision.

Juliette knelt beside him, and somehow her sweet voice cut through the blinding pain. "Oh, Sam." She leaned over him, and he focused on her beautiful face. Wondered if he was imagining the affection in her eyes.

With the hem of her gown, she dabbed at the blood dripping down his cheek. "I'm so sorry," she whispered. "Your arm?" she asked gently.

"Broken," he said through gritted teeth.

Her eyes welled with unshed tears. "The men are gone—they went inside the house. I'm going to take you to my sister's and summon a doctor." She turned and shouted toward the carriage, "Mr. Finch!"

The butler and a footman scurried toward them, but

Sam managed to sit up on his own. "I can walk," he said, with more confidence than he felt.

He held the elbow of his injured arm as Julie helped him stand. Mr. Finch directed the footman to rearrange some of the trunks and boxes stacked inside the carriage so they could squeeze in an additional passenger.

"Sam," Julie whispered. "Thank you. For what you tried to do. For fighting for Uncle Alistair and me. No one's ever done that before."

"You shouldn't be thanking me." He couldn't keep the bitterness out of his voice. "In case you didn't notice, I failed you."

"No," she said, adamant. "You didn't. You saved the portrait of Aunt Elspeth. I can't tell you what that means to me and my uncle—although you have a better idea than most."

Mr. Finch lifted the frame off the ground and carried the painting to the carriage almost reverently. He propped it behind the driver's seat and carefully draped a quilt over it.

Pain radiated up and down Sam's arm, from his fingertips to his shoulder, as he climbed into the coach and sat across from Alistair.

The old man leaned over and patted Sam's leg sympathetically. "Those miscreants had you outnumbered," he observed. "But you still managed to land a few good punches. Their behavior was utterly despicable, and they should be defamed of themselves."

Sam smiled for Alistair's sake. "How's the research going?"

He shrugged in response. "I miss my assistant . . . and

my study is in a bit of a shambles at the moment . . . but other than that, I'd say it's progressing dandily."

Julie stepped up into the cab, a silk pillow tucked under one arm. "I grabbed this out of one of the trunks," she said, gingerly placing it on his lap and taking care not to jostle his arm. "I thought it might help support your arm during the ride."

"Thank you," he said, touched. The pillow did help a little, but having her close helped more.

She slipped onto the seat beside him and pushed her mussed hair over her shoulder. Her dress was soiled with dust and his blood, and the dark smudges beneath her eyes made her face appear pale and fragile. But she'd never looked lovelier.

"Well," she said with forced brightness. "I think we have everything now. It's as though we're going to a house party—only it's in town."

"And the hosts are not at home," Sam added dryly.

"And there are no other guests," added Alistair, "save the doctor we'll be summoning."

Julie cast a slightly scolding glance at the pair of them. "But other than that, it's *precisely* the same." She pretended she was perfectly fine as the coach pulled away from the curb, and she didn't peer through the back window. Didn't spare a glance at the house where she'd lived most of her childhood.

But she didn't fool Sam. He saw the tremor of her chin and heard the catch in her voice.

He wanted to hold her and tell her that he'd find a way to make everything right.

Nigel may have won the round, but Sam wasn't about to give up the fight for the house.

And he sure as hell wasn't giving up the fight for Juliette.

Julie woke with a start. Her cheek rested on fresh, soft linen. Her hair was loose and still slightly damp at the roots from her bath. She wore a sumptuous silk dressing gown that definitely wasn't hers.

She sat up and gazed around the elegant bedchamber—dark but for the glow of a dim lamp. Ah, yes. She was at Meg and Will's townhouse. In their bed, no less.

Good heavens, how long had she slept? She sprang out of the bed and located a clock on Meg's desk.

Midnight.

Blast. She'd only meant to rest her eyes for a moment—but she'd slept the day away, leaving Sam to suffer alone. She hoped he was in the guest bedchamber where the doctor had attended him, sleeping peacefully, but perhaps he'd insisted on going home to his own bed.

There was only one way to find out.

She cinched the sash of her dressing gown, padded across the room, and slipped out the door to find the rest of the house blessedly quiet.

As she neared his room, she saw light seeping out from beneath his door, and her heart danced like it hadn't since . . . since . . . the last time she and Sam had been alone together.

She told herself she wouldn't disturb him. She'd only peek in to ensure he was as comfortable as possible. Tingling with anticipation, she turned the knob, cracked open the door, and glanced to the bed—the noticeably empty bed.

Julie sagged against the door frame. He'd left before

she'd had a chance to properly thank him. Before she'd had a chance to tell him how she felt.

"I thought you'd never come." The deep, masculine voice reverberated through her.

Sam sidled up to her, a wicked grin lighting his face. His right arm was bandaged and supported by a sling around his neck. His hair hung low over one eye, almost hiding the nasty cut. His shirt was open at the collar, with nary a cravat nor jacket in sight.

Desire pooled in her belly. The rogue was back.

With his good arm, he grasped her wrist, pulled her into the room, and closed the door. "But you were worth the wait."

Her cheeks flushed. "How is your arm?"

"Better." He led her to the bed, sat on the edge, and patted the mattress beside him. "Now that I have you to take my mind off it."

She climbed up and tucked her bare feet beneath her. "I wanted to stay with you while the doctor set your arm, but he wouldn't let me. And when he finished, he told me you were resting and shouldn't be disturbed.

"He prescribed a couple of shots of brandy prior to patching me up. I slept soundly for a couple of hours afterward."

"And now?" she asked. "Has the pain returned?"

"I'm a little sore," he said with a shrug. "No worse than you'd expect after your average pub brawl."

"How comforting," she teased.

"I'm glad you slept." He gazed at her with something akin to adoration. "Mr. Finch said you were packing trunks through the night last night. And you looked exhausted earlier. Now, some of the color has returned to your face. You're . . . radiant."

Warmth blossomed in her chest. "I want to thank you for what you did."

"I wish that the contract had been executed before Nigel learned I was the buyer. Then you could have kept your house."

"I cannot express how much I appreciate the gesture," she said, humbled. "But I could never accept such a generous gift."

"You weren't supposed to know that I had anything to do with the purchase of the property. And anyway, it wasn't truly a gift. The house was rightfully your uncle's," he said firmly. "I was only trying to ensure that you both could remain there—and that my brother couldn't unjustly manipulate you."

"What you did . . . it was beyond thoughtful." She tried not to stare at the smooth, tanned skin exposed by his open collar. "How did you manage to obtain the contract?"

"I sold a trinket or two to use as collateral for a loan," he said, as if it had been a routine thing. When she suspected it was anything but.

"Oh, Sam. Please say you didn't give up your father's pocket watch."

"He would have approved. I've no regrets."

Julie's throat constricted painfully. "You did that for us, even when you were unsure of my feelings for you?"

"I didn't need to know your feelings for me. Because I know what I feel for *you*." He caressed her cheek and brushed a thumb over her lips. "Sometime after I hid behind your settee, and before the night we first made love . . . I fell in love with you. Hard. Hopelessly. Every decision I've made since then has been easy. I simply ask myself what would make you smile. And then I do that thing."

"Then it's no wonder I cannot stop myself from smiling when you're near." Heart pounding, she reached for his hand and pressed a kiss to the palm. "I know what I feel for you too. I used to think home was a house, a solid structure. The singular place where a family dines together, where memories are made, and where babies are born. But it turns out that home isn't a place at all."

"It's not?" He arched a brow, amused.

"No." She leaned in and pressed her lips to his for a brief but heady kiss. "Home is the feeling you get when you're with the person you love. And no place would be home without you."

His handsome face turned sober. "I want to marry you, Juliette."

Her entire body thrummed with an odd mix of joy and disbelief. She opened her mouth to reply, but he stopped her.

"I don't possess a title or fortune. I can't offer you an elegant townhouse or a grand country estate. But I *can* promise you that I'll spend every damned day trying to make the best life I can for you and our family. My heart belongs solely to you, and I will care for you and protect you until my last dying breath." He swallowed and gazed at her earnestly. "Give me the chance to love you. Give me the chance to make you smile . . . now and always."

A lump formed in her throat and she blinked away tears. "I would be honored to marry you, Samuel Travis."

A slow, astonished grin spread across his face. "You would? You could definitely make a better match, you know." He pushed her hair behind her shoulder and playfully kissed her neck. "Any man would be lucky to have you. Are you certain you don't wish for a duke or an earl, like your sisters' husbands?"

Though his tone was light and teasing, she sensed that her answer mattered to him.

Very much.

"Sam." She stroked the rough edge of his jaw and waited till he met her gaze. "I confess I wanted what my sisters have. But it wasn't their husbands' titles or wealth I envied. I wanted someone who would be thoughtful and steady and true . . . *and* who could also make my heart race wildly. I wanted the fairytale, and I have that with you. I could never have it with anyone else."

He blew out a relieved breath. "We'll take care of your uncle. Once I find us a house, he can move in with us and continue his research. I know the move has taken a toll on him, but we'll help him return to his former, jovial self. I'll play another cricket match with him. Or maybe we'll try something different like archery or a fox hunt."

Julie choked back a sob—she couldn't help it. "Thank you," she managed.

"I like your uncle," he said, sincerely. "And I think he likes me. The true test will come when I request a meeting with him after breakfast tomorrow. He may like me more as a distant cousin than as your betrothed."

"Nonsense. He adores you. In fact, I confess to being a bit jealous at how quickly he warmed to you."

"I want us to be a family," he said, "but I also want to be a part of yours. Your sisters and uncle are important to you. That makes them important to me."

"What about your family? I'm sorry about Nigel. I know you'd hoped to reconcile with him. I don't want you to have any regrets."

"I could never, *will* never, regret loving you," he promised. "No matter what. My brother isn't the man I thought he was." He glanced down at his injured arm. "And yet, there's always a chance that someday he'll change."

They sat in silence for several moments, and Julie pondered all that Sam had said, wondering when it would truly sink in. They were betrothed.

"God, how I've missed you," he breathed, leaning his forehead against hers and cupping her cheek. "I can't believe you're here right now. In spite of all the day's catastrophes, I feel like the luckiest man in the world."

"You are very lucky, indeed." She braced a hand on his hard thigh and took care not to bump his arm as she slanted her mouth across his.

At last, the rogue was hers.

Chapter FORTY-THREE

Juliette probably had no idea that her silk dressing gown gaped open at the front, exposing the lush curves of her breasts. Sam would have sworn he'd died and gone to heaven—if the idea of him ending up in that place wasn't so damned farfetched.

Still, odder things had happened—like Juliette agreeing to marry him.

Her gleaming hair fell in soft waves around her shoulders as she closed the distance between them and pressed her lips to his.

The moment their mouths touched, he was gone.

She'd become the center of his world, and nothing had ever felt so right. Now she was here. Willing to give herself to him—heart, body, and soul.

The fragrant scent of her hair and the soft mewling sounds in her throat and the firm pressure of her hand on his thigh overwhelmed his senses in the best possible way.

"I want you, temptress," he murmured, already burning with desire.

"We cannot risk injuring your arm even more," she said regretfully.

"To hell with my arm." He squeezed a shapely hip through the satin of her robe and pulled her onto his lap, so her thighs straddled his.

"Goodness." She blushed adorably. "This isn't prudent, Sam. I'm certain the doctor wouldn't approve."

"I don't need the doctor's approval." He slipped a hand inside her dressing gown and cupped her breast, loving the way she melted into his hand. "Just yours."

"In that case," she sighed, "you may proceed."

With one tug on her sash, her robe slipped off her shoulders and fell away. He drank in the sight of her— proud, passionate, beautiful. *His.*

She was tentative at first, avoiding his injured arm as though the lightest touch would shatter it. But soon she was spearing her fingers through his hair and kissing his neck and rocking against him, greedy for more.

With a timid smile, she unbuttoned the front of his trousers and wrapped her fingers around his hard length, stroking him till he groaned.

"I can't wait, Julie. I need you. Now."

She frowned at his arm. "I'm not sure how . . ."

He grasped her hip and lifted her up and forward. "Just like this."

With a gasp, she lowered herself onto him. Tight, hot, wet . . . perfect. She cradled his head in her hands and stared at him, her eyes glazed with pleasure. "Are you all right?"

"I have never been better." He took a rosy tip of her

breast in his mouth as they slowly moved together, finding the rhythm that made her whimper with need. He reached between their bodies and touched her till her head fell back and she cried out his name.

The moment she came apart, he let go too. His release rolled toward him with the power of a thundercloud and surged through him like lightning.

Changing him, deep in his bones.

Afterward, he covered Julie with a quilt and tucked her close to his chest. "I love you, Juliette," he murmured against her temple. "Always."

And he knew it with utter certainty.

This was where he was meant to be.

It was *who* he was meant to be.

"How is your research progressing?" Sam poured hot tea into Alistair's cup before filling his own and sitting at the breakfast table, glad to have a few moments alone with him. Juliette must have fallen asleep again after she returned to her own bedchamber in the wee hours of the morning.

"My findings are hardly groundbreaking," the older man admitted. "But I've amassed quite a bit of evidence pointing to the adverse effects of dumping human waste and animal carcasses into the Thames. The sturgeon, salmon, and trout populations have all declined according to fishermen. And you don't need a scientist's powers of observation to smell the stench drifting off the mud banks."

Sam managed to swallow a mouthful of egg, then pushed his plate away. "Will you present your findings to the Royal Society? Your records could prove valuable."

Besides, Julie desperately wanted her uncle to gain acceptance in the scientific community. Perhaps more than Alistair wanted it for himself.

"I'm not certain." He pushed his ham around with his fork, looking wistful. "Maybe once I'm settled . . . somewhere. I'm feeling rather at loose ends since yesterday. But I know Juliette would like me to pursue membership, and I do like to make her happy."

Sam smiled. "That's something we have in common. I adore making your niece happy. In fact, there's something important I need to ask you."

The older man leaned forward. "Oh? What is it?"

Uncharacteristically nervous, Sam swallowed. "I'd like to humbly ask you for your niece's hand in marriage."

Alistair's fork clattered to his plate. "You wish to . . . to marry Juliette?"

Footsteps sounded in the corridor. Not the patter of dainty slippers, but the thud of large boots.

"Marry Juliette?" A masculine voice repeated, incredulous. "What the *hell* has been going on in my bloody house?"

Shit. Sam adjusted his sling, which suddenly had him in a stranglehold.

"Welcome home, William," Alistair beamed. "This is Cousin Samuel—and he wants to marry Juliette!"

More footsteps. This time of the dainty slipper variety. Julie appeared in the doorway of the dining room wearing a sunny yellow frock and blushing to the roots of her hair. "Good morning, everyone." Her eyes welled as she hugged her brother-in-law, the earl. "Thank you for coming. I'm so sorry to take you away from Meg, but I didn't know where else to turn."

"You should have sent for me earlier. I come back to town to find Alistair's been kicked out of his home and you're almost engaged to . . ."

"Samuel Travis." Sam stood and inclined his head since his sling didn't allow him to properly shake hands.

"He tried to help us," Julie explained. "But some dockworkers broke his arm."

The earl arched a brow, skeptical. "You can tell me the entire story over breakfast. But first I'm going to need coffee." Turning to Sam, he said, "Travis, I think it would be best if you left."

"Will!" Julie cried.

But Sam understood the earl's need to talk to his family privately and assess the situation from all angles—it's what he would have done too. He shot Julie an encouraging smile. "I'll go for now. I must stop by the office anyway. But I shall see you soon. I promise." On his way out, he scooped up her hand and pressed a kiss to the back of it.

"I say, Samuel," Alistair called after him. "Come back for dinner tonight. We'll toast your and Juliette's engagement."

"There is no engagement yet," Will said through gritted teeth. Unable to ignore Julie's pleading eyes, he added, "But do join us for dinner this evening."

Sam grinned. "I can't wait."

When Sam returned to the earl's townhouse that evening, the butler escorted him directly to Castleton's study.

As Sam entered the room, the earl, who sat with his boots propped on the corner of his massive desk, scowled. Without preamble, he said, "Why in God's name should I allow you to marry my sister-in-law?"

Not intimidated in the least, Sam looked him in the eye. "Because I love her—and she loves me."

Castleton snorted. "Forgive my skepticism, but you're a notorious rake. What do you hope to gain out of this match? Money? Status?"

"No. Just the chance to make Juliette happy and . . ."

"And?" The earl arched a brow, impatient.

"A family," Sam said simply. "I want to be part of a true family."

"Christ." Castleton raked a hand through his hair, stood, and paced behind his desk. "Julie wants to marry you too, though for the life of me, I can't imagine why. How will you provide for her?"

"I've taken a position in my friend's business. I may not have much to offer yet, but I will. I just never had anything worth working for . . . until now."

"I see," the earl said dryly. "So after meeting Julie, you're suddenly reformed?"

It wasn't far from the truth, damn it. "She made me believe I was more than a collection of salacious stories in the gossip rags—and for her, I want to be." He shrugged. "For myself too."

Castleton leveled a stare at him for several moments, thoughtful. "If you break her heart, Travis, you shall rue the day, so help me, God."

"I would sooner die than hurt her."

The earl snorted again. "Then we are of a like mind." He stalked to his sideboard, poured a couple of glasses of brandy, and handed one to Sam. "Welcome to the family. You should know that the Lacey sisters keep few secrets from each other. They're loyal and stubborn and passionate. And marrying into their unconventional, close-knit family makes you one of the luckiest bastards in the world."

Sam nodded soberly. "Trust me—I already know."

Chapter FORTY-FOUR

"How long have they been in Will's study?" Uncle Alistair asked.

Julie glanced at the clock perched on the mantel in the earl's drawing room, where they waited for Sam and Will to join them before going through to dinner. "A half hour." She paced in front of the scores of trunks and boxes from Uncle Alistair's house stacked neatly against one wall. She hadn't even begun to unpack all their things. "What could they be talking about?"

"I think it's safe to assume they're talking about *you*," her uncle said with a smile.

"I do hope Will's not being too hard on Sam."

"He looks well enough," Uncle Alistair replied with a chuckle. "Save the sling on his arm."

Julie looked up to see Sam and Will walking into the drawing room, shoulder to shoulder. The sight of Sam in a tailored dark-green jacket and snug trousers nearly took her breath away, and when a slow smile spread across his handsome face, she positively ached.

"Well?" she asked Will, perhaps a bit impatiently.

"If Alistair gives his blessing, then I give mine as well." He planted a congratulatory kiss on her cheek.

"I approve, wholeheartedly." Uncle Alistair slapped his knee for added emphasis. "I believe this calls for champagne at dinner."

Sam sat on the sofa beside him. "Thank you, sir. I don't yet know where Julie and I will live, but it will be your home too. We'll see that you have a fine study with plenty of shelves for books, river-water samples, and whatever else you wish."

"Thank you, Samuel," her uncle said, his voice more gravelly than usual.

Julie's heart squeezed in her chest. "But in the meantime, I wanted to make you feel more at home here." She scurried to the hall and waved a pair of footmen in.

"Oh, that's not necessary. I am fine. If I seem a bit ruffled, it's only because I miss . . . what's this?"

"Until we find a more permanent spot for it, Will agreed we could hang Aunt Elspeth's portrait in here." Julie hoped he'd feel less at sea with the portrait nearby. She helped the footmen navigate the room while holding the large painting, directing them away from small tables and vases that could easily topple.

"How thoughtful," Alistair murmured, lifting his spectacles to swipe at his eyes.

"I think the painting will look very nice here," Julie said, pointing to a spot beside the window, "and you'll be able to see it from either the sofa or the armchair."

"Wait," Sam said.

Julie blinked. "What's the matter?"

"Nothing. That is, there's something on the back of the picture—a small paper tucked into the upper-right corner."

The footmen set the portrait down and Julie went to look. "Have you any idea what this could be, Uncle Alistair?"

He shook his head, sending the white hair at his crown waving. "No, indeed—why don't you have a look?"

The yellowed paper was folded several times over and tucked securely into the corner of the frame. Julie took care not to tear the brittle paper as she slid it out and opened it.

"It looks rather official," she said, frowning. "Perhaps a note by the artist." She was about to toss it aside to examine later when a signature at the bottom of the paper caught her eye. *Currington*.

Good heavens. She swayed a little, and Sam rushed to her side, wrapping a strong arm around her waist. "What is it?"

She swallowed as she handed the note to him. "It looks like a letter . . . from your brother." Julie's heart hammered. Even there, in the safety of Meg and Will's home, Nigel had managed to intrude on their happiness.

"It's not from Nigel," Sam said slowly. "It's a letter from my father. To your Aunt Elspeth." As he scanned the paper, his face split into a smile. "It explains that he's giving the house on Hart Street to his cousin Elspeth and her fine husband as a belated wedding gift. And that though the house shall fully and legally belong to them, he intends to continue paying the taxes on the property, as it brings him a measure of joy to support a couple who clearly love each other as much as he loved . . . my mother."

Julie's eyes welled. "How beautiful."

"And generous," Will added.

Sam nodded thoughtfully. "That's the kind of man my father was."

Julie pressed a palm to his chest and tilted her head to his. "That's the kind of man you are too."

"The deed is enclosed as well," Sam said gruffly. "Signed, dated, and executed."

Curious, Julie turned to Alistair. "You never knew?"

"Elspeth may have feared I'd be too proud to accept such a gift. I confess to being a bit stubborn," he admitted, "particularly in my youth. But more recently I've learned to accept and appreciate the blessings life bestows on us. Some blessings come in the form of gifts, others as special people in our lives. Fate works in delirious ways," he said sagely.

"I couldn't agree more." Sam's words, so earnestly spoken, made Julie's chest squeeze. "We'll have a solicitor review the deed," he said, "but it would appear that the house on Hart Street doesn't belong to my brother after all. It's Alistair's."

"You're mistaken, Samuel," the old man said. "The house isn't mine—it's ours. *All* of ours. And Elspeth made sure of it."

Julie and her sisters could have celebrated Christmastide in any number of elegant households, from the Earl of Castleton's stately townhouse to the Duke of Blackshire's sprawling country estate.

But the Lacey sisters couldn't imagine Christmas Eve anywhere besides the old house on Hart Street, where Julie and Sam—hopelessly besotted newlyweds—now lived with Uncle Alistair. The house wasn't quite as ramshackle as it had once been, thanks to the renovations Julie had convinced her uncle to undertake, but it was still cozy.

And it was especially cozy tonight, because everyone had come home.

Meg and Will, their lively twins, Valerie and Diana, and their beautiful baby, born just two months ago, filled up the settee. The twins argued good-naturedly about whose turn it was to hold baby Daisy and who should have the next piggyback ride from their Uncle Alex.

Beth sat in the wobbly chair beside the sewing basket—which no one had touched in a year, but all agreed should not be disturbed since it lent the room a much-needed appearance of industriousness. Her eyes glowed with love as she watched her handsome husband entertaining the twins, and the secret smile she'd been wearing since returning from her honeymoon made Julie wonder if she would soon be an aunt again.

Alex's grandmother, the dowager duchess, sat beside Beth in a marginally sturdier chair. And, unless Julie was mistaken, the duchess was batting her eyes at Uncle Alistair, who, of course, sat in his favorite armchair.

The house was dressed in festive, fragrant greenery—holly, laurel, and evergreens that Beth had brought from the country. A Yule log burned in the parlor's fireplace, and mugs of potent wassail punch warmed their bellies.

All was as it should be—or, it would be, as soon as Sam returned home from work. His lips had lingered on hers as he'd said good-bye that morning. He'd tucked the sheets around her and promised to return before dinner . . . which was very soon.

Sighing happily, she said, "Uncle Alistair, you must tell everyone your news."

The dowager duchess perked up. "Oh? I confess I am intrigued, Alistair."

He waved a self-deprecating hand. "I'm taking up the cause of a group of fishermen, petitioning Parliament to restrict the dumping of waste in the Thames."

The duchess pursed her lips, impressed. "How very avant-garde."

"He's too humble to mention it, but his research makes a compelling case," Julie said proudly. "And because of Uncle Alistair's efforts, perhaps the Thames's waters will improve sufficiently so that our children may enjoy it."

"Did you say *children*?" Beth teased. "Have you an announcement you'd like to make, Julie?"

"I was speaking only of hypothetical children," she retorted. "Have *you* anything you'd like to announce?"

Beth blushed furiously. "No . . . that is . . . perhaps . . . soon." In an obvious attempt to change the subject, she turned to Uncle Alistair and said, "We couldn't be prouder of you, Uncle. Do you still intend to request membership in the Royal Society?"

"I promised Julie I would, and so I shall. But the Society selects only fifteen members a year. While it would be an honor to be named a fellow, I'd derive more satisfaction from a cleaner river, demonstrated in measurable results."

"Spoken like a true scientist," the duchess drawled. "However, I know several of the Society's fellows. I feel confident they shall be duly impressed with your research and cast their votes accordingly."

The duchess was accustomed to having her wishes granted—and she clearly wished to help Uncle Alistair. If she employed even a modicum of her influence, his acceptance among the ton's elite was all but ensured.

Julie's chest squeezed at the thought of it.

Her uncle had seemed happier lately. And though he still talked to Aunt Elspeth occasionally, he wasn't anxious or upset—rather, he spoke to her as if he were reminiscing with a dear, old friend.

"Girls," Meg said to the twins, "why don't you play the song I taught you on the pianoforte?" The suggestion was barely out of her mouth before Diana and Valerie scrambled to the bench, their blond curls bobbing. "Must everything be a race?" Meg asked rhetorically.

"No, but it's more fun that way," Valerie announced, matter of fact.

The girls climbed onto the seat and launched into song with exuberance reserved for seven-year-olds, giggling over each missed note. They were in the middle of the rousing chorus when a chilly gust swept into the parlor.

"Uncle Sam is home!" cried Diana.

Julie's knees went a little weak at the sight of him. A few snowflakes frosted his hair and the shoulders of his greatcoat, and his smile warmed the entire room. He carried a large wicker basket covered with a tartan blanket.

"What is *that*?" asked Valerie, bounding off the pianoforte bench.

"It's a gift for your Aunt Julie," he replied. "And she may open it now."

"Now?" Julie had assumed they'd exchange gifts later, in private. "Are you certain?"

"This present won't wait." Sam set the basket in front of the fireplace, and she knelt beside it.

"I can't imagine what it could be." It seemed she already had everything she ever wanted—respectability for Uncle Alistair, happy marriages for her sisters, and her own fairytale romance.

She lifted the corner of the plaid blanket and felt something cold and wet against her palm. Two furry black and white paws rested on the edge of the basket, and an adorably shaggy puppy peeked out.

A puppy that looked remarkably like . . . a mop.

Through sheer will, the curious creature hoisted herself out of the basket and landed squarely in Julie's lap.

Sam chuckled and scratched the pup between her floppy ears. "She certainly seems fond of you. What do you think of her?"

Her throat thick with emotion, Julie managed, "She's perfect." Her eyes welled as she nestled the puppy's warm, soft body to her chest. Pressing a kiss to her furry head, Julie murmured, "Welcome to the family, Moppet."

Hours later, after the guests had left and Uncle Alistair was sound asleep, Julie and Sam escaped to their bedchamber. The moment the door closed behind them, he hauled her body against his and pressed his lips to her neck. "I've been waiting all damned night to do this," he murmured, skimming his warm hands over her bare shoulders and down her back. His wicked fingers already tugged at the laces of her gown.

"Wait," she said, breathlessly. "I have gifts for you."

"This sounds promising, temptress."

Reluctantly, she broke off the kiss and retrieved two small packages from her armoire. "Here you are," she said, handing both to him. "Merry Christmas, Sam."

His expression quizzical, he tore the paper off the first box, removed the lid, and stared as though he couldn't believe his eyes. "My father's watch," he said with awe. "How did you . . ."

"It wasn't difficult to track down. You should never have given it up—it's far too precious."

"But not nearly as precious to me as you are." He brushed his lips over hers as he slipped the watch into his pocket, where it belonged. "Thank you."

"Now you must open the other gift," she instructed.

"As you wish, tigress." He unwrapped the other package and unfurled a long piece of snowy white linen. "A neckcloth?"

"Yes," she said saucily. "A cravat. So you shall never again have to rely on an embroidery cloth."

Sam slipped the cloth around her waist and tugged until their hips collided, making her heartbeat gallop in response.

"I like this gift," he growled, winding one end of the cravat loosely around her wrist. "I'm already imagining a number of other creative uses. Let's go to bed, siren." He scooped her up in his arms, stalked across the room, and drew up short at the sight of a black and white ball of fur sleeping in the dead center of their mattress.

"Don't disturb Moppet," Julie pleaded. "She's exhausted after carousing with the twins."

Sam gazed at the bedposts regretfully but carried her

to the thick rug in front of the fire. "Fine. We'll save the cravat for another night."

"We've no shortage of nights," she assured him.

"Thank God for that." He laid her back and stretched out beside her. Tracing lazy circles across the swells of her breasts, he said, "Merry Christmas, Juliette. I love you."

"I love you too." Her heart so full it could burst, she curled an arm around his neck. "But I have a confession."

He arched a brow. "Something wicked, I hope?"

"Quite. I confess I miss the cravatless rogue who first appeared on my doorstep. Is there any chance he might make an appearance tonight?"

Sam slid his hand beneath the hem of her dress and up the inside of her leg. "There is a one hundred percent chance," he confirmed. "In fact, I think he's here now."

"Yes," she sighed blissfully. The hitch of her breath and the tingling of her skin confirmed it was true.

Her rogue was back—to stay.

Thank you so much for reading *The Rogue Is Back in Town*—
I hope you enjoyed Julie and Sam's story!

- If you'd like to learn more about the *Wayward Wallflowers* books, please visit my website (http://annabennettauthor.com) and sign up for my newsletter (http://eepurl.com/bTInsb).

- I can usually be found procrastinating on social media and would love some company! Join me on Facebook (https://www.facebook.com/AnnaBennettAuthor) or Twitter (https://twitter.com/_AnnaBennett) where I share pictures of pretty ball gowns, historic tidbits, fun book quotes, and other writing inspiration.

- Lastly, reviews are a great way to spread the word about books. I'm always grateful for honest feedback from readers—even a quick rating or review on your favorite bookseller's site is incredibly helpful.

Thanks again for spending time with me and the Lacey sisters.
Until next time, happy reading!
—Anna

Read on for a teaser of the book that started it all

MY BROWN-EYED EARL

And don't miss out on the second Wayward Wallflowers novel

I DARED THE DUKE

Available from St. Martin's Paperbacks

Meg bristled. "I am quite capable of making the journey to my bedchamber without assistance."

"You almost swooned earlier," Will said.

"How gallant of you to remind me."

He shrugged. "And then you drank claret at dinner. Therefore, I will escort you to your room."

Feeling her blood heat, she crossed her arms. "I feel that I should have some say in this matter."

"I feel that I should be allowed to play the part of a gentleman. After all, you've already emasculated me once today."

Dear God. He was never going to let the incident go.

"Besides," he continued, "I won't have you tumbling down the stairs, creating yet another mess for Gibson to clean up." Ouch. He stepped closer, much closer than was proper, and offered his arm. "Indulge me this once . . . Meg."

Her name was a whisper on his lips. Soft. Seductive.

Meanwhile, his eyes gleamed mischievously, daring her to say yes.

Though she knew she shouldn't, she slipped her hand in the crook of his arm and let him slowly lead her from the room and down the corridor.

They made their way up the staircase in companionable silence, but she was much too aware of his long legs brushing her skirts and his powerful thighs flexing as he took each step. Swallowing, she averted her gaze.

Thankfully, this sweet torture was almost over. When at last they reached the landing, she whirled toward him, intending to bid him goodnight. Mistaking her sudden movement for tipsiness, he gasped and steadied her, his large hands encircling her waist.

They stared at each other for several seconds, and Meg noticed he was breathing almost as hard as she was.

"You weren't about to fall just then, were you?"

"No. I am generally able to manage a staircase without catastrophe." Although she'd tried for a breezy tone, it sounded more breathy.

He frowned at his hands, still firmly settled just above her hips, as though they'd betrayed him. "Well then, this is embarrassing."

Embarrassing, yes, but also exhilarating.

"There has been no shortage of humiliation today," she agreed.

His brow wrinkled. "But today wasn't *all* bad, was it?"

"I suppose not—if you discount Diana's near trampling and me breaking your crystal glass and kneeing you in the—" She threw up her hands and leaned her forehead against his chest. "It's been a horrid day," she mumbled into his waistcoat.

He chuckled, but Meg didn't care. It felt so good to stop sparring with him, to let down her defenses for a moment and simply absorb his strength. She was tired of fighting him and perhaps, more specifically, the attraction she felt toward him.

As though he understood, he wrapped an arm around her and pulled her flush against him. "Everyone is safe," he reminded her. "Diana, you, and even me." He held her there at the top of the stairs and lightly caressed her back and neck till she was certain her knees had turned to jelly.

"Come," he said softly in her ear, "sit down next to me."

He helped her sit right there, on the top step, settled himself beside her, and slipped an arm around her shoulders. "It's not a bad view from up here."

Meg had to agree. Moonlight streamed through the transom above the door in the foyer, making the polished marble floors glisten below them like a river. The chandelier's teardrop crystals twinkled above them like stars. And the stairs, covered in a plush runner, rose up to meet them like a grassy hill in the countryside.

In was easy to imagine that they were miles away from London, and that only the two of them existed. "It's lovely."

"Do you want to know my opinion about today?" he asked.

"Please."

"As far as days go, I'd say today was a very good one."

She shot him an incredulous look. "I fear your standards are rather low."

"I don't think so. First, it must be noted that in spite

of the near misses, all serious injuries were averted. Almost as remarkable, you and I reached a truce. But for me, the best part of today was dining with you and, well . . . right now." He reached for her hand and gave it a squeeze, which she felt somewhere in the vicinity of her chest.

She swallowed, then asked the question she simply had to know. "Why is now the best part?"

"I suppose I like having someone to share the view with."

Odd. He sounded almost lonely.

"And because," he continued, "while I do enjoy our little battles of wits, I also like to see you smile. Your smile is . . ." He rubbed the stubble on his chin as he searched for the words. "Bright, fleeting, rare. Like a comet shooting through the midnight sky."

She blinked slowly, letting his words sink into her skin and thrum throughout her body. Dumbfounded, she stared at the chiseled perfection of his face. "That's . . . beautiful. But my smiles are not so rare."

"No? The ones directed at me are rare." Cupping her face in his palm, he lightly brushed his thumb across her cheek. "I suspect you'll make me wait seven years to see it again."

She smiled at that, because it was ridiculous and sweet and because she couldn't stop herself if she tried.

His gaze dropped to her mouth, and his expression turned serious. "Meg," he breathed. It was a question. A plea.

In response, she leaned forward.

And then his lips were on hers.

It was the height of foolishness to allow the kiss, even

worse to invite it, but it seemed to be the predestined ending to their strange, emotional day. All of the fighting, the bargaining, and the revealing had led to this, the most unlikely of kisses.

And yet, here they were.

His mouth slanted across her lips, still parted in a soft smile. His hand cradled her cheek, pulling her closer and claiming her as his—at least for the moment. He growled and deepened the kiss, thrilling her with the knowledge that he wanted her. Desired her.

She wouldn't have believed it possible a few short hours ago, but there, on the earl's staircase in the evening's waning light, she could imagine that she was not a governess in a dowdy dress.

At that moment she was, as he'd said, a comet, bursting across the heavens in a shimmer of light.

A delicious shiver shot through her limbs as their faces bumped lightly, retreated, and came together again. He speared his fingers through her hair, cursing at the blockade presented by her tight bun. Changing course, he trailed his fingers lightly around her ear and down her neck, where the barrier of her modest neckline renewed his ire.

Unwilling to surrender, he teased the seam of her lips apart with his tongue, daring her to open to him. She did.

Never before had she been kissed like this—like it was meant to lead to something more.

Though her head was muddled with equal parts shock and bliss, she was certain of one thing: the earl could teach her all she needed to know about kissing. And other things as well, no doubt.

Yes, she was in excellent hands. And since the magical evening couldn't last forever, she might as well enjoy it while she could.

Tentatively, she curled a hand around his neck, lightly tugging the soft curls at his nape. When he groaned, she gave herself over to the kiss—and him.

The earth beneath her gave way, and she was floating, anchored only by his hand on her hip and his mouth on hers. She thought of nothing but the taste and feel of him, the pressure and heat of his body next to hers. Her breath came in short gasps and her skin heated. When the wall of his chest brushed against the front of her gown, her nipples tingled and hardened to tight, aching buds. As though he knew, he reached between them and caressed her breast, teasing its peak through the layers of lawn and wool, sending waves of pleasure through her body.

She cried out softly, but he swallowed the sound and murmured against her mouth. "I always knew."

Reluctantly, she broke off the kiss and pressed her forehead to his. "What did you know?"

His heavy-lidded eyes gleamed, reflecting her own desire. "That you were a magnificent, passionate creature."

In other circumstances, she might have been insulted, but since he clearly meant it as a compliment, she decided to accept it as such. "Thank you."

"I told you the day wasn't all bad. We managed to salvage the end."

He pressed a kiss to her palm and held her hand in his lap for a minute, giving her pulse a chance to return to normal. With each beat of her heart, she felt the spell between them slowly breaking, and the stark reality of their situation intruding once more.

She had *everything* to lose. Her virtue, her pride, her job. . . . her heart.

Suddenly self-conscious, she pulled her hand away and smoothed a tendril of hair behind her ear. She required time and space to think about what had just happened and to figure out what, if anything, it had meant. "This day did have some things to recommend it. However, I think that now I shall truly retire for the evening."

When she reached for the balustrade to pull herself up, he immediately stood and offered his hand, lifting her to her feet. With his hair disheveled and cravat askew he looked vaguely lost. Almost vulnerable. "Until tomorrow," he said, his words holding the hint of a question.

"Of course." However, she wasn't really sure of anything. Not while her lips were still swollen and her mind was still reeling from his kiss. "Tomorrow."

He walked beside her as she made her way to her bedchamber, crossing his arms as though he didn't quite trust his hands to be free. As she opened the door, he stepped aside but lingered.

Perhaps he wanted to say something, like *I shouldn't have kissed you*. Or ask her a question, like *Could we pretend this interlude never happened?*

Or maybe he wanted to kiss her again.

Her skin tingled at the thought.

He leaned his long frame against the doorjamb, reached for the curl resting on her shoulder, and twirled it around his finger as though mesmerized. His gaze drifted to her mouth, and she knew. He *was* going to kiss her again.

But instead of coming closer, he dropped the curl and backed away solemnly. "Good night, Meg."

She closed the door to her room and rushed to the mirror above her washstand to check her reflection. She wanted to see if her face looked as flushed and her lips appeared as swollen as they felt. In short, she wanted to see if she had the look of a woman who'd been ravished.

But no. The change, it seemed, was primarily on the inside.

It was only after she'd washed, changed into her night rail, and slipped beneath the covers of her sumptuous bed that she realized the irony of the evening she'd spent with Will.

She'd gone to see him intending to turn in her resignation, but had ended up *kissing* him.

Even worse, she'd begun to think of him not as *the earl* or *Lord Castleton*, but as *Will*.

Clear signs she had begun the steady and inexorable descent into madness.